PENGUIN BOOKS

SCARRED

Monica Dickens, great-granddaughter of Charles Dickens, has written over forty novels, autobiographical books and children's books. Her first book, *One Pair of Hands*, which arose out of her experiences as a cook and general servant, made her a best-seller at twenty-two and is still in great demand. Her books reflect the varied aspects of a full and eventful life. Three years' wartime nursing led to *One Pair of Feet* and *The Happy Prisoner*. After a year in an aircraft factory she wrote *The Fancy*, and this was followed by *My Turn to Make the Tea* about her job as a reporter on a local newspaper in the 1950s.

Marriage in America was fictionalized as *No More Meadows*, while *Kate and Emma* was the result of her involvement with the NSPCC. Her lifelong love of horses and all animals produced fourteen children's books, one of which became the successful Yorkshire TV series *Follyfoot*. *The Listeners* developed from her work with the Samaritans, and in 1974 she started the first Samaritan branch in America in Boston, Massachusetts, near Cape Cod, where she lived for thirty-three years with her husband Commander Roy Stratton, US Navy.

She now lives in England in a thatched cottage on the Berkshire Downs. She has two daughters. Penguin has published her autobiography, *An Open Book*, and many of her other works including, most recently, *Closed at Dusk*.

MONICA DICKENS

SCARRED

PENGUIN BOOKS

PENGUIN BOOKS

Published by the Penguin Group
Penguin Books Ltd, 27 Wrights Lane, London W8 5TZ, England
Penguin Books USA Inc., 375 Hudson Street, New York, New York 10014, USA
Penguin Books Australia Ltd, Ringwood, Victoria, Australia
Penguin Books Canada Ltd, 10 Alcorn Avenue, Toronto, Ontario, Canada M4V 3B2
Penguin Books (NZ) Ltd, 182–190 Wairau Road, Auckland 10, New Zealand

Penguin Books Ltd, Registered Offices: Harmondsworth, Middlesex, England

First published by Viking 1991
Published in Penguin Books 1992
1 3 5 7 9 10 8 6 4 2

Printed in England by Clays Ltd, St Ives plc

In admiration, and gratitude for their help to
John Kirk, FRCS
and
Doreen Trust, Founder and Director of
the Disfigurement Guidance Centre, Guild House,
1 George Street, Cellardyke, Fife KY10 3AS

Chapter One

It's mine!'

'Annette gave it to *me*!'

'You jerk – give it back!'

The aggressive small cousins from Canada were going home before Christmas, so twelve-year-old Annette had dug out of the attic her grandmother's long red dressing gown and put it on to play Father Christmas.

As they fought over a mutilated red and gold parcel, Annette reached forward to take it from the furious younger boy. He snatched it away, and she tripped on the long flapping robe, staggering against the oil heater. She saw the bottom edge catch fire and, as she pulled it free of the grille, the flames rushed up and engulfed her.

An instant's oblivion. No sight, no sound, no breath. Her

life stopped. Then the screaming started, and she saw her hands held out like claws, her melting arms, what used to be her body. Someone knocked her to the floor, and she was smothered in the harsh suffocating rug – let me free!

Beyond the clamour of cries and shouts, a terrible voice shrieked, on and on into the black night.

'Il mio pe-e-en . . . sier!'

The rising bravado of Violetta's celebration of life shrieked up to reach (only just) and hold top C, and the audience was delivered into the interval.

A visiting opera company at Kingscombe's Majestic Theatre was a rare delight, even with this cliff-hanging soprano. Peter and Catherine went contentedly to the bar.

'He*llo*, Mr Freeman!' The woman in the tight red dress seemed familiar. She was surprised to see him at the opera, so she was probably a patient.

Yes, a few years ago. Excision of basal cell tumour on cheek. In her smile, Peter could see the faint line of the scar.

'Nice to see you.' He knew her scar but not her name. Catherine might remember it, but she had turned away to talk to someone else.

'Antonia and John Baker. This is Peter Freeman.' The basal cell woman introduced him to her friends. Antonia was attractive and vivacious. She chattered about her design studio and her husband's job with a chain of West Country hotels.

'And what do *you* do, Peter?' Her eyes sparkled at him.

'I'm at the Royal.' The Royal Victoria Hospital, on one of the hills that framed this Devon seacoast town, needed no other name.

'A doctor?'

'A surgeon.'

'Oh, goodness.' Antonia was impressed, and the basal cell woman told her, 'He's a plastic surgeon.'

'*Are* you? How fascinating. Face lifts and nose jobs. I've always hated my nose,' Antonia said gaily, screwing up her face round a perfectly acceptable nose. 'I might be calling on you some day!'

'Actually' – behind his smile Peter could feel his face stiffening into retreat – 'I'm mostly in reconstructive surgery, not cosmetic.'

'Oh – but I need reconstructing, don't I, Johnny?'

'Totally.' Her husband grinned. 'The whole lot.'

'I'm a freak.' They both laughed loudly enough over the noise of the bar to make Catherine turn her head inquiringly.

The laughter stopped.

Peter's wife Catherine spread her wonderful innocent wide smile that drew the eye away from the portwine birthmark that covered her left cheek. 'Don't worry,' she told Antonia warmly, 'I've lived with this all my life.'

Before Antonia could decide whether to look, or look away, the three-minute bell saved her.

When they were back in their seats for the second act of *La Traviata*, Catherine asked Peter, 'Should I have explained that I didn't have time to put on make-up?'

He shrugged. 'You're the expert.'

The beautiful melodies of the opera took over and eased out the tensions of a long day of routine and small difficulties. Violetta and Alfredo were pouring their hearts out to each other when Peter's jacket pocket bleeped discreetly.

There was no telephone in the lobby, but a girl in the box office let him in to make the call.

It was Noel Grant, his senior registrar.

'Young girl about twelve, very badly burned. The ambulance brought her to our unit, and the house officer saw her and then called me in. I've got an IV drip going, and she's had morphine and penicillin.'

'You want me to come up?'

'I don't want to bother you . . .' Perhaps Noel would like to handle this alone, but it was Peter's rule to be told of all emergencies.

'What's the burn area?'

'About sixty per cent, I'd say. Hands, arms and chest, neck, legs, some very deep.'

'I'll be there.' If Peter did not go back to his seat, Catherine would take a taxi home.

He swung the car out along the sea front and drove fast up through the outskirts of the town, to the jumble of hospital buildings piled on the hill at different levels. At the far side, the Milner Plastic Surgery Unit had been built from wartime military huts: three long wings radiating from a two-storey central block.

In the clinic Mary Knight, the house officer, was writing up notes, long back curved wearily, hair straggling forward. She looked up and put the hair behind her ears.

'Where is she?'

'First single room on B, sir. Mr Grant is with her, and one of the night nurses. I got a nurse from one of the general wards to cover.'

'Good. Parents?'

'Waiting.' Mary made a sympathetic grimace. Her young face was thin and bony, and often prematurely haggard at night.

'What do you think?' Peter would form his own opinion, but juniors should always be asked for theirs.

Mary shook her head. 'I don't see that she has much chance.'

In the brightly lit room, reeking of burned flesh, they had removed the girl's clothes and wrapped her in a sterile sheet under a cotton blanket. Short curly hair damply plastered, eyes swollen, no facial burns, but in the middle of the small white face her childish nose was painted red.

Noel Grant, in blue jeans and T-shirt under a white jacket, had bandaged the needle arm to a splint. 'I couldn't get a peripheral vein,' he said. 'Too contracted from shock. I had to cut through burn to get a deeper vessel.'

'Hello, Annette, let's have a look at you.'

Although the child was shivering and in shock, she moved her lips towards a smile. She did not realize how badly hurt she was. Since the nerve ends were damaged, she would not be feeling the pain of the deep burns . . . yet.

As the nurse helped Peter gently to unwrap the sheet, he murmured to the girl, 'Why the nose?'

Over the blob of red, her eyes opened, a startling clear grey blue washed with tears, the iris translucent round the dilated pupils.

'Father Christmas. She wouldn't let me wash it off,' the nurse said. 'Thank God she wasn't wearing a beard.'

'It was my fault.' In the waiting room the father, a stubby man with glasses and cropped Airedale hair, said this, and then was silent while Peter gave the main information about his daughter. Detail was no use at this crisis stage. People could listen and nod and ask questions, but they could not take much in.

'My fault.' The man took off his glasses and rubbed his eyes harshly, screwing up his face.

'Don't keep *saying* that.' His wife, tense on the edge of her seat, trying to be whatever she thought the doctor thought she ought to be, looked at her husband as if he were a stranger.

'What happened, Mrs Leigh?'

The woman shook her head. The man jerked out, 'The contact point in the electric fire needed soldering. The room was cold. I brought in the old oil heater we used to use in the greenhouse. It was turned up too high and the guard on the front was bent. The long robe caught in it, and she – ' He steadied his mouth with his hand. 'When we had her smothered in the rug, she was screaming like an animal. I'll always hear that.'

'Don't, Ted.' His wife licked her lips and looked at Peter. 'Will she be – she's a lovely girl – will she be badly scarred?'

'Don't worry about that now, Mrs Leigh.'

'Oh.' She looked down at her hands, clenched in her lap. 'She's going to die, then.'

The father winced and jerked his head. His eyes were raw and weak without the glasses.

'She's desperately ill,' Peter said carefully. 'If I can clean up the burns tomorrow, I'll be able to tell you more. The next few days are critical.' The man's eyes were screwed shut. The mother kept nodding, her eyes tied to Peter's like a lifeline. 'But you know we'll do all we can.'

How often he had said that, or something like it. Not worth much, but what else could be said?

They thanked him blankly, as people did in the first shock. Sobbing and anger and why, why, why? – that came later, and usually not at the hospital, where courage and good behaviour were struggled for.

They stood up when Peter did. Deirdre Leigh was taller than her husband, with thin legs and long feet. Off the sofa, they were unsteady. They moved closer and propped each other up. Peter arranged for coffee and sandwiches, and asked one of the nurses to put up camp beds in the day room. After he checked with Noel the volume of four-hourly plasma transfusions and the amount of whole blood to be crossmatched, he drove the few miles home, thinking about the shocked, flayed girl, and planning tomorrow. If she died, he would have to let go of Annette and her parents, never having known them. If she lived, he would know them very well, through months and years of skin grafts.

He ate what Catherine had left out for him, standing at the kitchen table, glancing briefly at the newspaper. Upstairs, he looked into the chaotic rooms of his children, Evangeline and Philip, vigorously asleep, immune from disaster, as any parent expects his child to be until it comes.

Catherine was reading in bed. While Peter moved about the room, getting ready to join her, he told her about Annette.

'Can you save her?'

'I don't know. Noel asked me that: "Can we save her?", rather insecurely for him. I don't think he's ever seen such bad burns. Lovely child, a bit like an older Evie – only not perfect now.'

In the mirror, with Catherine and her soft thick hair reflected on the bed behind him, he saw his tired, serious face. How was it that at nearly fifty, tired, thinking about tragedy, he still looked like a boy in pyjamas? He got into bed and sighed, and they held hands in the dark, their faces turned towards each other on the pillows. Peter reached behind him to pick up the luminous alarm clock.

'What time are you setting it for?'

'Seven. I've got an early cleft lip, and a palate to do. Then I'm hoping this poor child will be stable enough to start cleaning the burns. I'll drop Phil and Evie at school.'

He slept. He had learned years ago as a house officer to fall asleep when there was time for sleep, whatever had happened or might happen. Soon he half woke and reached out a hand. 'You're awake, Cath. Are you all right?'

'Yes.' Catherine had not told him after they met at the theatre, and she did not tell him now, that Evie had said uncomfortably today, for the first time, 'You don't have to pick me up at school, Mum, when you're not at work. The bus is all right.'

Peter woke again suddenly before two, expecting the phone to ring. This sometimes happened, especially when he had a critical patient. The telephone woke him just before it rang, as if he had heard it draw breath.

It rang. 'Mr Freeman? You said to ring you about the burns girl?' Night sister was from Australia. Her statements were questions.

'How is she?'

'Fair. She was very restless. Mr Grant has given her a little more diamorphine.'

'Is he still there?'

'He's gone to get some sleep.'

'Keep her going for me, Joyce. Tomorrow – today, we'll start putting her back together again.'

'We will.' She had been doing that with him for seven years. She knew almost as much about burns as he did.

The children fought over their breakfast like savages. Catherine picked up what they spilled and scolded them amiably, while they continued to exchange abuse. They were eight and nine. They loved each other. Peter went out to get the car.

He was anxious to get to the hospital, but at the school he waited to see them through the gate into the walled yard. Philip headed off intently into his own world. Evie grabbed a girl who was flouncing along, all white socks and purple anorak, and pulled her back towards the car.

'Mandy,' she said hoarsely, 'this is my father.'

Peter said, 'Hello,' cheerily.

Mandy blanked him out with a brief look and jerked her arm free to turn away.

'New friend?' Peter asked Evie.

'Yes . . . No.'

'Which?'

His daughter did not answer, so he said, 'Goodbye, darling,' and put the car in gear, and Evie ran ahead. He tried to wave to her as he passed, but she was swallowed up in the jostle at the gate.

Peter found Annette fairly stable. Colin Kemp, his anaesthetist, was with her. There seemed to be no throat or lung damage from the fire, so after Peter had repaired the cleft lip and the palate, Annette was brought into the theatre, and he began to clean up the terrible damage to the small victimized body.

The deeper burns were mostly on her chest and waist where the clothing had been tighter, although there was severe injury to her arms and legs. On almost half the damaged area he would have to excise deeply burned tissue within the next few days to avoid infection and septicaemia.

'Does your son still believe in Father Christmas?' he asked Sally, his theatre nurse.

'After today' – with the next probe ready, she watched him swab out blistered tissue from under Annette's ribs – 'I won't want him to.'

As he worked slowly and patiently with the Cetavlon and saline, Peter began to plan aloud his programme of major skin grafting, and one of the medical students took notes.

Noel came in before Peter had finished, and they discussed interim treatment. Noel, who did not always agree with Peter, which was refreshing, since the last registrar had been a yes man, agreed on exposure for some of the burned areas.

'Lucky one of the low-air-loss beds is free.' Peter went out to the basins, taking off his gloves.

'We need at least two more,' Noel grumbled. 'And two more nurses to go with them.'

'Dream on.' Peter did not complain openly any more about lack of money and equipment and staff and space. There were better ways of using energy, like getting on with the job with what you had.

In the day room, where a couple of bandaged patients played chess, one with one hand, the other with one eye, Annette's parents waited, looking exhausted. Peter took them into his consulting room.

'She came through it well.' They looked up at him with hope. This was not the time to remind them that they could still lose Annette. 'If she goes on all right, I'll start the excising and grafting in a few days. There will have to be several quite major operations.'

'She's very healthy,' the mother offered.

'That will help, Mrs Leigh. She's going to have to go through a lot.'

The father shook his head of short dense hair and groaned, still haunted by 'My fault'.

'And it will be very hard for both of you too,' Peter said.

The man looked upwards from a lowered face, like a puzzled dog.

The mother said, 'We'll be all right.' She had a reckless, vulnerable face that juggled expressions of pain, inquiry and a sort of 'here goes nothing' bravado. She squared her shoulders and ran long knuckly fingers through her hair. The father was built more sturdily, but he might go under. It *had* been his fault, for taking a risk with an unsafe heater, and it was always harder for men, because they kept themselves closed off. The mother was strung up and skinny, but she was tough, like string.

Later in Annette's room, where the nurses came and went, he found Mrs Leigh sitting alone by the wide high bed that filtered air through the soft mattress to keep the body's under-surface dry and avoid constant rubbing. Motionless, with the blank face of sorrow, she watched her daughter sleeping, attached to oxygen and intravenous tubes.

'I've sent Ted home to shave and go to work,' she said. 'He's manager of the Apex appliance shop in the precinct, and it's a battlefield, what with Christmas. Better than sitting here wringing his hands.'

'I suppose.' But Annette was still very ill. Her temperature was high, and her pulse racing and feeble. If she were going to die, her father should be here. He would not be able to stand that extra guilt.

Richard Valentine, the other plastic surgeon, was in the

Torquay clinic today, so Noel, who was already very skilled, was doing some excisions of skin tumours and a microsurgical repair of a hand ripped apart in a knife brawl.

Peter saw outpatients all afternoon: two new cleft palate infants, a hypertrophic knee scar for revision, a strawberry mark beginning on a baby's cheek, a dog-bite man with a graft of skin to replace what the dog had torn out of his calf, and several other skin grafts at various stages.

When he went back to Annette's room, the child was dimly awake but not speaking. Her eyes were half shut, her pale mouth slack, the corners dribbling a little froth. Mrs Leigh sat by the bed with a lapful of swabs and wiped it away attentively, pleased to have something to do.

'Her father coming in?' Peter asked her.

'After work for a bit. Our younger child is with my mother. Ted may fetch him home with him to sleep. I've told Ted on the phone, Annette will be' – she looked across the bed at Peter – 'all right?'

'We have to believe that.'

Outside the room Peter asked the nurse, 'Does she want to keep things from the father?'

'She told me she's had to protect him all through their marriage.' The nurse shrugged and made a face. 'Her business, I suppose.'

Annette had been given a pint of whole blood and would have more plasma in four hours. Peter went over her treatment with Mary Knight, walked across to Intensive Care in the children's building to look at this morning's cleft lip babies, sprawled scraps under bandages and tubes, and then drove across the high bridge over the river gully to the smart new Restora Hospital, where he treated his private patients.

The entrance hall was thickly carpeted, the chairs comfortable, the flowers professionally arranged, the receptionist groomed and glossy. The lift walls had tinted mirrors, so that you could observe yourself en route to consultation or admission without seeing how ill you looked. Peter was tired, but the lift showed him a healthily coloured face and interesting reddish glints in the brown hair that was not yet receding, like that of most of his contemporaries.

On the second floor the corridors were lush and hushed. Heavy doors closed soundlessly, cream walls displayed expensive prints instead of the daubs and masterpieces put out by the children's wards to decorate the long noisy corridors at the Royal. The consulting room he shared with other doctors was furnished and carpeted like a hotel business suite, with the examining couch behind a panelled partition.

Did it all make patients feel that they were getting more for their own or their insurance company's money? People loved the old rambling Royal, where the piecemeal rebuilding programme could never keep ahead of the decline. Nobody came back to the Restora after they were discharged, just for a visit.

Catherine was working in the cool indirect light of the secretary's lair off the consulting room. With her warmth and her soft plumping figure and the friendly smile that crinkled up the lids of her candid brown eyes, she brought normality to the Restora.

She had lightened her covering make-up as she travelled through her thirties, and she wore none here, or when she was helping Peter at the Royal, because she hoped it would be encouraging for disfigured patients to see that she was one of them, and had survived.

Peter visited the patients who had been admitted for early operations tomorrow, and kept a few appointments in the consulting room: a haemangioma, a dissatisfied woman he could not put right because there was nothing wrong with her, and a recent rhinoplasty patient who had brought in the nose that Peter had created for her a month ago.

Her first post-operative euphoria at finally getting rid of the long bumpy tuber she had hated for years had worn off during the aftermath of pain and swelling. Her eyes were still too small. She felt cheated of miracles, worried about her sense of smell, even more worried by guilt.

'Was it *wrong* to have it done – vain, silly? My daughter disapproves, I think. My husband liked me all right the way I was.'

'There are no right and wrong operations,' Peter reminded her. 'Only wrong reasons for having them. You wanted this desperately, remember? And if it makes *you* feel better . . .'
He often had to shore up confidence with that small phrase, not less true for being simple.

'When I first dared to ask my GP about it,' the patient said, 'he told me, "I don't see anything the matter. What are you worried about?" '

Peter went to a file and showed her the full-face and profile pictures he had taken when he first saw her.

'Oh, my God!' She gave a little shriek. 'I should have come to you long ago.'

'But to ask for help is to admit how bad it is. That's hard. Enjoy my nose. When I see it next month, it will be perfect. The scarring is all inside.'

In the waiting room his wife was talking to the haemangioma patient, who still had scars from a skin graft on part of a portwine stain less deeply pigmented than Catherine's.

Having learned how to live with her own widespread blemish, Catherine was now able to advise and support other sufferers. Eleven years ago, a very young twenty-seven, she had sidled into Peter's room at the new Milner building, decked out unsuccessfully in a flamboyant broad-brimmed hat, her hair a jazzy blonde and her mouth crimson.

'Why do you get yourself up like that?' Peter had asked with polite interest. When a disfigured patient finally took the giant step of asking for help, you could usually get down to the truth pretty fast.

'It distracts from my face,' Catherine had said and wept, knocking off the dreadful hat, hanging the disastrous hair over her blazing cheek.

A biopsy had shown that the widespread discoloration was so deep that even partial excision and grafting would leave scars worse than the existing purple-red blemish. But Peter had seen her again, and again outside the hospital, for pleasure, and had sent her to learn about camouflage. Now she was able to help many of his disfigured patients, not because she was disfigured herself, but because she was a natural ally who just happened to be disfigured.

Chapter Two

'Mark!' Mrs Andrea Temple, Field Sales Manager in the Advertising Department of the *Grafton Weekly Chronicle*, put down the phone and called across Lois and Joan's desks to where Mark Emerson was tidying up so that he could slip away early. 'They want you back in Graphics.'

'What about?' Mark did not look up.

'The Edgemoor visual.'

'That's all done.' Mark picked up a pen and made marks on a piece of paper.

'I hope so. They still want you. Mark!' Mrs Temple raised her voice sharply, as he did not get out of his chair.

'In a moment.' Mark frowned busily at the scrap paper.

'Now!'

He got up slowly, and stopped by Joan's desk on his way

to the door to ask, 'Why doesn't she yell at *you*? Why always me?'

'Because it's usually your fault.'

'You've got a point there,' Mark said, with the comfortable grin of someone who is always right, so can afford to take the blame. He ambled down the corridor and stood in the Graphics doorway.

Jake, the scruffiest of the artists, had Mark's Edgemoor Hotel copy out on the table, with the layout. 'Is this what the client wants?'

'Looks like it. Very nice. Special evening out . . . singers, dancing, first glass of wine free . . .'

'What are they going to eat?'

'I shan't know till I get there. I'm hoping they'll give me and Judy a special rate.'

'No, look.' Jake ran the business end of a pencil through his hair. 'You've got here that they want "Menu" as a heading at the side, with fancy scrolls round. But your notes don't say what.'

'Don't they?' Mark tried innocence.

'You know they don't, and I should have got this finished and off to Production an hour ago. For God's *sake*, Mark – '

'No problem, no problem. Get it for you right away.'

Mark went back to his desk, rehearsing face-saving lines.

'Edgemoor? Manager, please . . . Oh, hullo, Mr Dean. I'm, er – Mark Emerson here, *Chronicle* Sales.'

'What's up?' Mr Dean sounded busy. 'I thought the advertisement was all settled.'

'Just checking.' Mark smiled, to put a smile into his voice. 'About the menu. I just want to make sure it's exactly the way you want it . . . Yes, if you would . . . Yes, Parma ham and honeydew melon. *Potage maison*, or . . .' By the time he could say genially, 'Nice talking to you, Mr Dean,' and put the phone down, his prickling scalp told him that the dreaded Temple was standing behind his chair.

He hunched his shoulders and did not turn round, so she came and leaned her bony hip against his desk.

'What was all that about, then? I thought your visuals were all done.'

'Just double-checking. The client is very particular.'

'And you missed a few details.' The voice would cut teak. 'Not been very thorough, have we?'

It was a good thing Mark knew she had a soft spot for him. The cold grey eye and little twitch at the side of the mouth did not reveal it.

'Come over to my desk and let's go through the drill.'

After he took the menu notes to Graphics, Mrs Temple made him go over all the niggling points of a display ad, as if he were a raw beginner, not a seasoned salesman, well known around this Somerset town.

'Exact placing of the logo. Did you get that from Mr Dean?'

'Well, I did ask that, of course, but he – he sort of left it up to me.'

'Mark.' Andrea Temple leaned back in her chair and looked at him pessimistically. 'Do you think you're in the right job?'

'Oh, yes.' Mark gave her disarming candour. 'My father always hoped I'd be an accountant, like him, but people and sales are more my thing.'

'Want to stay in this business?'

'If I can get ahead.'

'Of course,' said Mrs Temple, who knew that Mark had been in and out of half a dozen jobs since he dropped out of his first year at the technical college. 'But I'm fed up with mistakes. I think next time you call on a new client, I'll come with you and make sure you get it right.'

'No, please.' Mark stood up. 'I'm not a kid. I do a good job. The clients think so anyway.'

'I'm glad.' She had a nice line in ironic eyebrows.

'Confidence, Mrs Temple. Remember when you took me on, you said I needed more confidence.' Mark had been unusually nervous at his interview a year ago, so he had hammed it up a bit, but Andrea had seen through him. 'So I'm getting it, thanks to you.'

'That's enough.' Partial to him, as he believed she really was, she was like a mother refusing to be wooed by her children smarming round for sweets. 'Go back to work. And remember, you have been warned.'

Because she stayed at her corner desk facing him, Mark could not sneak off home. He made a few phone calls to set up appointments, and pottered industriously with his notes for tomorrow: the garden centre, the new chiropractor, half-price oil change and double coupons at the Esso station. The Temple warning was no joke. Mark made lists of basic points to cover, keeping his arm over the paper so that Lois could not see his kindergarten homework. If he lost this job, he would lose the company car, and at the moment that meant more to him than carving out a success in advertising and public relations.

The white Sierra was cold, but he removed his jacket to show his striped shirt and gaudy braces, although it was dark. It was six already. He had been at work since eight minutes past nine. Andrea Temple had greeted him with a finger of fate pointed at the clock. Slavery.

'Sorry I'm late, dear,' he would call out to Judy in the comfortable domestic voice he sometimes used to mock their fiery up-and-down relationship. 'Had to help the boss with a tricky bit of copy.'

'You drive yourself too hard,' Judy would say. 'I worry about you.'

The blue Toyota they shared wasn't in the car park. Judy wasn't in the flat. Mark had a beer and a salami sandwich. They would probably get a lot of stuff later at Bill and Marion's.

Judy came home late in her skimpy black business dress, looking even smaller about the body and face, as she did when she was tired.

'Where the hell have *you* been?' Mark called out, not angrily, more from ritual, like a wife who knows the old man stopped off at the pub.

'I had to stay for a supplier who came in late.' Judy was the buyer for a large gift shop near the abbey ruins. 'And stock-taking. It's been a hell of a day.'

'Go and have a shower.' One of Mark's panaceas. Sometimes he took three or four showers a day. 'You'll feel better when you take off that funeral outfit and put some proper clothes on.'

'Why?'

'We're going out, remember? Bill and Marion's party.'

'You go if you want. I'm exhausted.'

'You're coming!' Mark shouted at her.

'Okay.' She shook her ears like a dog bothered by a high-pitched smoke alarm. Sometimes she gave in quickly. Sometimes she shouted back, and they screamed and threw things and pretended to kill each other. Sometimes she opposed him silently. She was five years older than Mark. She was a lovely woman.

The party was like most parties, fair enough, but never up to expectations. Mark charged in and gave it his all, making a lot of noise, laughing and joking and playing the crowd of familiars and strangers until he thought he had delighted everyone worth delighting. In the kitchen a minor television actor was attracting attention. Mark poured himself a drink and joined the group. The actor was dull, with a mild round face and glasses. Restless, Mark padded into the other room and pulled Judy up from the floor.

'Time to go.'

'Hang on.' She sat down again and finished her conversation with a woman in a sari, then got up and followed Mark out to the crowded hall, where he was making the evening worth while for a vapid girl who couldn't breathe through her nose.

'I'm ready.' Judy's geometrically cut head appeared on the level of Mark's shoulder.

'I'm not.' He continued with the adenoid girl, although he was longing to escape, and Judy leaned against the door frame and closed her eyes.

'Where are we going?' she asked, as Mark turned the car away from home.

'Look in at the Fountainhead, see what's doing.'

'I'll sit in the car park.'

'Not safe.' At the pub he pulled her out and put his arm through hers, so that they went into the noisy bar as a couple, welcomed, popular. There were a few friends there, and some loose jokes and insults as Mark integrated himself into the surroundings, and into the attention of a plump blonde girl he recognized as Debbie, secretary to the *Chronicle*'s Advertising Manager.

When Judy went to sit down with orange juice, Debbie advanced on Mark, throwing her yellow hair about and pushing out well-lubricated lips.

'Hello, big boy.' They had met occasionally in the *Chronicle* corridors, but her boss was far above Mark, who was trapped in lowly thrall to Andrea Temple. Debbie put hot hands on his arms and drooled at him. 'You are a luscious piece of meat, Markie. You are so good-looking, it kills me every time I see you in the office. Perfect, you know, except for this.' She put up a finger and touched the rough crooked scar on his cheek.

Mark took the hand and kissed it. It smelled of shrimp crisps. 'Who wants to be perfect?'

'Not you, darlin'.' She was well away. 'You're battle-scarred. Like one of them, you know, German students. Got slashed in a duel, didn't you?'

The man she was with pulled her away, and there was some scuffling. The sensible people had left, and before the others got thrown out at closing time, there was a scrap, half serious, half clowning. Mark hit someone in the chest – he wasn't sure who – spilled a drink, got punched, punched back, tripped someone up, and roared into an argument with the landlord, who didn't see the joke.

Outside, it was:

'Good old Mark.'

'Take him away, Judy.'

'See you tomorrow, Debbie.'

'If they let you in.'

'Who cares?'

'Don't give a damn about anything, do you, big boy?'

'Night, then, Dicky – night Joe!'

'Night, Scarface!'

Mark laughed – he always laughed at the nickname Joe threw at him – and yelled a last fading insult as the noise thinned out and the silly little crowd scattered.

'Why do you have to be like that?' Judy asked Mark at home.

'Like what?'

'Noisy, showing off, getting into scenes.'

'No one else complains.'

'I do.'

'I've been like that since you've known me.'

'It's losing some of its charm.' Judy went into the bedroom of the flat and took off her sweater and jeans.

'Then why do you stay with me?' he asked comfortably, pulling her roughly to him. In her bra and underpants, she was like a child pretending to need a bra.

'Who knows?'

'You know.' Mark bent her backwards and leaned over her, growling, and she put up her hand to touch the scar on his right cheek that made his smile slightly crooked. 'You think it's ugly,' he accused her.

'No – it's part of you.'

'My warrior's tribal badge. Scarred at the initiation rites. That fat girl at the pub – '

'What girl?'

'I saw you watching over your orange juice. She thought this was a duelling scar.'

'Did you tell her about a drunken teenager turning his Dad's car upside down?'

He pushed Judy on to the bed and fell on top of her, but

she wriggled away from under him, and put on the frayed blue shirt Mark used to wear when he was working with the boat builder.

'Your mother rang after you left this morning,' Judy said.

'What did she want?' Mark pictured his mother at the kitchen wall phone in the Birmingham suburb, perched impatiently on the edge of the counter, smiling as she waited to hear his voice, raising her thick eyebrows when Judy answered, and dropping the smile.

'You should send something for your father's birthday.'

'Why?'

'You always have.'

'Under pressure.' A book, a pen, a gadget the old man didn't need. 'Oh, hell, I'll send a bloody card.'

Seeing that Mark was dropping into a sulk, Judy began to coax him out of it, brisk as an older sister, because a short sex session was easier than letting Mark develop his sulk into a full-blown grievance.

Judy saw sex as a simple practical pleasure, especially when she was tired. Mark tightened his hands round her frail wrists, and wanted her to play Caliph and Slave.

'Put your legs together, so I can force them apart.'

'I want them apart. Come on, Mark. Don't mess about.'

'Slut!' he hissed.

All right, she would say it. 'Violator!' All was going quite well, until Judy turned her head to stifle a yawn against his arm, and then took the lead efficiently, to dispatch the business so that she could go to sleep.

'That does it!' With excruciating agony to himself, Mark got off and flung away and fell on the sofa in the other room, because if it couldn't be done his way, then the hell with it.

Chapter Three

On the first morning of the New Year, Peter was at the hospital to see his patients – burns, windscreen lacerations, a multiple sclerosis pressure sore – and to examine Annette, who was due for her first major skin grafts the next day.

'Happy New Year, Mr Freeman.' Annette's father, not an elegant figure at any time, was a rumpled chunk in the green hospital gown.

'And a hopeful one for your family.'

Annette was holding her own. How she would weather the long series of demanding operations remained to be seen, but the start of the carefully planned graft programme brought to Peter a confidence and strength that he could already feel in his hands.

'We're going to start with that right upper forearm and

elbow, and then go step by step from there, aren't we, Annette?'

She could not nod, because of the pain and the padded collar of dressings on her neck, but she gave him a tight smile and her usual trusting stare out of those arresting slate-blue eyes. The nurses said she sometimes whispered to them, but she had not spoken to Peter since she was brought in. He talked to her constantly when he was working on her small suffering body, and told her everything he was going to do; and because of those clear, direct eyes, her silence, like an animal's, communicated with him.

No favourites had been one of the aphorisms of the great Thomas Sutcliffe, Peter's teacher at Guy's. 'Love all your surgery, but not one patient above another.'

Oracular advice, but feelings were inescapable: Annette is *mine*.

'Step by step, that's right, Mr Freeman.' The child's mother answered for her through the cotton mask tied round the bunchy paper cap that covered her hair. 'We know it's going to be a long journey, but Annette is a brave girl. I've brought both my children up to understand that life isn't easy, but faith conquers all, isn't that right, Ted?'

Mr Leigh took this kind of stuff stoically, and no doubt his struggling, anxious wife would come down to earth as the first crisis settled into the long day-to-day life of the Milner Unit, to which this family had been condemned by that moment when the red dressing gown caught and flared in the treacherous heater.

After stopping in at the Restora to see his old naval captain, whose new wife had insisted on excision of a misguided youthful tattoo, Peter drove twenty miles along the coast to his small white house at the edge of the Farne estuary. It was their summer place, but they spent some weekends here all the year round, and always New Year's Eve. When the tide was high, the angry winter seas boiled up almost to the top of the rock wall that held the old coastguard cottage on its grass ledge. At low tide the deep, narrow river channel followed its ancient pattern through the long sands that shone far out beyond the headland, golden in the low sun, streaked silver under the moon.

Catherine was down on the beach with Philip and Evie, who was throwing an orange ball for Archie to swim after through the channel. The yellow Labrador's barking echoed from cliff to cliff across the estuary.

Peter kicked off his respectable doctor shoes and socks, rolled up his trousers and climbed down the rock steps to join them. Phil and his Nigerian friend, Njoba, the son of a physician at the Royal, were plaguing Evie, snatching the ball from her and running away, shouting, with the dog into the icy offshore wind.

'They are rotten boys.' Catherine's thick hair was wild, her cheek whipped into a darker red glow.

'Who cares? Dad and I will look for saltwood.'

Peter and his daughter were collectors of small pieces of wood rubbed smooth and blunt by years in the sea, tossed up, dragged out again, thrown up at last to lodge by a rock or above the tidemark. They painted tiny figures on them of people and animals they thought might have drowned at sea.

As they wandered off with their heads down, picking up scraps of wood and rejecting them, for they were very particular about their collection, Evie asked her father, 'Is Mum's face like that because you hit her?'

'No – what on earth are you saying? You know Mum's mark was born with her.'

'There's a girl at school – she said Mum was a battered wife.'

'I'll batter *her*. You want me to talk to her?'

'Oh, no!' Crouched by a rock pool, Evie turned to look at him, her wet salty hair whipped across her scowling face.

'Darling, what *is* the matter? Is something wrong at school?' The child had few but likeable friends. He remembered the offensive girl in the purple anorak. Why had Evie wanted her to meet him? 'Is anybody giving you a hard time?'

Evie shook her head violently, and pounced on a short piece of curved wood that might once have been part of a barrel stave.

'Nice shape but too splintery,' Peter said. 'I could sand it down, if you like.'

His daughter threw the piece of wood away.

As the stormy light left the sky, they climbed up the rocks and sat round the kitchen table for tea and toasted buns before setting off for home.

Peter asked the boys casually, 'Does anyone tease Evie at school?'

'I don't know.' A year and a half older, Phil's world of school was far removed. 'Why should they?'

'Who is it that thinks this is a bruise,' Catherine put a hand over her left cheek, still darkly reddened from the cold wind on the beach, 'not a birthmark?'

Evie shot a glance at her father that said he shouldn't have told. To protect her mother, or to exclude her from the secret? Sometimes she panicked because her mother and father were not together enough. Sometimes she tried to divide them.

'What do you mean? I don't know.' Philip and his friend were clearing out the biscuit tins, because biscuits would get soft here by the sea before they came again. 'No one says anything to me.'

'I was teased at school,' Catherine told Njoba. 'When I was small, I don't remember minding, but when I was Evie's age, and Phil's, I hated myself.' She and Peter had always been quite matter-of-fact with the children and their friends about her disfigurement. 'My mother pretended the mark didn't exist. That made it worse. I used to brush my hair without looking in the mirror, because if she couldn't face it, nor could I.'

The Nigerian boy stared at her intently. Had he too suffered because of his skin?

'On the wall in the dining room, there was a picture of me aged about four or five, posed in a studio in my best dress. I looked like a little angel. She'd had the birthmark brush-stroked out. When I was angry, I used to turn that picture round to face the wall.'

She laughed, and Phil and Njoba laughed too, eating. Philip asked, 'Is that why you married a plastic surgeon – because he's seen it all before?' and Njoba wanted to know, 'What does a birthmark look like on a black person?'

'Dark purple, less noticeable than mine.'

Peter was going to add something, but Evangeline turned pointedly to him and ordered, 'Tell me some more about the Father Christmas girl.' Annette was in his mind all the time, and he had been talking about her on the beach. 'Where are you going to take the graft from?' Evie demanded. 'How big will it have to be? Show me here, on my arm.'

Mark and Judy went to a New Year's Eve party where everybody wore a mask. Judy had brought home two funny animal faces from the gift shop. She was a cat with earrings. Mark was a fox, with triangular eye slits and a thick swag of coarse hair under the snout, like a terrorist moustache, only ginger.

At midnight masks came off. Surprise! It did not make much difference to the way people behaved. Mark wanted to keep the fox mask on, but someone snatched it off, and he instinctively put up a hand to the scar on his cheek. After that he was noisier, because he had more breath. Judy continued to talk long and seriously to a man she knew who worked for the BBC in Bristol. He had arrived with another man, and both wore black demonic masks and tight black clothes; Mark supposed they were poofs.

After 'Auld Lang Syne' and all the inane jokes, they played a game called 'Resolutions', in which New Year's resolutions were written on pieces of paper and thrown into a bowl, for people to pick at random and read out as if they had written them themselves. 'Wash my feet more than once a week', 'Stop picking my nose in traffic jams', 'Keep my legs together' were fair examples.

Judy got 'Lose forty pounds by March', which was ludicrous, because she was so tiny. Poor old Robert, whose only son was doing time for drugs in Kuala Lumpur, had to read out 'Keep my paternity payments up to date', which fell flat.

Mark hoped he could get a good easy laugh out of

whatever he picked. He dug to the bottom of the bowl and held the folded paper in his hand for a moment before he looked at it.

Some total idiot had written 'Be kind to children and old ladies – keep my mask on all year'. Ha ha. He held the paper close up to his eyes and invented 'Save a homeless man from freezing – set fire to his cardboard box'.

'Bit raw that,' someone said. 'Who wrote it?'

No one owned up. Mark crumpled the 'children and old ladies' paper in his pocket and put on his fox mask again, to enfold Judy in a fierce New Year embrace.

She screamed and struggled and choked on the bristly moustache. He tried to get her off by herself, but there were couples in all the bedrooms, so they went into a small place of coats and muddy boots, and he pulled the mask down to hang round his neck and told her earnestly, 'I'll be better to you this year, I promise.'

'You said that last year.' Judy could keep a straight face and laugh at him with her eyes.

'And I was, wasn't I? I agreed to sharing the flat. I got a job. I was nice to your parents. A lovely boy, they think I am.'

'Do they?'

'Don't laugh at me. I'll work for a rise. I'll humble myself before the Temple of tyranny and sell more advertising space than anyone on the paper. Than anyone who's ever *been* on the paper.'

The door from the kitchen opened and several people barged out through the back door, pushing Mark and Judy into the coats.

'Let's go too, Mark.'

'I'll get your jacket.' Another revolutionary reform. He pulled up the mask.

'Don't put that thing on again.'

'A new me, a new face.'

Going to work after a break was always a struggle, but the new Mark got up when Judy woke him on Monday, and was in the Grafton *Chronicle* office before Andrea Temple, who ruffled his hair as she came in.

'Get your hair cut, Emerson.'

'No way.' His clean strong dark brown hair was a good length. He liked pushing it back when it fell forward, and running his hands through it, and coming up from a dive in the pool with it plastered round his face.

The week was like any other. Why did everyone get so excited when the year changed? Nothing happened, except that Mark had another fight with Judy about sloppy habits. Perhaps his parents were right about not getting mixed up with an older woman. This ancient Somerset town, fighting to keep its country and mystical image in the teeth of high-tech development, was a dead end. Work was boring. Clients were nobodies. The paper was rubbish. But by Friday the big new conference hotel was ready to announce: 'Opening in the Spring!'

'This is important,' he told Andrea Temple. 'Several big teaser ads now, then Grand Opening – full page with all the trimmings – and it should grow into a red-hot regular account.'

'Perhaps I'd better go and see them, then.'

'Thanks, Mrs Temple,' Mark said, as if she had offered him a favour, not an insult. 'I've already talked to Mr Dietz a couple of times. I'll stick with it.'

'Well, don't mess it up.'

Mark came behind her chair and pressed a hand on her shoulder pad. 'Thanks for caring.'

The meeting went well. The hotel manager knew what he wanted and had detailed copy ready. It all looked so promising that Mark took him out to lunch to talk about the future campaign over whisky.

'I pulled it off,' he told the unimpressed personnel of Field and Telesales, who had been to lunch later than him and come back earlier.

'You'll pull yourself right out of this job if you aren't careful,' Andrea said without looking up. 'You had an appointment with Datronics at two. They rang twice. If you don't get out there right away, they'll ring the manager next time.'

Rushing out, Mark met the manager's secretary in the corridor, big blonde Debbie, and skidded to a stop to chat her up.

'I thought we were going to have a date,' she said succulently, one hip out, sweater like a twin hammock.

'Oh, are – yes, aren't we?' Better keep in with her.

'Maybe we is, maybe we ain't.' She switched her weight to the other hip, appraising his agitation and flushed face.

Before Annette's operation, Peter had marked the donor sites on areas of her back that had not been damaged by the fire, low enough to hide the scars in later years of low dresses and swimsuits. Her chances were not amazingly good, but he had to approach each of these crucial operations as if they were a hundred per cent certain of success.

For the long ragged burn on the upper arm, he removed

a partial-thickness slice of skin tissue about six by four inches. He dressed the raw site, and while he and theatre sister cleaned and trimmed the deep arm wound, Noel processed the skin in the meshing machine into a web of fine strips, like a string vest, to expand it to three times its size.

When the graft was sutured and a thick pressure dressing in place, Annette was carefully turned again. Sister handed Peter the dermatome, an instrument like a cheese slicer, and he harvested another patch of skin to make a mesh graft for the right elbow. This graft took longer, because of the delicacy of trying to ensure that the joint would keep full mobility.

You could never be absolutely certain. Grafts could contract, wrinkle, form ugly scars, distort surrounding tissue. But this one had gone well, and when the pad of antiseptic dressing was in place and the whole arm splinted to prevent any movement while healing began, Peter realized that he had begun to hum softly, a sign that he was relaxed and hopeful.

Sally, his trusted and dependable theatre sister who never said much, nodded at him. Noel, whose voice was always heard, said briskly, 'Looks very good, sir.'

The note of slightly patronizing surprise did not bother Peter. He was too glad and relieved that the first step toward reconstructing Annette had gone so well.

Annette's mother was in the hospital all the time. When Annette began to surface from the no-man's-land where sleeping merged with waking, and night and day did not exist beyond a vague tendency to be light or dark, she wondered, 'Why aren't you at work?' Her mother was supposed to be out of the house before Annette and Campbell left for school.

'They can get along without me.'

Annette whispered, 'You'll lose the Council job,' and her mother said, 'Who cares?' It seemed to be all right for her to be permanently in this room, coaxing Annette's dry lips with ice-cream and lemonade, washing her face and brushing her hair, talking comfortable nonsense through the terror times of pain and the black howling voices.

After what they said was the operation, which Annette could not remember, she became aware that her father was sometimes there, stuffed into his dark business suit. Mum carried on about his shirts.

'You sell washing-machines, Ted. You ought to know how to use one.'

One day Annette's grandmother brought her brother in to see her. He was paralysed with fear. Annette wanted to tell him, 'It's all right, Cammy, it's only me,' but he would not come close to the bed, and she could not even whisper.

Poor Cammy shuffled in with his track-suit trousers tied too loose, the strings hanging down, the top bunched up, and a gap of skin in the middle, falling over his big feet on the way to the windowsill, where he felt safer with the furry animals.

'Don't stay too long,' Mum told Gran.

'We've only just come.'

'She's very frail.'

'I can see that for myself.'

'How's the boy been?' From the bedside Mum looked round and held out her hand, but Cammy would not come to her.

'He's no trouble to *me*,' Gran said, as if poor Campbell were a bad lot. 'But Ted says he's been carrying on with nerves and nightmares. Though what *he's* got to carry on about, when my little Annette – '

'Keep your voice low,' Mum whispered. 'Don't upset her.'

'I'm upsetting myself. To see that little one lying . . .' Gran had a bit of a cry. Mum passed her a tissue.

She was getting ready to leave when Mr Freeman looked in.

'Come in, Doctor.' Mum was in charge of the room. 'My mother, Mrs Last.'

Gran had on her green knitted suit and the black high-heeled boots that clung round the bulge of her legs. 'Campbell.' She gave him her Mrs Thatcher voice. 'Come and shake hands.' She tried to make him move forward, but he only stared with his ugliest dumb face, holding the floppy pop-singer doll from the windowsill.

'Come along.' Gran tugged at his loose track-suit. 'Put the doll down. It belongs to Annette.'

'She don't want it,' Cammy muttered.

'It was brought for your sister,' Mum said in the fair's-fair voice that drove her children round the bend when they wanted to shout and argue.

Annette wanted to shout now, 'Let him take it!' but her voice was somewhere else.

'Why don't you let him have it?' Mr Freeman, examining her puffy hand, raised his head and said it for her. He and she understood each other so well, without words between them.

A week after the first surgery, Peter and his colleague Richard Valentine did two more excisions and grafts on Annette's other elbow and on the badly burned area of her neck, from chin to clavicle. It was a long and difficult operation, and Annette did not recover as well as from the first one. Her temperature stayed up, there were signs of septicaemia, and, after a few days, some kidney dysfunction.

Richard and Noel wanted her in the main hospital Intensive Care, but it was too far from the Milner Unit, and Peter wanted Annette here, under his eye, and in the care of his hand-picked nurses. Annette was extremely ill. He told her parents that, but did not add that she might be nearer to death than at any time since the night of the fire. With some you could, with others you couldn't.

Deirdre Leigh, although tense and exhausted, with the colour drained from her skin and hair, had developed a stoic surface, as hospital mothers did, through long vigils. Ted was shaky. He did not come in as often.

'He can't take it,' Deirdre told Peter.

'Not everyone can.'

But this was just the beginning. If Annette got through, there were still months of trauma and anxiety ahead for all the family.

And for the surgeon. Peter had lost patients – burned, crushed, mutilated, too far consumed by cancer to survive excision and reconstruction – and had had to detach himself from disappointment and grief to do his best for other patients. The living pulled you away from the dead; but each loss remained as a shadow on the vista of memory.

Annette (*No favourites*) he could not lose. And if she continued in life, it must be in a body as near perfect as he could give her. No one should ever look away from Annette Leigh in shock or embarrassment. *There are no miracles* was another of Tom Sutcliffe's maxims. But with skill and great care, scars might eventually be faint or cunningly hidden, skin tone and texture almost exact.

Annette is mine to save.

Soaking the dressings off the first grafts was so painful and traumatic that Sister Janet asked Deirdre to be there with Annette while it was done. Deirdre talked, nonsense mostly, in a soothing monotone. She would not look at what Janet and the student nurse were doing. But when the pad of bandage was eased off the right elbow, she saw, and, with the breath knocked out of her, could only croak, 'Cover it up before she sees.'

Janet glanced at Annette, mercifully sedated. 'Mr Freeman will be here in a moment to examine the grafts.'

'*What has he done?*'

The inside of the delicate elbow flared, discoloured purple-red like raw liver. The grafted skin was an angry grid of crusts and blisters.

'Don't worry, my dear.' Big husky Janet strove to be gentle and tactful with families, although her natural style was gruff and blunt. 'This looks quite normal.'

'There's something wrong.' Deirdre raised her voice angrily. 'What has he *done?*'

'Hush, please. The surgeon', Janet said rather stuffily, 'has excised or repaired deeply damaged tissue and ligaments and performed a satisfactory mesh graft to the antecubital fossa, the inside of the elbow.'

Annette began to open her eyes blearily, so Janet put a sterile towel over the graft, and the mother bit her lips and sat down and waited, stoic again, for Mr Freeman.

When Annette's condition improved, the doctor told her exhausted mother to spend a night or two at home.

'Is that an order?'

'Well – yes, if you like. Annette and I need you. We can't let you collapse.'

'No fear of that.' She flexed a stringy arm. 'My strength is as the strength of ten.'

'There are limits.'

'If you ask for fortitude, Mr Freeman, it is given to you.'

'Then please ask for the fortitude to spend a few nights in your own bed.'

Deirdre came home to see what Ted and Campbell had been up to. They had prepared the house for her. Ted had washed dishes, bleached the sink, swept the kitchen floor, put the rubbish outside, and thrown away the pile of junk mail on the hall table, so that Deirdre could not blame him for not taking up special offers that might have won her thirty thousand pounds. Cammy had dusted with a dirty vest, magnetized a cartoon joke about a doctor to the refrigerator door, changed his pillowcase and tidied some of the clutter of his room into the drawer under his bunk bed.

'Right.' When Deirdre got home, she rolled up her sleeves. 'I'll just have a whizz round.'

'Now Deedree, don't start,' Ted begged. 'I thought you were dead beat. There's a stew in the oven, and I've got a bottle of wine to celebrate.'

'Celebrate what? Me here and my Annette in the hospital?'

'Don't carry on, dear,' Ted said. 'Pull down your sleeves and pull up a chair. Nothing to fret over, Edward is here.' One of his feeble verses might relax her.

But Deirdre took a tour of the house before she would sit down, sniffing into the refrigerator, running up the stairs, opening windows, flushing the lavatory twice.

'Everything all right?' Ted put his bowl of sloppy stew on the table, the thumb of the crusty oven glove in the gravy. He stood back on his heels and smiled at his wife, blinking and pushing his glasses back on his short thick nose.

'You did your best.' Deirdre threw chocolate wrappers from her son's room into the bin. She sat down at the table by the kitchen window and tested the dry earth of the plants on the sill with her knuckle.

Ted said, 'Piping hot, that's your lot,' and ladled out stew cheerfully. 'Isn't it nice for the family to be together again?'

'It's not the family without Annette.' Deirdre rested her head on her long bony hand and pushed the food about with a fork.

'When's she coming home?' Cammy ate with his chair pushed back from the table and his large feet on the rung, leaning forward on his elbows to shovel in stew and bread.

'Take off that dreadful cap,' his mother said. But the maroon and white baseball cap that said ROVERS 88 was as necessary as hair to the eleven-year-old boy. She must know that.

Cammy jerked his head away and asked again, sulkily, 'When's Annette coming home?'

'Who knows, Campbell, who knows?'

'Nev – never?' The boy choked on the word.

'No, of course not.' His father leaned across to pile potatoes on his plate.

His mother said, 'All those operations, it's more than flesh and blood can stand. They slice bits of healthy skin from her back,' she told Cammy, who pulled the peak of the cap lower over his eyes, 'and sew them over the burned places. And a terrible mess they've made of her elbow.' She took her hand away from her bunched-up hair and clenched it into a fist, and made a fist of the other hand that held the fork, prongs up, pounding the table on either side of her plate. 'I wouldn't want you to see it, Ted. It looks horrible.'

'What does Mr Freeman say?'

'Oh, he's pleased with it, of course. They always are. I was in shock. That big Janet, who looks like a man dressed up as a nurse, gave me the business. ''Mr Freeman has performed a satisfactory mesh graft to the antecubital fossa.'' ' She mimicked the nurse's professional tone. 'Annette was doing all right before the second operation.' Deirdre's eyes were fixed on something beyond the silver and grey striped wallpaper and the Gauguin prints that she set such store by.

'It had to be done, Dee.'

'Not so soon.' Deirdre was an expert now, after all the time in the hospital.

'But he's so many grafts still to do if she's not to be disfigured for life. Hands, thighs, her stomach, Mr Freeman said. The job's got to be done.'

'But does he know his job?' She looked at Ted bleakly, her eyes watery, her mouth screwed into a bitter shape.

'Deedree!' Ted flushed up red into his low-growing hair. 'He's the best there is, you know that. I thought he was your god.'

'Well, you've got to suck up to them.' Deirdre sat back and lit a cigarette. 'They're all vain. If you don't lick their boots, they take it out on the patient.'

'That's paranoid. Calm down.' Ted was nervous. 'Don't start.'

'Don't *you* start. Haven't I had enough?' She simmered, smoking one cigarette after another, staring at nothing while Ted cleared the table round her. Campbell had taken three choc-ices out of the freezer and banged out of the house.

After school next day the boy did his homework as requested, because it was easier than telling his mother that Dad let him do it at ten pm, after the guns-and-guts shows. When Mum had folded piles of laundry and paired a dozen socks and prepared a shepherd's pie to be heated up for supper, she left the cooking things in the sink and put on her boots and big brown coat with the cape effect that made her look like a highwayman.

'Where are you going?'

'To the hospital. Dad will be home in about an hour.'

'I hate the hospital.' Campbell punched the air.

'You never go there.'

'Because I hate it.'

'Poor Annette.'

'How can *I* help her?'

'You can't. The shepherd's needs twenty minutes at two hundred and you can have frozen carrots.'

'Thanks for nothing. When are you coming back?'

'I'll see. I might sleep there.'

'You're supposed to stay here!' Cammy jumped up and grabbed the wide skirt of her coat and dragged her back, so that she staggered, and dropped on the sofa. He got on top of her and pounded her, but she was still stronger than him – just – and she struggled to her feet and slapped him. He swore at her.

'Don't be rude, with that ugly face.'

He couldn't help his face, but he could make it uglier. 'You're to come back.' He glowered. 'I can't sleep.'

'What rubbish. Gran said she couldn't get you up for school.'

'I had the nightmares.'

'Big boy like you. She give you a fried supper?'

She ran her hands through her straight limp hair, tucking it behind her ears, and put on bright pink lipstick, beyond the edges of her narrow mouth. In the hall she turned back to him to say, 'I'm sorry about this, son, I really am, but you do understand, don't you?'

He was deaf and mute.

'Gi's a kiss, then.'

He would not kiss her, with or without the lipstick.

Annette's next grafts were delayed until she had slowly fought her way back to some strength and stability. She was still anaemic, and very subdued. She talked intermittently to her family and the nurses and cleaners, and to the senior registrar, Noel, who could make her laugh, which she had to do without moving her jaw, because of the neck graft. Peter could not always even make her smile. She followed him with her clear blue Icelandic eyes, but in their six weeks of close involvement in the unit she still had not spoken to him.

One afternoon in February Peter saw that one of the names on his clinic list was Dawn Dodd.

Peter had known Dawn for all of her six years of life, and she had spent almost as much of them in the hospital as at home. Home had been a shifting affair in any case.

Dawn had been born with a frontal encephalocele. The front

of her skull was not joined, and the brain, which had formed in the womb before the bone, was pushed forward through the gap into a huge ballooning sac of brain tissue and fluid. From the first drastic operation at three weeks, the baby and her mother had survived years of interminable risky surgery to close the skull and gradually reduce the mass of tissue and leaking fluid that dominated the upper part of her face.

Her father, a come-and-go character at the best of times, had passed out in Maternity when he saw the baby, and disappeared for good after the second or third operation, protesting that he could take no more meningitis crises and horrified looks in the street from people who were old enough and ugly enough to know better.

Dawn and her mother Beverly, with no visible family, had lived in bed-sits, hostels, high-rise ghettos, basements, and on the sagging sofas of friends and brief acquaintances who were not much better off. Bev was a bit of a rogue, who drank and gambled when she could, and took up with drifting scoundrels, but she had stuck by Dawn, while the monstrous deformity had gradually metamorphosed under Peter's hands to a sunny, beaming face with bright black eyes whose inner corners were obscured by the lump of thickened nose. More delicate operations into her teens would almost completely correct the blemish.

In Peter's consulting room the child held up her face to be kissed, then went straight to the biscuit tin on the bookshelf.

'Everything all right?' Peter had not seen Dawn for months, but she was as important to him and the whole unit as if she were still the constant customer she used to be.

'As such, Mr Freeman.' Beverly had gone brunette. Her

cheeky starveling face looked perkily out between curtains of straight-cut hair.

'Her next check-up isn't for a few months, is it?'

'This is different. I'm broke.'

'Do you want to see someone from Social Services?'

'No, look, I've had my lot – and more, thanks to this hospital. It's just that I can never quite manage.'

'You don't seem worried, Bev.'

'No, because I came to tell you – I've had fantastic luck!'

She had met a man in a pub. Worked on a paper, nice fellow, bright, interested, the kind you could really talk to. They had gone back to the damp basement room where Bev and Dawn were living, 'Until that cow runs dry of the milk of human compassion and puts us out, because of how much I owe her.

'This guy, Denis his name is, I told him some of the story and he was very fascinated with Dawn. Wanted to see her old pictures, especially the baby ones, where she looked – well, *you* should know.'

'I was born with a balloon on my face,' Dawn said chattily, coming to lean on the desk beside Peter and make a picture on the pad on which he drew simple surgical diagrams for patients.

Denis worked for a tabloid newspaper. 'Next day, he talked it all up to whoever cooks up the heart-tug stuff.' Beverly paused and sucked in her breath, then leaned forward and looked intently at Peter. *'They want to do Dawn's story.* Can you imagine? "A Miracle Dawns – When she was born, we prayed she wouldn't live." Well – my mother did say something like that, you know, after I sent her a picture to Australia.'

'Well now,' Peter said cautiously, 'do you really want them to do this?'

'For ten thousand pounds? You bet I do. Good, eh? So, since Dawn is, like, sort of your creation, I came to ask you, what do you say?'

'It needs some careful thought.'

'They want a decision tomorrow.'

'That sort of paper – they do mess – do, er – take liberties with the facts, you know.'

'Den says there'll be nothing in it I don't want.'

'What about Dawn? What do you think of being in a newspaper?' he asked the child.

She shrugged the shoulder nearest to him, absorbed in her coloured drawing.

'Dawnie? She's a ham. You know how she loves attention.'

'Well . . . Thanks for telling me, anyway.'

'I'm glad you approve.'

'It's your business, Bev, not mine.'

'No, listen. Why I came was, they want pictures, of course. You've got dozens in Dawn's file, and I thought, perhaps you could get them released.'

'It would have to go through the Health Department.'

'Plus they've got to talk to you. Not Denis, he's not doing the story. One of their top writers, he said.' Beverly leaned forward, nodding at Peter encouragingly.

'Oh, but I don't think –'

Beverly leaned back into herself, her face closed into secrecy, and Peter guessed that she had already accepted the paper's offer.

'And if I said no?'

'You won't, Mr Freeman.'

Dawn straightened up and slid her coloured picture in front of him. 'For the board.' That was where the unit had pinned up snapshots of small patients for the last twelve years, and their works of art and love letters.

What could he tell Beverly? 'I suppose I don't mind,' he said slowly.

'Yes, you do,' she said sharply. 'You're so bloody modest. Remember those American surgeons, and you didn't know what to do with the praise? "Just a repairman." Yanks say thanks if they get a compliment. If you're thinking,' she added craftily, ' "Haven't I done enough for them?", you don't need to do this for me really, you know.'

Peter laughed at her. 'I don't mind you putting me on the spot, but I don't want it to look like advertising. There are hundreds of surgeons doing what I do.'

'But only one Dawn Dodd.'

'Perhaps a few quotes so they get the technical stuff more or less right . . . I suppose there's nothing wrong with a bit of good public relations for reconstructive surgery and our unit.'

'Friends of the Milner.' Beverly had helped them to raise money, although she never had any herself. 'The committee would love you.' She stood up. 'And so would me and Dawn.'

'You do already.'

She nodded. She had often told him. 'And now it's worth ten grand.'

When they had gone, he asked the secretary for Dawn Dodd's photograph file. All the patients had pictures taken when Peter or Richard first saw them, and again at every stage of the reconstruction, before and after.

He looked through some of those early pictures: the great blinding balloon of membrane, the wide distorted skull, the suffocated nose and misshapen lips, Beverly in a hospital dressing gown holding the newborn with the tender pride of a mother with her 'perfect baby'. Although Peter remembered all the stages, all the disappointments and setbacks and small triumphs of healing and renewal, it was hard to believe that the pitiful little grotesque was the origin of the charming sprite who had gone straight to the biscuit tin and then to his pad and the mug of coloured pencils.

Annette was alone in her room. Her colour was better. She was listening to the tape recorder and keeping a gentle beat with one of her bandaged hands.

'I think we can start the grafts on your left thigh in a few days,' Peter told her. 'All right with you?'

She hated the operations. She cried when she had to be lifted on to the trolley. But she gave him a small nod, eyes fixed on his, mouth uncertain.

'You're doing very well, you know. I'm putting you on my honour roll of heroes and heroines.'

He told her about Dawn. 'Born with even worse damage than has been done to you. Her face was all wrong and she's had dozens of operations, and been so brave, and put up with children calling her names. She's won her reward for courage. She's almost perfect now.'

Annette's dry lips opened, and she spoke to Peter for the first time.

'Will you make me perfect?'

'I'll do my best.' He could hardly answer.

'Promise?'

'Promise.' He turned his head away, and met the inquiring glance of Janet, coming through the door with the quick light movements that some big women achieve.

Chapter Four

After all the Christmas and New Year rubbish had been cleared out of the *Chronicle*, there were January sales to clutter up Mark Emerson's life, with regular retail customers coming in to update their advertisements, and Andrea Temple chivvying him out of the office to bully promising clients into a bigger display ad this year. After that, it would be sodding Saint Valentine.

Occasionally, if he had a client across the canal not too far from the flat he shared with Judy in one of the new blocks, Mark would nip home for a beer and five minutes' feet-up to see what kind of television was watched by people who stayed at home all day. No harm in that. He could still get in all his client calls, or leave them for next day.

'Town and Country?' Mrs Temple had a sceptical habit

of going through his list every morning. 'I thought you saw them yesterday. And that was a close shave, for a half page. If they want to change their image, Graphics will need extra time.'

'I did go,' Mark said, wide-eyed, innocent. 'The chap wasn't there.'

'What chap?'

'The new man – what's-his-name.'

'Hadn't you made an appointment?'

'Yes, but it takes two to keep it.'

On Valentine's Day Mark Emerson brought chocolates to all the women in the Advertising Department, and flowers for the divine Andrea. It cost a lot, but they were really pleased, and even Andrea seemed more indulgent.

A few weeks later, one extra busy afternoon when Lois had stayed home sick – literally sick, Mark supposed, since the immoderate woman was pregnant – he nipped off home to have a shower, fell on to the sofa wrapped in a towel, and nodded off.

The telephone woke him. Without thinking, he picked it up. It was Andrea Temple. He couldn't hang up, because he had already said, 'Hullo, Mark Emerson,' in the brisk salesman's style he had carried home from the office.

It was a bit awkward. Andrea had checked the messages that Telesales had taken for him, seen that one was urgent, and rung Homecraft Furniture, where he was supposed to be.

'When they said they'd not seen you, I tried the clients on either side of that appointment, and then rang this number, on a chance.'

'I got pizza on my shirt. I just – '

'You've had two warnings,' Andrea said. 'This is two and a half.'

She had left when Mark got back to the office at the end of the afternoon, in his last clean shirt, to prove the pizza story, so he would have to wait until tomorrow to see if she still loved him. When Debbie, the manager's secretary, came in to put a note on the sacred Temple desk, Mark said, 'How about having that drink I promised you?'

'*You* promised *me*?' Debbie lifted the corner of a glistening coral lip, but then shrugged. 'All right, then.' They went to the Feathers, and Mark had three Bacardi and Cokes and Debbie had two.

She had two ways of using her eyes. She either swivelled them round about to see what she was missing or fixed them on you intently. Her low-cut black jersey top was made for leaning forward. The skin above her breasts was like soapy silk.

She was still fascinated by the scar on Mark's right cheek. 'It's a trademark,' she said. 'Like my dimple. God touched me with his finger, my mum used to say. How did you get yours?'

'I told you. In a duel.'

'Come off it. I'm one who likes to talk seriously.' Her eyes wandered round the bar again.

To recover her attention, Mark said, 'Actually, I got it in a car crash when I was seventeen. Not my fault.'

'It never is.' Debbie turned back to him. 'Who was driving?'

'Me, but it was the other guy's fault. He stopped dead.'

'And you went through the windscreen?'

'The car skidded and turned over. I was thrown out on

to stones.' Mark fingered the scar. 'It was outside Birmingham, and they took me to some tinpot hospital and stitched me up. After it healed, I could see what a lousy job they'd made of it. I ought to sue.'

'No, it's nice, darlin'.' Debbie put out her warm fleshy hand. 'It's given you that cute crooked smile, and it's got a dear little lump here at one end.' She tipped her head on one side and pushed out her lips, as if she were stroking a pet.

Mark grabbed the hand. It was hot and exciting. He pulled it into his lap, and Debbie jerked it away, and shook off the contamination.

'Do you want to come and have something to eat?' Mark was hungry.

'Not now, treasure.' Debbie had lost interest. They parted without her agreeing to another date.

Mark felt depressed. The Bacardi had slid away, and the fatigue of the day caught up with him. Telling the story of that stupid car crash had brought back the confusion and fear of that time. He had been stitched up in Casualty by an Asian woman who told him, 'You'll be as good as new.'

Driving home from the Feathers, with the feel of Debbie's hot damp fingers on his cheek, Mark looked again into the pit of emotion into which he had dropped when the wound was healed, and he realized that he would always carry a scar. As good as new! He had despaired of it fading; but no one went, 'A-a-agh!' or vomited when he appeared, so as time went by he had to accept the scar as part of himself, although he never got used to it.

Now, years later, he hated being called Scarface, but it was supposed to be funny, so he had to laugh. When girls like Debbie stared at the scar and fingered it, they got a kinky sort of thrill, as if there were nothing else sexual about him.

Moodily, he drove without attention. He missed a repairs diversion sign and found a barrier and flashing lights across the bridge. He backed out too carelessly, crumpled the left rear end of the *Chronicle*'s white Sierra against a bollard and sat limply, listening to the cheerless tinkle of glass on the road.

For the rest of the week he parked the car a few streets away from the office, so that no one would see it.

'I'll leave it with Roger to fix while I'm in Birmingham,' he told Judy. 'He'll do a rush job if I promise him a good rate for his next ads.'

Mark's father was recovering from a hip operation, and his mother had put pressure on him to come home at the weekend.

'You're coming, Jude.'

'No. They don't like me. They think I hold you back.'

Mark laughed. 'What from? You're the one thing that holds me together. And they like it that you work so hard.'

'But at an inferior job. I ought to be one of those high-powered women who makes money. Anyway, I'm going to Suffolk to look at a new glass factory, so I'll need the Toyota.'

'You can't. I want it.'

'It's half mine.'

'It's in my name.'

'It's half my money. Look,' Judy said reasonably, because they had been having too many rows, 'I can only get to Bury in a car. You can go to Birmingham by train.'

'Then I won't go.'

'You promised your parents you would.'

'How can I tell them?'

'You can't,' Judy said, still reasonably.

Sulking, Mark told her about going to the Feathers with Debbie. Judy was disappointingly unmoved.

Mark called through to the kitchen, where she was clattering. 'What would you do if I had a bit on the side?'

'I'd live, I suppose.' She turned from the sink with a saucepan in her hand. 'What would you do if *I* did?'

'You wouldn't live, because I'd kill you,' Mark said. 'Before or after killing myself.'

It must be nice to be one of those lucky people who were always convinced the best would happen. If it didn't, they had to face that, like everybody else, but meanwhile they hadn't wasted time and energy worrying about the worst.

Mark's train journey was blighted with anxiety. At the garage Roger had said, 'No problem about the Sierra,' but that could mean anything. If Roger didn't get the car repaired, it would have to wait another week. What if someone from the *Chronicle* spotted the damage, which Mark had failed to report? Andrea Temple had been in remission for a while, watching Mark, but not pouncing. If she found that he had smashed the car, would she jump on that as the last straw?

Never any luck. Some people got ahead. Others were constantly being knocked down. Lois and Joan were not inspired saleswomen. Why were they always preferred over Mark? If Mr Frayn left and Andrea Temple moved up to Advertising Manager, Joan, with her luck, would get the top Field Sales job.

To stop himself thinking, Mark opened the paper he had bought at the station. A government scandal on the front page, and a sex-crazed vicar in a flapping cassock. If the *Chronicle* were a daily tabloid, the job would be much more exciting. On the middle pages, a double spread was headlined MIRACLE OF A NEW DAWN. There was a picture of a baby with a ghastly deformity on its face, a sort of miniature elephant man, and another of a pretty little girl with her smiling mother. Boxes in bold type said 'We prayed she wouldn't live' and 'I've been given a miracle. The magic he's performed for Dawn can never be repaid or forgotten'.

This baby, Dawn Dodd, had been born with its brain ballooning out through a gap in the front of the skull. Without an immediate operation the brain would have grown and burst through the membrane.

After emergency surgery to close the gap, fluid had continued to leak, so there was still a huge unsightly lump under the skin. 'But then,' said Beverly, the mother, 'she was desperately ill with meningitis, so it didn't matter what she looked like, because she might have died.

'I was so happy when I finally took her home. I'd got used to how she looked, but my sister-in-law came into the house and fainted.' Neighbours talked about a monster. 'I didn't take her out any more. I couldn't stand the terrible looks we got.'

When the baby's head began to swell, as well as the lump, it was back to the Royal Victoria Hospital in Devon, and a dozen operations by the renowned chief of the Milner Plastic Surgery Unit, Mr Peter Freeman. It was years before Dawn began to look anything like a normal child. Everyone thought she never would, and it was only the remarkable skill and dedication of the surgeon, and the courage of the child and her plucky, exhausted mother, that were in the end to prove them wrong.

In contrast to the care and devotion of Mr Freeman and his staff, Beverly's life outside the hospital had been one of great hardship. Her live-in lover, the father of the child, abandoned them during the first year. Mark skimmed through the sordid recital of calamity and struggle to the last two columns where, under a picture of a beaming little girl who did not look half bad, except for a miniature boxer's nose, the mother proclaimed, 'Nothing matters beside the miracle of my beautiful daughter.'

Mr Freeman, the paper said, would be operating in a few years to bring Dawn's eyes closer together, by altering the bony sockets, and to level the eyebrows and insert silicone in the bridge of the nose. When she was sixteen, this brilliai consultant, whose department at the Royal Victoria was nationally renowned, would use cosmetic surgery to improve the scars on Dawn's nose and forehead, and the wide 'hot-cross bun' scar under her hair where he had had to open up the skull to remove infection.

Beverly said simply, 'He is my hero.' There was a picture of Peter Freeman, not dressed like a television doctor, but in white Arran sweater and polneck on a beach with his hair blowing, looking normal.

Life should be like that. Drama and emotion. Disaster and rescue. Not constant boring little worries and frustration. Doctors were not high in Mark's esteem, but it was good to know that they were not all bungling crooks. He tore out the middle pages of the paper, folded them and put them in his pocket.

His mother was waiting for him in a winter coat of a curious ginger colour which made her look like a brandysnap. She was a high-coloured woman, with the dark eyes and lashes she had passed on to Mark. The scarlet wool hat she wore in the draughty station was the same red as her cheeks.

'You're cold,' she told Mark. Mothers went on saying that all your life. 'Why no coat?'

'I've got a jacket.' It was a bulky bomber jacket with a sports motif that made him look like an outdoors man, with the jumbo trainers that had soles like tractor treads.

In the car she pulled off the hat and shook out her strong dark hair, which she had also given him. 'I can always tell when you're cold. Your scar goes blue.'

You would have expected her to be used to the scar after seven years, but she never lost an opportunity to comment on it.

As they approached the suburb which had once been a country town, Mark looked for the familiar places with the mixture of pleasure and pain that is childhood remembered. The narrow strip of wood that he and Joe Gurney used to explore manfully with compass and provisions, as if it were a forest; the bridge over the river where his father had once taken him to fish, for two hours before the old man got fed up with it; the farmhouse where Mark and his sister Georgina played with the children who took them to watch sheep bonking, the matted old ewe wandering off to eat, her rump stained with blue or red dye from the ram.

He knew that the farmhouse had been remodelled and enlarged for apartments. Its land was clustered with red brick houses where the sheep meadows had been.

'Sad to see it all go,' Mark said.

'People have got to live somewhere.' His mother spoke very fast, as if she had more things to say than could be fitted into a lifetime.

'I loved Elm Farm the way it was. It had a sort of magic.'

'Those Gurney children were always fighting, and the mother gave you liver for lunch. Her husband went off with a woman they met in Spain. She had five fingers on one hand, six if you count the thumb. You and Georgie would only eat the mashed potatoes and gravy. When you came home, you always wished you hadn't gone.'

The Emersons' white stucco house was square from all sides. The doors and non-functional shutters and window trim were green, which gave it a slightly Scandinavian look. So last summer Mrs Emerson had brought home from Denmark a gaily painted round plaque, which Mark was surprised to see still decorating the wall by the front door. Dad's hip must have been too bad for him to bother to remove it.

Although she had two heavy shopping bags to unload, Mark's mother drove the car into the garage. Her husband did not care for cars standing on the gravel outside the house. It was not that he was a bullying tyrant, but for subtle, often indefinable reasons, it was easier to let him have his own way. Many people thought he was a sweet man, quiet and unassuming, with a garrulous bossy wife, a tough daughter and an irresponsible show-off son. You had to know Marcus Emerson quite well before you detected that by a passive smile and withholding public decisions or opinions, he manipulated his family into being the worst of themselves. His wife was forced into a loquacious taking charge: somebody had to say *something*. His son turned somersaults to get his attention. His daughter had grown a defensive shell against criticism of her marriage and children, which he actually never voiced.

Carrying the shopping bags, Mark asked, 'So Dad's going

to be all right, then?' They had not talked much about him on the journey.

'I hope so. It was a bigger operation than it need have been, because he put off doing anything about it for months and months. I even went myself to the orthopaedic surgeon to discuss it, but your father wouldn't. "You go if you like," he told me, "if it makes you feel better." He had a very hard time, and it's painful still, but he's as strong as an ox.'

So why had she said on the phone, with that catch in the breath, 'I think you ought to come,' as if his father were at death's door?

She went through into the kitchen with the shopping. Mark looked in the hall mirror at the scar on his cheek. It was slightly blue. His mother kept the car heater down, because of her blood pressure.

His father was sitting stiffly in a straight chair, not his usual armchair. Mark gave him a hearty greeting, grinning towards the closed smile, saying things like 'Well – how *are* you? I've been worried' and 'You look great, Dad, it's good to see you!' As long as he was here, he was going to be as nice as he could. He never gave up the fantasy that when he had left, his father might think of him with love.

After supper, when his mother had washed and Mark had dried the dishes – she did not believe in plate racks – she went on fiddling and messing about the kitchen and the house, making unnecessary phone calls, not in comfort, but in the kitchen, standing up. She hardly ever sat down and did nothing. That was why she had high blood pressure. Or because.

Although there were a couple of programmes that Mark would have watched, there was nothing on television, according to his father, so Mark poured whisky and sodas and sat on his old small stool by the fire, because he did not feel grown up.

'How does the hip feel?'

'Bloody painful.'

'No tennis this summer, then, Dad?'

'Don't get your hopes up. I'll be playing in a few months. I can still beat the hell out of you.'

He had coached Mark as a boy, encouraged him, forced him out to practise when he wanted to do something else. Mark was supposed to beat opponents in junior tournaments, but not his father in a singles. When they played doubles together, they had to win, but the sniping and subtle poaching and muttered criticism could rattle Mark into mistakes. When they lost, even with his father playing his infuriatingly unshakeable best, it was Mark's fault.

He stared into the wood fire, one of the things he missed in his spaceless flat, which did not even have a fake hearth for an electric fire. Poor old man, he thought. Stuck up here with a dummy hip at only fifty-five, not able to drive, or play golf or tennis, or prune every bush within an inch of its life or go to his beloved office.

Mark had planned to entertain his father with tales of life in the south-west, and the comedies and dramas of working on a newspaper. He had told a girl on the train that he was an investigative reporter, and the girl had said, 'Do what?'

He chatted a bit about the job, until his father asked when he was going to get a rise. Mark's standard defence was that he cared more about job satisfaction than money, to which his father replied, on cue, 'People only say that when they haven't got any.'

It was too early to go to bed, so Mark moved on to childhood memories. 'When we crossed the river on the way from the station, I thought of that Sunday you took me fishing.'

'And you got bored.'

Why couldn't one shout at this man, 'No, *you* did'?

'Why didn't you drive up?' his father wanted to know.

'My car's being serviced.'

'Serviced or repaired? Had another argument with a van?'

'Listen – that man stopped dead on a wet road.'

'You were too close.'

'That was seven years ago.'

'And it was my car.'

Would he ever let go of this? Mark had paid off the debt two years ago. He had taken his father's car without asking, and it was not insured for him to drive.

'I thought we were talking about why I came by train.' Mark shifted ground. 'Judy needed the other car to go to Suffolk.'

'Ah, Judy.' Pause. 'The cradle-snatcher.'

'Shut up.' If the old bastard was not going to behave like an invalid, Mark was not going to treat him like one.

Marcus Emerson raised his eyebrows. His face, which did not show anger or irritation, took on a detached curiosity.

'Why do those shoes have an enormous padded flap halfway up your leg?'

Mark stuck out his giant-size Reeboks. 'In Somerset, people kick you in the ankles.'

'Why?'

'Ask *them*.'

His mother came in with pills and a glass of water. His father took the capsules eagerly and crammed them into his mouth with the palm of his hand, to demonstrate that he had

been bravely concealing pain while his wife forgot about him
and his son exhausted him with prattle.

'Georgie's bringing the children over tomorrow,' Mark's
mother said, 'so I'm glad you two had the chance of a good
talk this evening.'

Georgina was her usual bouncy self, putting on weight. Her
children were self-possessed and cheeky. Mark could not
remember being so bold with grown-ups at that age. The little
boy went confidently to his puckishly smiling grandfather –
'Mind my leg, you villain' – and was allowed to rifle his
pockets for toffees.

'The old man is slipping.' Mark went to slice vegetables
for his mother. 'He was never so easy-going with me.'

'He did his best,' Jean Emerson said quickly. 'Children
never notice that, of course. They're too self-absorbed. They
have to be, if they're not going to grow up with stunted egos.
And times have changed, d'you see. We used to believe we
mustn't relax discipline, but children have more freedom
nowadays, and it doesn't seem to do them any harm.'

'Why did I miss out?' Mark cut carrots into two-inch
lengths, then into strips. 'If I were a child now, would he leave
me alone to be what I wanted?'

'No, no, I shouldn't think so.' She gabbled at him breathlessly, with her head inside the refrigerator. 'There's always
been something about you that – that irritates your father.
Not your fault, I suppose. Just the way it is, d'you see.' Her
usual formula of acceptance.

After lunch, when the children were out in the garden,
Mark's father asked him to help with his therapeutic stagger
along the hall six times, and up and down the stairs. Back

in his chair, biting his bravely smiling lips, he looked at his watch, and, because it was not time for painkillers, ordained a few hands of Racing Demon.

The card table was brought up to his chair, and the four of them laid out their packs. Even with a butchered hip, Marcus played with the quiet, deadly speed that invariably pushed his score ahead.

Georgina swore at him for using both hands. Her mother said, 'It's no use, he always wins. I don't know why we play.'

Mark, who had been cheating at family games since he was a child, risked counting out less than the thirteen cards he had to get rid of. When he went out first, Georgina shouted, 'Cheat!'

'You always say that if I win.'

'Because you can only win by cheating.'

Their father sat uninvolved, separating the cards in the middle into different packs. Their mother plunged hectically in, out of her depth in the rights and wrongs of it, fussing at them, 'Georgina, don't shout, Mark, you're not to cheat.'

'I wasn't.'

'He didn't put out enough cards.'

'Prove it.'

Georgie couldn't, but in the next game she reached over to count his pile of thirteen cards. He knocked her hand away, scattered his cards on the floor and stamped up to his room, as he had done countless times as a desperate boy.

The room had not changed much. The posters and rock concert souvenirs and football pennants were gone, and his tennis photographs and small silver plated cups, but the wallpaper and curtains and rugs and furniture had been there since the beginning of time.

Sitting on the bed, kicking his heels against the box of toys and books his mother was storing 'for your own children', Mark could still feel like a child in this room, impotent and resentful. He could still feel seventeen, hiding here with his tapes and car magazines, because he could not be downstairs with that face of his father's unspoken anger, which would not look at him.

Unable to talk about what had happened, he had lain up here and played the car crash over and over in his mind like a bad film. The speed, the corner, the braking skid, the world out of control, the ground coming at him. Days later, he had looked at what was left of the car with a pang of self-destructive recognition that he could remember now was almost like love.

He got up and looked at himself in the mirror over the chest of drawers. The scar, the indelible keepsake of the accident, had reddened, the small lump at the lower end flushed and swollen.

'We're going!' Georgina called up the stairs.

'I'll come down. You can drop me at the station.'

Downstairs Mark turned the scarred side of his face away as his mother hugged him. At what age did the feel of your mother's breasts change from paradise to an embarrassment?

'Feeling better, old silly?'

'Don't baby him,' Georgina said.

'He always used to go into a sulk if he couldn't have his own way,' Jean Emerson said. 'Don't you remember?'

She had given Mark one of her paperback whodunnits for the train. She was in love with the mean, lean, sensitive chief inspector in the series, but after the early lure of a garish murder on the fourth page, Mark could not be bothered to follow the clues or disentangle the suspects. He shut the book and sighed. It was dark outside now. In the carriage window his eyes were shadows in a blurred face against the black evening. Mark sighed again and took the newspaper story of Dawn Dodd out of his pocket and unfolded it.

'I've been given a miracle,' the mother had said.

Some people had all the luck.

Chapter Five

*P*eter and Catherine lived with their children in a comfortable, conventional Victorian red brick house in a small market town five miles inland from the hospital.

It stood in a quiet tree-lined avenue, set back with a garden all round. The front door was inside a glass porch with geraniums on shelves and a small stone lion given to Peter by a dupuytren's contracture patient who had had to move into a flat. A fanlight bore the name: LIBERTY HOUSE. The name had pleased Peter and Catherine as much as anything when they moved here from their first small place in the town and began to liberate the pleasant lines of the house from years of obliterating ivy.

Indoors, rooms were square and ceilings high. Tall windows and a glass garden door gave light and airiness to a house once suffocated by velvet curtains and brown paint. The large kitchen at the back was also their dining room. The basement where the kitchen used to be was now a garden flat rented by a young trainee eye surgeon and his French wife.

Claudine could usually come upstairs in the evening and stay with the children if Peter and Catherine went out. Returning from a dinner party, they found her with Evangeline, still awake and watching television.

'She couldn't sleep,' Claudine said. 'Something bothers her, but she doesn't say what.'

Evie liked to see her mother with the covering make-up she wore more for other people's sake than her own. Sitting on Catherine's knee after Claudine had left, she touched the raised, rippled birthmark on her cheek and jaw with the flat of her hand.

'Still a problem for you, Evie?' Peter asked. The child did not answer.

'Someone saying things at school,' Catherine guessed. Evie shook her head violently. 'If they do, tell them, "Lots of people have birthmarks, and a big twit like you ought to know that!" '

Evie grunted, frowning. Easy to tell her what to say. Catherine ached to go down to the school and say it for her. Her daughter slid off her knee and stood apart in her short nightdress, bare toes turned in.

'If Daddy can change people's faces all the time,' she said aggressively, 'why not yours?'

'I've explained it to you, darling. Come on, I'll take you back to bed.'

'Tell me *now*.'

Peter saw her small square face set like Annette's when she

was expecting pain, delicate brows drawn down, eyes seeking yours as if she were grabbing for your hand.

They went through it again, patiently but briefly. 'He couldn't take it away because the colour went too deep,' Catherine told the child standing by her knee, bones so vulnerable within her enfolding arm. 'But he helped me not to mind it. And I don't. Honest. So you needn't.'

Unresponsive, Evie trailed towards the stairs, putting on a flat drone: 'Mu-um – come on.'

'The old story,' Catherine said when she came down. 'You can help other children more than your own.'

'Shall we tell them about the possibility of laser treatment?'

'Not yet. If the waiting list is so long, why disappoint them?'

'I'm hopeful,' Peter said.

'I'm not. Why disappoint myself?'

'You're tough.'

'No. Blemished. It gets through to the soul.'

When the article about Dawn Dodd appeared in the paper, Evangeline was famous at school for a day, and life looked better. The teachers said, 'You must be very proud of your clever father,' and Mrs Knowles, who had been to the Milner last year for a mole removal, put the newspaper story on the bulletin board in the main corridor.

Evie *was* proud of her father. When she was younger, she used to tell incredible stories about him sewing on severed legs and heads to anyone who would listen. When he drove her to school, she had pulled Mandy over to the car so that the bitch could see that Evie had a super father. Now she could also see that he was a hero.

But Mandy, swaggering by with her creepy friends in the

cloakroom passage, had pushed Evie hard against the wall and said, 'If all your father's patients look like that freak in the paper, perhaps he doesn't mind you being so ugly.'

At the Royal it seemed that everyone had seen the newspaper story. When Peter went across to the main hospital to talk to the head of dental surgery about a post-operative patient who was going to need reconstruction, he was stopped in the corridors for jokes and praise, and hailed by the mothers and nurses in the children's Oncology ward.

In the Milner Unit all the patients were thrilled. Annette was brighter and more talkative. She had taped Peter's picture to the edge of her bed table. Deirdre Leigh looked at him speculatively and said, 'They could have written about Annette. Why didn't you tell them about Annette?'

Peter was like a Grand National winner returning to its village training stable. He was admired and teased by all the nurses, porters, cleaners, secretaries and technicians. The house officer, Mary Knight, whose time with them as part of her surgical rotation was nearly over, said, 'I wish I was staying here. No one will ever get their picture in the paper on Gynae.'

Noel asked the other plastic surgeon, Richard Valentine, while the three of them were scrubbing up for an operation, 'Are you in shape for a miracle?'

'Shut up,' Peter said. Noel had already greeted him as 'Miracle Man' this morning. Tom Sutcliffe must be whirling in his grave.

'Yes, I know.' Noel grinned. ' "There are no miracles", courtesy Thomas Sutcliffe of Guy's. Me, I never had that sort of great teacher. Except you, of course, sir.' He smiled at Peter engagingly.

Noel Grant was the best registrar they'd had, and he was going to be one of the people who took plastic surgery brilliantly into the next century, but he had a way of taking digs at you, and then soaping you up before you could get seriously annoyed.

'Mr Freeman is my hero,' he said solemnly to Richard Valentine.

After the morning surgery, a photographer from the local paper was waiting to get a picture of the renowned consultant on an ordinary working day. In theatre gown and mask? No. With a patient then – bandaged perhaps? No.

'I talked to a gentleman in the day room,' the photographer said, 'and he's willing.'

So Peter had his picture taken with William Mack in the white turban, under which his bat ears had been repositioned closer to his head.

There were a few patients to see at the Restora, and more acclaim, then back to the Royal for a committee meeting with 'Friends of the Milner'. They were involved in a major fund-raising drive which would culminate in a dazzling theatre benefit and reception at the end of the summer.

The unit needed many things: another low-air-loss bed, a new saline bath, extra equipment for the microscope, including a wall screen so that everyone in the theatre could see what the surgeon saw. Peter's dream was that one day they would have a special burns unit, and lab facilities to develop techniques in culturing new skin for grafts.

'Keep up the publicity,' the chairman said. 'You're doing well so far.' He had brought photocopies of the newspaper article. The committee were delighted with Peter. Would he speak at the Chamber of Commerce lunch?

Driving home at last, he yawned and blinked. His eyes were watery and sore after hours of peering through the microscope, or his magnifying fly-tying spectacles. After supper he was going to Trinity Church for choir practice.

'Can't you miss rehearsal this week?' Catherine was worried because he looked so tired.

'They're always short of tenors. And I want to go.' Singing with the Fidelis Choir, which practised in the church and gave recitals all over the area, was one of his private joys, challenging and relaxing at the same time.

'Haven't you got that Down's Syndrome boy first thing tomorrow? If it were my child,' Catherine said craftily, 'I would want the surgeon to have an early night.'

'That's not fair.'

'It's not meant to be. You're stubborn; I'm underhand.'

Apple pie and coffee and a quick game of draughts with Evie were interrupted by a call from Noel. An emergency had been brought in, a hand crushed in machinery. Peter listened carefully and then said, 'Do you want to take care of it? Fine. Ring me later and tell me how it went. Who's the theatre sister on call? Good. Go ahead.'

'Because you want to go to choir practice.' Evie was listening.

'Because Noel can handle it very well. And he needs the responsibility.'

'Is that fair to the patient?' Catherine came in with more coffee.

'I wouldn't let him do it if it weren't. What is all this moralizing? I can do that for myself without any help from you. I'm trying to be fair to all the patients Noel will reassemble in the future.'

'Are you quarrelling?' Evie knew that other people's parents had terrible fights, with bottles thrown and windows smashed.

'Sorry to disappoint you,' Peter said shortly.

He arrived late at the church. 'Ah – the famous Mr Freeman.' The conductor, a stern, dedicated character with prawn eyebrows, had tapped his baton to halt the big chorus from *Carmina Burana*. 'Where have you been?' He never made allowances for anyone's life outside the choir.

'Working miracles,' one of the sopranos said cheekily. They all laughed and smiled at Peter, and the pianist gave him a thumbs-up. He went quickly to his place, mentally turning up his coat collar. Enjoy the ten thousand pounds, Beverly. Peter was tired of being famous.

Chapter Six

*M*ark had folded small the magical newspaper stor[y]
Dawn with the transfigured face. He kept it in his v[allet]
a talisman to show that, in spite of all evidence, go[od,]
true things could happen in the world.

Something good did eventually happen even at the C[ollege.]
There was to be a huge antique fair at the town ha[ll. It]
would attract exhibitors and visitors from all over So[merset,]
and Andrea Temple decided to let Mark han[dle the]
advertising.

'You could do with a bit of culture,' was how she [put it.]

The organizers were a couple of hard-bitten deale[rs who]
knew what they wanted and were willing to splash o[ut on]
large advertisements and some smaller ones with photo[graphs,]
made up so cleverly by Mark to look like news stori[es.]

they had to have 'advert' in tiny print at the bottom. For the final full-page display, a few days before the fair, he met the two women in their office to go over details and decide on the layout.

Mrs Burns and Lady Daly were quite pleased with Mark, who had handled their business with efficiency and good will.

'Thanks very much,' Lady Daly said, in her curt, strangled way.

'Come and see us on May 2nd.' Mrs Burns shook his hand. 'Bring all your friends.'

Most of Mark's friends would not see an antique fair as their heart's desire on a Saturday, but he enthused, 'Sure, great!' and drove back to the office in quite a glow to write up his copy.

The *Chronicle* came out on a Wednesday morning. At eleven thirty, when Mark came in to fetch his next client's file, which he had forgotten, Andrea Temple's heels clattered down the stairs from the second floor as Mark bounded up from ground level.

Mrs Temple grabbed the back of his jacket and propelled him up another flight, and pushed him, protesting and prickling with a nameless fear, along the corridor to the office of Mr Simms, the Managing Director.

This stuffed rotund man, to whom Mark had spoken only once in more than a year with the *Chronicle*, rose from behind his desk with a cry like a stricken buffalo.

'*This* is – ' He could hardly articulate.

'This is.' Mrs Temple gave Mark a final push, and he stood on the executive carpet alone before the desk, a man in the dock.

The charge? The final full-page advertisement for the Great Somerset Antique Fair had the wrong date.

Lady Daly had rung Mr Simms in a blistering rage. Grimly, Mr Simms had checked back. The advertisement had gone through production, typesetting, proofreading, with no queries. The proofreader had indeed checked the date with Mark's facts form, which was still attached to the file copy.

'May 9th.' The Managing Director's forefinger stabbed into the open newspaper, a damning accusation on his desk.

May 9th? No – May 2nd, surely, next Saturday. 'May 9th?' There it was in print. 'Yes – er, yes, that's right.' Mark fought to swallow down his panic. 'That – that's the date they gave me.'

'Show me the client's notes.'

'I – oh, my God, I shredded them. I always do when I'm finished with something. We're supposed to – ' Mark looked wildly back at Andrea Temple. She stood silent by the door with her arms folded, a prison guard posted to prevent his escape.

'The town's most important event, and our readers won't be there. The Antique Fair is on May 2nd,' Mr Simms enunciated, as if he were speaking to a foreigner or an idiot. 'Three . . . days . . . from . . . now.'

'Can't we – '

'*Mister* Emerson.' Mark felt the flush suffuse his face, and automatically put his fingers over the scar on his cheek. 'We are a weekly, not a daily paper, in case you hadn't noticed.'

At some expense the paper made a twelve-by-sixteen bromide, correcting the mistake, and printed forty copies on thick shiny paper. Mark had to take the posters round to hotels, banks, the town hall, the library, bus station, railway station – anywhere where they could be put up immediately.

'*Chronicle* screwed up again, ha, ha.'

The unfunny quips drove Mark to hollow repartee. 'Big surprise. Our Production Department got it wrong, as usual.'

Whatever feeble loyalty he might have had to the paper had been squelched by Debbie, stopping him in the lobby on his way out with the posters to tell him that she had just typed his letter of dismissal from Mr Frayn, the Advertising Manager.

Before the letter could reach him, Mark told Andrea Temple, 'I'm resigning.' He would have liked to follow that with a summary of what was wrong with the Field Sales Department, but found himself saying, because he and Andrea had almost been friends in a weird sort of way, 'Sorry if I'm leaving you in the lurch.'

'Don't worry.' She looked beyond, not at him. 'I have a back-up file of people who want to work here.'

Bitch.

Mark felt his system deserved a breather before rushing into another job. He played a bit of tennis with the cunning lob-and-cut geriatrics who were the only people at the club on weekdays, flipped through the Situations Vacant columns in the *Chronicle*, noting typos with grim satisfaction, and wrote off a few vague letters, which did not get a reply. He had not yet nerved himself to find out whether Mrs Temple would give him a reference.

At Judy's insistence, although he hated the Social Security office, he signed on as available for work. Summer was coming. Perhaps he would find an outside job with a landscaper or a garden centre. He could coach at the tennis club.

Blaisebrough Castle was open for the season. It might be fun
to be the man who sat astride the miniature engine and pulled
children through the park.

He put his cap on backwards to see how he would look as
a railwayman. No, it was better the right way round, with
the peak tilted to one side to shadow the scar. As the Antique
Fair disaster faded before the memory of all his good work
at the *Chronicle*, Mark began to see himself more and more
as a victim of discrimination. Andrea Temple and Mr Frayn
and Lois and Joan and even Debbie, with her yes – no style,
had all been down on him because he was disfigured. Working
on his own outdoors might give him a better chance.

Once or twice, he looked at the story of Dawn Dodd and
the surgeon, as one might read a Bible passage to contemplate
the possibility of salvation.

'When Mr Freeman first came to examine the baby in
Intensive Care,' Beverly Dodd had said, 'I knew at once that
here was a man I could trust.'

Peter Freeman had given the child a new face. Mark gazed
often in the mirror. Shaving was more difficult on his right
cheek, because of the scar's irregular edge. Should he grow
a moustache and beard? Judy said beards were like pubic hair.
Was it his imagination, or was the scar really growing uglier?

'Judy, come here. Judy, look, in the mirror, in this light,
don't you think my scar looks worse?'

'You imagine things.'

'I'm a leper. I'm a freak. Oi be Pru Sarn.' He had seen
Precious Bane on television: a beautiful actress made up with
a dark hare lip, like snot coming out of her nose. 'I turn people
off.'

Mark had thought a lot about his mother's candid

statement: 'There's always been something about you that irritates your father.' And the scar, of course, reminder of that damn car crash, would add to the irritation. He stood in front of the mirror on the wall between the windows, with his hands in his thick hair, holding it back, pushing it forward, searching for the attractive young man he used to see.

'By contemplation of his own face,' Judy quoted, 'Narcissus was driven to suicide.'

'Don't be clever.'

Judy seemed restless. Feeling the spring. Uncertain of what Mark was going to do. Fed up with this flat and its limited choices of where the furniture could go.

'You need a change,' he said. 'We should go out more often, see more people. Let's have someone in for a meal, if you can be bothered to cook.'

Judy invited the two BBC men from Bristol. She came home early from work, and, while she was preparing the food, her younger sister Daisy turned up, unexpectedly as always. She dropped a large floppy bag in the hall, kicked off her heavy boots in the middle of the living room floor and pushed Mark off the sofa with her questionable bare feet, so that she could stretch out in her faded Indian cotton dress, inside which she might or might not be pregnant.

'What are you doing here?' Judy, in her neat striped apron, looked down on her sister with distaste.

'Sharing myself with you.' Daisy smiled up through a web of hair, sunnily.

They were quite different. Judy was spruce, quick, conventional, grown-up. Daisy was a slob. If Judy went without a bra, it was because she hardly needed one. With

Daisy, it was because she was an anarchist, and liked things flopping around, out of control. She was a female yob – a yobbette? She drifted, joining riots, throwing bricks.

'What for?'

'Not *for* anything. Against. Against whatever the riot's about.'

'Does she have to stay to supper?' Mark asked.

'Supper, hell,' Daisy yawned. Even her tonsils were sloppy. 'I'm going to spend the night.'

Judy let her come and go. She never stayed long, and it was easier than fighting.

The smaller of the two BBC men quite took to Daisy. She talked about a Bangladeshi ghetto in South Wales, and about a guru she had lived with for a while in a bus on Dartmoor, and he listened to her seriously. The men were both queer, Mark did not change his mind on that. The taller one, Duncan, was quiet and clever. He and Judy talked about books, theatre, television documentaries. Mark did not try to keep up with them. He was urbane, and made jokes.

When they had gone, taking Daisy with them, thank God, Mark and Judy agreed it had been a good evening. Judy was wound up. Mark thought she was going to tackle the pile of dishes in the kitchen, but she poured herself another drink and paced about the flat talking, in bare feet smaller and more appetizing than her sister's.

'Either go and wash up,' Mark said, 'or come to bed. You've had your excitement.'

'I still want – oh, what do I want?'

'You want things to change, like I do.'

'Should we split up?' Judy asked.

'*No!* What a rotten thing to say. How could you leave me now when I'm an unemployed victim of the system.'

When she had recovered from the third series of skin grafts on her thighs and knees, Annette was able to go home, in a wheelchair, because the leg grafts must be quite stable before she could stand on her feet. She would come back to be checked frequently, and would need some more grafting at the end of the summer.

Meanwhile she wore tight-fitting pressure garments over the grafts to avoid scar contraction. They were uncomfortable and Annette fussed, although she had never whined at the hospital.

'It's different at home,' her mother told her, 'not having all those nurses at your beck and call. You'll have to make do with poor old me.'

'I can manage,' Deirdre told Mr Freeman stoutly. She had been a star mother at the Milner Unit, with privileges and gratitude for her help. Now she would be a star mother at home, but the only privilege was being on call twenty-four hours a day, and there was not much gratitude. Campbell was difficult, although he should have been happy to have Annette at home. Ted was uneasy, because he did not know how to help. If you gave him something to do, he did it wrong.

Annette's pressure garments were supposed to be worn all the time, but they became tight and hot, and when she was too miserable, her mother would take them off for a short while. She and Annette would both find it hard to be patient during the slow, painful job of getting them on again over the ugly irritable scars, often in the middle of the night.

'God forgive me, Ted.' Deirdre woke him up when she

finally fell back into bed, as the first grey light oozed round the edges of the blind. 'He has His mysterious ways, but I sometimes wonder whether it was right for that poor child to survive.'

'Hush now, Deedree. You should let the district nurse do more for you. You should let me help you more. I don't mind getting up in the night.'

'You?' Deirdre's bottomless sigh said all the things that Ted knew. Clumsy. Thick fingers. Not trained by the hospital as she had been.

Campbell, rude and unsociable, took over some of the jobs for Annette that Ted could have done. A teacher came in once a week, and the boy fetched books from Annette's school on his bike and took her work back. He pushed her chair from room to room, whistling, his latest aggravation, and along the paths in the park, since the palms of her hands were not healed enough to turn the wheels. On Sundays Ted would have been proud to push the chair round the neighbourhood and show off his heroine, but Cammy would not let anyone else have it. If he was on his mother's nerves, and she said he couldn't take Annette out, he would scream like a baby, and she would lock him in his room, which made him worse and made Annette cry, because she was unable to let him out.

The boy still called out sometimes in the night, or came stumbling to his parents' room, babbling and screeching about fire, to be told, 'Anyone would think you were the one got burned, not Annette. What are you doing, waking the poor girl up just when she's got to sleep?'

It would be Ted who took the boy back to his room and held his shivering body tight and talked to him.

'You spoil him,' Deirdre stayed awake to tell him when he came back to bed. 'He's playing for attention.'

Whatever people thought of Ted's negligence about the unmended heater and the dangerous oil stove – and he knew that he would be blamed for a long time – everyone did think Annette was a heroine. At first friends and neighbours came in quite a lot, and there had to be tea and biscuits on the go, until they got used to her being there, and to the wheelchair, and the knowledge that her healing was going to be a long, slow, undramatic process.

Deirdre's mother came nearly every day with presents and things to eat. She vacuumed and ironed, and would have stayed with Annette while Deirdre went to the shops, but Deirdre would not have that, so Mrs Last went out and did the shopping for her. If she was at the house when Ted came home, he would have to keep his shoes on, and not go to the cupboard under the sideboard for a beer until she had gone. Mrs Last thought that Deirdre had married beneath her. So she had, but Deirdre and Ted got on all right, and he could not see that it mattered.

'I've got this friend,' Mark said to Joe in the pub, which was increasingly boring now that he could drop in there any time, instead of only at weekends and after work. 'He's got this kind of gross mole or something on his face. He wants it cut out, but he hasn't a clue how you get to see a surgeon. Do you know?'

'Simple. You go to your GP, and he refers you to a consultant.'

Mark's doctor was an uninspired man, who simply hoped to get all the work done each day, with no time for niceties.

Mark had seen him two or three times for a back problem, but the doctor looked at him blankly when he came in.

Mark had nerved himself for the expected opinion, which he got.

'This isn't anything to worry about.'

'But I do worry.' Doctors always missed the point that this was why you'd come. 'It's unsightly. I want to have it taken away.'

'Plastic surgery, you mean?'

'Yes. There's a man at the Royal Victoria at Kingscombe. Mr Peter Freeman.' There, the name was out, his private obsession made public.

'You're not in their catchment area.' The doctor showed no reaction to the magic name. 'You'd have to see someone in Bristol.'

I don't want to see anyone in Bristol.

'Since it's not an emergency, and' – the doctor frowned at Mark's scar and shook his head – 'not really necessary, it would be a long wait even to talk about it.'

'How long?'

'A year – two years.'

'If I went as a private patient' (the money would come from somewhere) 'I could see Mr Freeman, couldn't I?'

'Whether he could help you or not, that's his business. My business is that I can see nothing wrong with you, and anyway I don't like making referrals to private consultants.'

Why? Mark could not ask that righteous moose face.

'My advice to you, young man, is to stop looking in the mirror and get on with your life.'

The effect of this was to increase Mark's determination to see Peter Freeman. The next time Judy let him take their car, a growing cause of fights now that Mark had been stripped of the white Sierra, he drove the sixty miles to the Royal Victoria, and found his way to the Plastic Surgery Department. It was a two-storey building across a slope of grass from the muddle of the main hospital buildings, with low wings stretching out from it on three sides. Its name, MILNER UNIT, was set into the brickwork over the main door, and in the small, spotless lobby a bronze plaque on the wall immortalized Sir Joseph Milner and his splendid gift.

The receptionist told Mark where he could find Mr Freeman's secretary. Two narrow boards by her door said MR P. FREEMAN and MR R. VALENTINE. It was so easy. No desperate search, no disappointment. Never mind R. Valentine, Peter Freeman was here.

Mark was excited. His heart beat fast. His scar would be reddened. The secretary would look up from her desk and see at once that he was a patient in urgent need of help.

She was talking on the phone. When she put it down, Mark started to speak breathlessly, but it rang again. At last she was free, and smiling helpfully. Small and cropped-haired like Judy, she was a good omen.

'You haven't got an appointment. Have you got a letter from your GP? No, I'm afraid it's impossible for you to see Mr Freeman.'

'Just for two minutes.' Mark leaned on the shining counter.

'I'm sorry.' She shook her small head and her bright lips did not smile. She waited for him to go away.

Mark felt that he might throw up over the counter. 'But please – ' he swallowed with difficulty. 'I mean, I'd pay for it. Doesn't he see private patients?'

'Mr Freeman has a private practice, yes. So does Mr

Valentine. But you'd have to make an appointment through the other secretary, at the Restora Hospital.'

'Where's that?' Mark pushed himself upright.

She told him. 'But you can only be referred by your GP. Are you all right?' she added as an afterthought.

Mark left her. Outside the closed door, balanced on his toes, he looked towards the lobby. No one about, and he was out of sight of the receptionist. No one in the other direction. He slipped along the passage and turned left, following signs that said OUTPATIENTS, CLINICS, DAY WARD. Peter Freeman was somewhere in this building. Mark was so close. He would not be denied by bureaucrats.

There were people about, nurses, a woman in a white overall with a basket of bottles and test tubes. Mark slowed down and moved casually, through an archway and along a polished corridor. Ahead, a door opened. A tall fair-haired young doctor, complete with loosely worn white jacket and stethoscope, held the door for a nurse propelling a wheelchair. Mark hardly saw the child in the chair, for just behind, shorter than he had expected, calm and serious, his light brown hair tidy, but otherwise looking just like his clear-eyed beach picture, was Mr Freeman.

Mark stepped forward, but the surgeon had turned away to walk beside the wheelchair, bending down to the child, who was crying. Mark was going to follow, but the tall young man put a restraining hand on his arm.

'Can I help you?'

'I want to speak to Mr Freeman.' He tugged his arm free, and almost hit out with it.

'He's busy now. If you want to make an appointment, you will have to be referred – '

'I know, I know. By my GP.'

'Well, then.' The young doctor, who had an old-fashioned haughty look, like people in 1920s television films, did not seem to notice Mark's despair. 'You know. And you should know that you can't wander about all over the unit. The way out is in the other direction.' He turned Mark round. *Take your hands off me*. 'That way.'

'If I were to ask you to lend me some money,' Mark said casually to Judy, 'what would you say?'

'It would depend what you wanted it for.'

'If I couldn't say, if it was a sort of secret, but definitely connected with me getting a decent job?'

'Special training, you mean?'

'Sort of.'

'Why couldn't you tell me?'

Because she did not mind his scar, Judy would think the surgery a waste of money.

'I'd just hope you'd understand afterwards.'

'Don't be mysterious, love. How much are we talking about anyway?'

'Oh . . . five hundred – a thousand pounds?'

Judy shook her head and put her bottom teeth over her top lip. 'Can't be done.'

Mark sounded out a couple of pals, with foreseeable results. In any normal family he would have rung his mother. She had gone back to teaching part-time for the last ten years. She had her own bank account. But she would still say, 'I'll have to ask your father.'

Mark had not told her yet about being fired from the newspaper.

Gordon Dietz, the breezy manager of the new conference hotel, had become something of a friend, since they had discussed the advertising campaign over food and drink. They occasionally had lunch, or Mark would drop in to the hotel for a drink, and chat to Gordon when he came through the lounge.

Gordon was a businessman. Mark made him a proposition. A thousand pounds cash, repayable in three months at two per cent above base. Mark did not know where he would get a thousand pounds plus interest, but that could wait. Peter Freeman's miracle surgery was all that mattered. When that was done, the world was going to be Mark's oyster.

Gordon Dietz didn't say yes, but he didn't say no either. He would probably come round. With that in mind, Mark followed up a discreet telephone inquiry to his doctor's surgery by making an appointment with one of the other GPs in the practice, on a Saturday morning when his own doctor was off.

Dr Lawford turned out to be a woman, messily dressed and running to fat, but with a sharp, intelligent eye.

'What's the problem?' She summed Mark up. 'Something that can't wait until Monday?'

Impaled by the eye, Mark stammered a bit, then told her his story and asked her for a private patient referral.

'Saturday morning is our busiest time of the week.' She stood up. Mark stood up too. 'I would have been glad to help you with a genuine problem, but you are taking up time with an insulting suggestion that I should go behind a colleague's back.'

'Will you – ' Mark put his soul into his eyes. 'Will you please not tell my own doctor that I came to you?' She was a woman, after all, even in that lumpy green woollie and broad brown trousers.

'All right.' She looked more kindly at Mark. 'I won't, then. It was a mistake.'

Mark could not be deterred from the pursuit of his holy grail: the man who had become a kind of god in his mind, a god who had all the answers. The right answers, not the ones lesser mortals dished out.

He would go to the Restora Hospital anyway, and try his luck. He speculated for a while on a convincing story to tell, then in a revelation so pure and swift that he knew it was infallible, the idea came that he must simply tell the truth.

To avoid explanations about why he wanted the car and where he was going, he went to Kingscombe by train and taxi. He travelled up in the Restora's delicately tinted lift and along a soft corridor to the pleasant little office where a gracious woman with lovely legs sat sideways at a desk, not defensively behind it. After the first shock Mark did not know whether to look, or not look, or pretend not to notice the violent purple stain that was splashed all over one side of her warmly welcoming face. Did she feel the same about his disfiguring scar?

She asked about a referral. Mark had been going to say, 'It's in the post', the cliché of our times, but he looked into her friendly brown eyes and told her the whole truth.

This woman was no bureaucrat. She sighed, still smiling, then said, 'I'm sorry your own doctor couldn't refer you.'

'But would it matter?'

'I think we may be able to work round it. Now, Mark Emerson, you're very anxious to see Mr Freeman?'

'I must see him.'

'Since this is not a doctor's referral, may I ask who recommended that you come here? A patient of Mr Freeman's perhaps?'

'No, well, yes, in a way. I read the newspaper piece, you see, and I thought, at last, here's someone who can help me.'

'Yes. I see. We had quite a lot of inquiries after the story.'

'So you mean, I'm just one of hundreds who've got nothing better to do than bother a busy doctor?'

'No, of course not.' Her gentleness dispelled his flash of defensiveness. 'Now, let's see where I can fit you in.' She opened the desk diary. 'Next week, week after – when would be convenient for you?'

'As soon as possible,' Mark said huskily. He felt like the man in the cartoons, crawling over the desert sand with the oasis at last in sight.

His appointment with Peter Freeman was for the end of the following week. He spared a passing thought for National Health patients with their two-year wait.

He had still not confided in Judy. He would tell her after the operation was arranged, too late for her to argue him out of it. She'd see how much it meant to him, and would mean to her. With a new face, there would be a new Mark.

He told her he needed the car for a job interview in Newton Abbot. He left too early. His appointment was for two thirty. By one thirty, he was already in the car park of the Restora Hospital, a new concrete building with three floors of big windows and tubs of tulips and wallflowers outside the wide blue entrance door.

Not wanting to sit nervously in the waiting room, Mark went to the snackbar and bought a cup of coffee and a doughnut. There were no empty tables, so he sat with a mother and her little boy, who was there for a check and blood tests.

Everything was going right today. Judy and he had woken early and made love, and when he dropped her at the gift shop, she kissed him very sweetly and wished him luck with the non-existent job interview. He would buy her a present.

The roads had been clear, the sun shining on the pasture slopes whose walls traced the curves of the small humpy hills. Turning off through the outskirts of Kingscombe, he had seen fresh paint on houses, pink blossom frothing along the streets, front gardens rioting with tulips and aubrietia. Free of the cold winds, people walked more upright, looking round them, pushing babies and shopping trolleys as if they enjoyed it. To crown the luck, this slim, well-dressed mother at Mark's table told him that her son was a patient of Mr Freeman's.

'Oh.' Mark beamed, and liked the way the boy bit carefully round the edges of his sandwich. 'So am I.'

'He's wonderful, isn't he?'

Mark agreed enthusiastically, forgetting to keep his face half turned, to hide the scar.

'He's done so much for David.' She was glad to talk about it. The little boy had been born with a cleft palate and bilateral hare lip, a very serious condition.

'They didn't know if he would ever speak properly. But because of Mr Freeman – he's done all the surgery – we're really pleased with his talking now, aren't we, David? Take that sandwich away from your face for a minute. I think he's extremely handsome, don't you?'

Mark liked to hear a parent admire a child, without the nonsense about making him vain. He could have done with a little vanity himself at that age.

'They say that Mr Peter Freeman is one of the top plastic surgeons in his profession.' Mark wanted to keep talking about the doctor.

'Oh, absolutely. No question.' She gave Mark a steady look of fellowship across the table. He had not told her why he was here, and she was too well-mannered to ask. 'I think he's a very great man.'

Charged up by this encounter, Mark floated upstairs in the rose crystal casket to report to the secretary.

'Oh, there you are, Mr Emerson. I was trying to get you on the phone, but you must have left early.'

This was not an accusation, but Mark parried automatically, 'I had some stops to make,' as if it were.

'I'm so sorry. Mr Freeman has been called away to an emergency at the Torquay clinic.'

Oh, my *God*. The drop from high expectation was so physical that it felt like a thud.

'I was going to give you another appointment, but since you're here, Mr Grant, Mr Freeman's registrar, is seeing patients today. Is that all right?'

No!

Mark could hardly move or speak. He registered dully that a small brass plate on the secretary's desk named her as CATHERINE FREEMAN. Perhaps the coincidence had cancelled out the birthmark and got her the job with the 'very great man'.

Noel was tired and resentful. He did sometimes help Peter with his private practice, outside his hospital working hours, and for a fee. But last night he and Peter had been up long after midnight with two burns emergencies, and although he had time off this afternoon, he did not want to see patients at the Restora. He wanted to go to his hospital flat and sleep, but he could not let the man down.

When Catherine announced a new patient, 'Mark Emerson', on the intercom, Noel turned an indifferent face towards the door. The young man who came in looked as if he didn't want to be there. *That makes two of us.*

They recognized each other at the same time. It was that crazy bastard who had tried to waylay Peter at the Milner when Annette was crying after the dressings.

Noel would have liked to buzz through to Catherine and say, 'Why did you let him in here?', but he kept his face non-committal, which he was good at, because he did not believe a doctor should reveal anything of himself to the patient, and told Mark Emerson politely to sit down.

The young man, who was well-built and good-looking, sat rather awkwardly in the comfortable patient's chair and would not look at Noel. The scar on his right cheek where an injury had been rather inefficiently repaired was surely not enough for the wild-eyed desperation he had shown in the corridor at the Milner.

'What can I do for you?' Noel asked again.

At last Mark felt able to look at the supercilious doctor whose straight fair hair, brushed back, made his face naked and narrow, like a reptile, with those cold professional eyes.

'Mr Grant will report to Mr Freeman,' the secretary had said. So Mark fixed his mind on Peter Freeman reading this report and began, with difficulty, to tell his story.

Mr Grant listened, his lids half lowered. Then he got up and shone a thin torch on Mark's scar, muttered something about slight sarcoidosis, and sat down again.

When he asked, 'What are you hoping for?' Mark plunged in with regained eagerness.

'I want him to operate on it and take it away.'

'Do you think he can?'

'I know he can. I know he can help me.'

'Let me say,' Mr Grant said carefully, 'that the surgeon cannot exactly "take away" a scar. The scalpel is not a magic wand. Your cheek could never be exactly as it was before the accident, since plastic surgery, like any other surgery, must leave its own scar. For you, it would be a different, a lesser scar.'

'That's what I want.' Whatever the operation left, it would not be as bad as this. Mark felt the flush move up his face. The scar would be reddening. This man must see that.

'You know.' Mr Grant sat back and put the tips of his slender fingers together like an older practitioner. 'It's actually not that bad.'

It is, it is.

'It's not as unsightly as you think. You're a good-looking chap,' the doctor said. 'Do you believe that?'

Mark shook his head. 'People don't like how I look.'

'I do.'

What was he doing? Was he trying to keep Mark from seeing Peter Freeman?

'It disgusts people. I'm a freak.' He could not help raising his voice. 'I hate myself like this. I've lost my job because of it.'

He was shouting. He was making a fool of himself, sweating and breathing fast. Oh, if I could only have seen Peter Freeman, it wouldn't have been like this!

So now he had disgusted someone else, this privileged quack who stood between him and the only man who could help.

'Hang on,' Mr Grant said in his laid-back upper-crust voice. 'I'll have a word with the boss. We'll be in touch with you.'

'When?' Mark stood up.

'Oh – not too long.' The doctor manufactured sincere eyes. His voice was smooth and harmonious. As he opened the door of the consulting room for Mark, he gave him a pat on the shoulder.

'Take it easy.'

Chapter Seven

*W*hen you have built something up to a peak of excitement, you are asking for a let-down; but when Mark was actually in the consulting room with Peter Freeman, the only surprise was that he looked so young for a man of about fifty who had done what he had done. To sit down opposite the doctor's undemanding smile was everything he had needed and hoped for. It was journey's end.

'I know you've had some difficulty about a referral,' Mr Freeman said. 'That's all right. But I wondered why you had chosen to come to me?'

Instinct told Mark not to say, 'Because of the newspaper story.' Mr Freeman might not have liked it. He wasn't the sort of man who would read that paper. The secretary had talked about a lot of calls and inquiries. Mark must show himself to be not just an impulsive fan, not one of many. A special case.

He said, 'Because I knew you were the best plastic surgeon.'

Mr Freeman let that go. 'Why don't you start by telling me how you got the scar?'

Mark told the story, leaving out the bit about it being the van driver's fault for stopping dead, because his father was right: he had been too close.

'I was taken to a hospital, not the Birmingham Accident, but a smaller place in a town near where I crashed. They X-rayed my head, and a young surgeon stitched up my face in Casualty. They kept me overnight, and I went home next morning.'

His mother had collected him. 'Oh dear,' she said, when she saw the big white pad taped to his cheek, 'is that going to spoil your beauty?'

'Sorry, Mum,' he had managed to say in the car.

'Oh, well, it's happened.'

'How's Dad?'

'Raging. You know what he's like.'

'That was about seven years ago,' Mark told Mr Freeman.

'And you think they didn't do a very good job?'

'What do *you* think?' Mark leaned forward.

Mr Freeman had been studying Mark's face while he was speaking. 'It's possible that the wound wasn't cleaned thoroughly. If some small fragments of road dirt caused infection, that would affect the formation of the scar. Who looked at it while it was healing?'

'No one. I didn't want to go back there, and I wouldn't go to our family doctor, because he and my father – well, I'd had enough lectures. The stitches dissolved and after a bit I left the bandage off, and I thought that in time the scar would fade. It didn't. I think it's getting worse. I know it is. Does that happen sometimes?'

Mr Freeman did not answer. He asked, 'What about your father?'

'You can imagine. He was raving mad. He'd always been down on me, but this was it. I've tried, I really have, but he won't forget, and I've never been able to get along with him since.'

'What do your mother and father think about the scar now?'

'That's another thing.' It was a relief to tell this man everything, an unfamiliar luxury. 'It reminds my father of the car crash. It gets on his nerves.'

'Have you asked them what they would think about surgical revision now?'

'I'm nearly twenty-five. It's not their business.'

'Mr Grant told me you share a flat with a girlfriend. What would she think?'

'She pretends not to mind the scar, but I'm sure she hates me being disfigured.'

'You've not discussed it?'

'Oh, yes,' Mark lied. He was not going to tell Judy until the operation was arranged. 'But Judy's rather cagey. I don't always know what she's thinking.' He had not planned to tell his life story, but Peter Freeman was easy to talk to and he seemed to have plenty of time. 'So we have a lot of misunderstandings. Fights, you could say. She's very independent. Sometimes I think I need her more than she needs me.' He had not consciously thought about this before, but the truth hit him now, with a terrifying glimpse into the dark abyss that would open up beneath him if he were left alone.

'Everything,' he told the doctor, 'everything will be all right if only I can look all right.'

He was struggling to stay calm, but his head was crying out, I've got to get it done – nothing will be all right if you won't help me!

He had shouted in this room with Mr Grant. He desperately wanted Mr Freeman to know how bad it was, but he was not going to make a fool of himself in front of his hero.

The doctor was thoughtful. Mark, not comfortable with silence, asked, 'What would you do to get rid of the scar?'

'Let's say if I decided to operate. If you and I decided that surgery would be the best thing for you.' Mark had decided long ago. 'The scar goes diagonally down your cheek to the corner of your mouth. Smile for me. Right.' He took a hand mirror from a drawer and held it up for Mark to see. 'It crosses the crease lines and has stretched. That's why it seems more obvious.'

He had not said, like everybody else, 'It's not so bad.' Mark loved him for that.

'Any treatment I might do would involve very careful realignment into the crease lines. This would mean breaking up the line of the scar in the form of zigzags. Z-plasty, it's called.'

'Can you do that soon?'

'You have to understand that all surgery leaves some scarring. You wouldn't have a completely smooth cheek, but the marks would be less visible.'

'I know. The other doctor told me.' Mark had not totally believed it. Even now, he still imagined a perfect unblemished self. Peter Freeman could do miracles, couldn't he?

'I want it done,' he said confidently. 'You'll do it, won't you?'

'I'm going to think over the pros and cons, and I want you to as well, and I'll see you next week.'

I need to know now. Mark frowned and clenched his fists.

'Make an appointment with Catherine before you go. Right?' Mr Freeman stood up and shook hands. He was shorter and slighter than Mark, but he had the power. 'I'll look forward to talking to you next week.'

As Mark left the secretary's office, he saw another patient, a woman, going through the door between the waiting room and the consulting room. Mark's day was over. But he would be back.

In one of his informal discussions with Richard Valentine and Noel Grant, Peter brought up the subject of young Mark Emerson. He and Richard consulted with each other about their private patients, as well as about the people being treated at the Milner Unit.

'I'm in two minds whether to take this young man or not. Noel found him very tense and excited,' he told Richard. 'With me, he was more controlled, but there was an under-lying urgency. He wants a surgical revision of an old facial scar.'

'And he wants it *now*,' Noel said. 'Which is his attitude to many things in life, I would suspect.'

'There seems to be plenty of trouble in that life, besides the scar. Indeed, the scar may be the least of his problems.'

'It's not so bad, in any case.' Noel went over to the coffee-maker.

'It is to *him*,' Peter said. 'You or I might think we could live quite comfortably with a scar or a double chin, but it's what the patient thinks . . .'

'I know. First rule of cosmetic surgery,' Noel droned. 'But it does pain me to see a young layabout like that carrying on like a woman with bags under her eyes, when there may be someone in the next room who's had half his face burned away. More coffee?'

'Thanks. You didn't like Mark Emerson, then?'

'No, to be honest.'

'Don't worry.' Richard Valentine stirred his bulk in the chair to reach the coffee cup Noel had put on the table. 'You'll be knocking yourself out all your professional life to help and cherish people you wouldn't normally have anything to do with. Your patient, Peter – any history of psychiatric problems?'

'Not as far as I know. He's been in and out of several undemanding jobs, and recently lost his last one, which might have led somewhere. Thinks he's a freak. Can't get on with his father. Fights with his girlfriend. Scared she'll move out.'

'How long have they been together?' Noel asked.

'About two years, I think.'

'That'll usually do it.' Noel spoke from a disillusioned past. He was shortly to marry a new and untried love called Alison, very young and idealistic.

'So what do you think you'll do?' Richard Valentine asked.

'I'm not sure,' Peter said slowly.

'If he were mine,' Noel said, 'I'd do the revision for the sake of peace.'

'It would be difficult to make a success of it, and it could make his problems worse, you know. If he's been using the scar as a crutch, an excuse for failure and inadequacy – nobody likes me because I look like this – I wouldn't be doing him a favour. The scar would be improved, but he'd still lose jobs and girlfriends, and he'd have nothing to blame.'

'Except himself.' Richard nodded.

'What do you think, then?' Peter asked.

'I'd probably operate. But you'll make your own decision anyway.'

'It's a help to discuss it.'

'Why don't you have a word with Joseph Bremmer?'

Dr Bremmer was a clinical psychologist at the Royal, an energetic man with a head of bubbly curls and the face of a bright-eyed monkey, who was quite often seen sounding off ebulliently on television talk shows and panels.

Peter gave him a brief summary of Mark Emerson. 'I'm trying to understand this young man.' He was still undecided.

'Look, the doctor can't ever know how the patient feels. You can only listen to his suffering, however illogical. You know I'm not sold on cosmetic surgery, and he may be, as you suggest, using the scar for secondary gains, but if you want a quick answer, and I'm late, I've got to run, I'd say, do the surgery and make him happy. But I'll add one thing, Peter.' Dr Bremmer paused at the door. 'Watch that knife. With this kind of emotional immaturity, you'd better do a hundred-per-cent perfect job, or you're in for deep trouble.'

At home Peter discussed Mark with Catherine, who often made more sense than anyone else.

'Joe Bremmer gave me one of his snap judgements. He's the only shrink I know who's secure enough to do that. Tell me, Cath, if laser treatment had been available, or if I could have operated on you twelve years ago, if I could have removed at least part of the stain and given you a graft, would it have made you completely happy?'

'Well, I was beginning to be happy anyway, because you and I had found each other. But without that . . . I suppose

I still would have gone on thinking my parents wished I were somebody else. I still think that, in any case, except that now I quite like them. But if you'd been just a surgeon who operated, instead of my true love, I would still have been addicted to hiding my real self. This thing,' she cupped a hand over her chin and cheek, a familiar protective gesture, 'had always given me the excuse to do that. I'd quite have missed it. It was my excuse not to compete. Like people who hang on to a depression that cripples them, like the very fat girl who can't be accused of trying and failing.'

'Mmm. Thanks.' Peter went out to the garden, where Evangeline was working in her small vegetable plot, bending over with her legs apart and her neat bottom in the air, like a small child at the beach.

'What do, Daddy?' Her baby question, which he and she hung on to.

'Thinking.' He crouched down and began to pull out grass from the short row of early carrots, just beginning to shoulder their way out of the earth.

'What about?'

'Oh – you know. A patient.'

'The burns girl?' Evie and Philip knew about Annette, and had taken her tangerines and Smarties when they were in the unit.

'No, for once. I'm anxious about how she's doing at home, but she's all right. Are you all right, ducky? No more difficulty at school?'

Evie and Philip had not talked about it any more, so he assumed it had run out of steam, as problems did at school, unless you kept fomenting them.

*

When she was leaving for work, Judy asked Mark what he was going to do with his day. He almost told her that he was going to Kingscombe again by train for his second appointment with Peter Freeman, because she would not have time to stop and argue it out with him.

Instead he found himself jeering, 'Do you really give a damn?'

This evening would go better anyway. He planned a sensational announcement: 'June 15th! (Or whenever.) Take the day off. I'll need you to be with me when I go under the knife, to be made beautiful – all for you!'

Today he would have to ask Mr Freeman how much it was all going to cost. Gordon Dietz was still hanging in there, because 'No one can say that I won't do a favour for a friend,' and Mark's sister Georgina had laughed, but not flatly turned down his request for a small loan for 'a project which looks like a real winner'.

Mark greeted the blemished secretary like an old friend and went into the consulting room, smiling. Mr Freeman looked serious.

'Sit down, Mark.' He had not called him Mark before. 'I'll come straight to the point.'

Mark sat still, his hands gripping the knees of his salesman's suit which he had worn for the occasion.

'I'm sorry to disappoint you, but I'm afraid I can't take you on for surgery.'

It was brutally honest. It knocked the breath out of Mark, and pinned him against the back of his chair like a frog on a specimen board.

'There are two main reasons. The first, to elaborate on what I said last week, is that I believe revision of this particular scar would be – not impossible but quite difficult. I think you have high expectations of what I can do, and you might be disappointed. It would take twelve to eighteen months to see any real benefit, and the scar can never be completely eliminated.'

He paused to give Mark a chance to speak, but Mark could only stare at him.

'The second reason, and one you probably won't agree with, is that, apart from the physical result, my intervention can't give you what I think it is you want.'

With a thick tongue and a paralysed throat, Mark managed to mumble some sort of question.

'There are some problems in your life, I know, but this wouldn't solve any of them.'

Mark's anger, distant from the scene in the presence of Mr Freeman, returned with a rush. 'Aren't I the best judge of that?'

'Of course. I can only tell you what I think.'

'Doctors can't refuse treatment. You can't tell me no.'

'I can only tell you that I can't treat you, and there'll be no charge for the consultations, of course. There's nothing to stop you going somewhere else, the plastic surgery unit at the Frenchay Hospital in Bristol, for instance.'

Mark shook his head hopelessly. Didn't Peter Freeman understand that *he* was the one? The anger had receded, and now Mark felt like weeping. He could not hate this man. He had made him into a god, and now he had been cast out by him upon the outer darkness, where he could only howl his anguish.

Mark stood up and pushed his chair back clumsily.

'If it would help to see a counsellor or a therapist,' Mr Freeman was saying, as if from a distance, 'I could arrange for you to see someone here, or refer you to someone nearer your home.'

Mark stumbled out and ran down the hushed corridor to the stairs. Behind him he heard the voice of his hero, the seductive voice of the magician, calling his name from far away.

At the end of a long Friday Peter was thankful, as always, to go with his family to the cliff cottage on the estuary at Farne.

Waking early next morning, he raised himself to lean on the windowsill and look out at the high tide of water which made the house feel like a boat, already noisy with gulls, and sparkling in the sun. He had all day. He could go back to sleep, or go out and take Archie for a run along the top of the cliff.

He snatched up the phone at the first ring, but Catherine was already awake. It was Harry Baker, the new houseman.

'I'm sorry to – I'm sorry, Mr Freeman.' Harry was anxious, but he would learn not to apologize for calling a consultant. If it was a situation to apologize for, then he shouldn't have made the call. 'Casualty thought you should know. A young man tried to – well, he was brought in last night after trying to drown himself off one of the disused docks. Someone put a boat out and rescued him. After he was resuscitated, he wouldn't say who he was. He has now. I've just come on, and the psychologist – Dr Bremmer, is it? – thinks he's a patient you saw yesterday. He thought you should know.'

Chapter Eight

Mark had to stay in the hospital for a few days, to make sure there was no lung damage.

After he had half jumped, half fallen, from the dock and hit the water hard, like diving through concrete, he had swum out into rough water. He was going to swim for ever. He swallowed a lot of water, coughing and retching. It was very cold. He could not have gone on much longer when the fisherman with the wall eye pulled him out into his boat.

'You're lucky, boy.' He came to visit Mark on the ward. 'There's never anyone about on that derelict wharf, but two women on the path above saw you go in and went for help. You'd disappeared. "He's a goner," they said, but I thought I'd put the boat out in case. Good thing I did. You *were* far gone, boy. What were you up to? Didn't really want to drown yourself, did you?'

'Yes.' From the bed Mark watched the rise and fall of the man's paunch under the tight sticky jersey. 'Yes, I did.'

'People who try to kill theirselves really want to be rescued, isn't that right?'

'No,' Mark said, 'but thanks anyway.'

Same old story. No one believed the terminal depth of his agony. Even the frothy-haired psychologist he had to see in the hospital talked to him about impulsive gestures and attention-getting.

'You almost drowned yourself, Mark. You don't want to risk *that* again, I'm sure, so we'd better do something about it. I'll talk to you again this evening.'

Dr Bremmer gave Peter a snap diagnosis.

'Probably borderline personality.'

'Surely not, Joe. Basically sane but insecure and unstable, and with unreal expectations.'

'And very low tolerance of being thwarted. There are closet psychotics, you know, Peter. Outwardly functioning, but off the wall if things get too intense. I'd like to talk to his girlfriend.'

'He's obsessed with the scar as the reason for things that go wrong with his life.'

'That's why I think you should operate.'

'That's why I *don't* want to operate.'

'I think he should have the surgery as soon as possible,' Joseph Bremmer said. 'He's in a calm enough state now, after the orgasm of a suicide attempt.'

'As a private patient? He's got no money. He's talked

vaguely about a loan from friends or family, but it sounds as unrealistic as a lot of his ideas.'

'No, in your unit. I'm sure you can jump the queue with him, as an emergency. I'll square it with the Health Authority.'

'I don't like to do that, Joe. It's not fair to other patients.'

'How many have you got waiting for a scar revision?'

'None at the moment. But my reasons for not operating on this young man are still valid.' Yet how reliable had his judgement proved to be, after all? 'And now that he's done this, I certainly don't like being blackmailed into surgery.'

'You'd rather he goes straight out of this hospital and under a bus? He's my patient too, Peter, don't forget.'

Judy came into the ward in a very short skirt and dark glasses, as if she were visiting her lover in gaol. She wore a loose shirt of Mark's in a sort of bereaved, penitential way, and wept when she saw him sitting in a cotton dressing gown with the old men in the solarium. It was not her style to weep. When they had wounding fights, Mark was the one who cried. Judy threw things.

There must be some advantage to be gained from her vulnerability, but Mark wasn't sure what. He told her about his visits to the surgeon and his hopes for a new face, and how, once more, life had thwarted him.

'Remember when you said to me, Judy, "By contemplation of his own face, Narcissus was driven to suicide"?'

Judy looked up, her eyes fired with their old spirit, 'Oh, so it's my fault you jumped off the dock.'

'Narcissus drowned himself.'

'But you didn't.'

'I wish I had.'

'No, you don't. It's got you what you want, if Mr Freeman is really going to do the operation for you now.'

Mark Emerson's surgery was to be fitted in as a priority, and he was moved to the Milner Unit. Ethical or not, Peter would be glad to be done with it and get the unpredictable young man out of the hospital. 'And out of our hair,' Noel said.

Annette was still doing quite well at home. When the pain and discomfort increased with the warm weather, she was found to have grown, so a slightly larger collar and new pressure bandages had been fitted. In about a month she would be back in the unit for further grafting to her right elbow and groin, where there was beginning to be some restriction of movement.

'There goes my job,' Deirdre Leigh said. 'They gave me eight months' leave at the most.'

'Surely they wouldn't sack you?' Janet, the big Sister, said in the outpatient treatment room.

'Wouldn't they? You think a sick, maimed little girl comes before the affairs of the Planning Department?'

'You go back to them, Mum,' Annette said. 'I'll be all right in here with Janet and Mr Freeman and all my friends.'

'You *won't*. Not without me.'

At Peter's home, his daughter Evangeline seemed less nervous. She was well-behaved and quiet, which worried her mother as much as if she were rude. If school had gone stale for her, the summer term was almost over. Catherine would take three weeks off and be with the children by the sea at Farne, and Peter would join them whenever he could.

When the headmistress called, it was not Evangeline who was in trouble but Philip.

'He hit a girl?' Uncomplicated, sociable Phil – Peter could not believe it when Catherine told him.

'He punched her against the edge of a door and hurt her head.'

'It doesn't make sense, Phil.' He had to tackle his son.

'Doesn't have to.' The boy was not stubborn or defiant, just closed off.

'Who was the girl?'

'I don't have to say.'

'Why did you hit her?'

Philip shrugged, fiddling restlessly with a toy car in his hand, feet half out of his shoes, grubby shrunken T-shirt announcing CHAOS!

I don't know him, Peter thought in a flicker of panic. Is this what happens to boys? He tried to remember himself at ten, but could not distinguish any significant development from the general mêlée of fighting and fear and intermittent euphoria.

'What are you going to do?' Catherine asked afterwards.

'Nothing?'

'All right. Is he supposed to apologize? What shall we do if the girl's parents make a fuss?'

'I don't know, do you?'

Catherine shook her head. They looked at each other uncertainly, as if they were children caught out themselves.

Revision of a scar was usually carried out under local anaesthesia, but with a face wound, and given the nature of the patient, Peter had asked Colin Kemp to give a general anaesthetic.

For the microsurgery needed for the precise, delicate work, Peter used the theatre microscope, which could peer into any tiny area, and take pictures and videos. It had an extra arm with its own binocular magnification and focus, so that Noel could see what Peter saw and assist in joining blood vessels and nerves.

The tricky operation took about an hour and a half. Peter's back was giving him trouble after a heavy surgical list, so, with Noel assisting, he worked sitting on a stool at the microscope, humming to himself as he excised the old scar and broke up the line of the wound with zigzag cuts to bring it into the natural vertical creases. The scar was quite deep. Near the mouth, Peter found the reason for the slight roughness there. It could have been enormously worse.

'Obviously,' he said to Noel, 'they didn't clean the wound thoroughly enough. Look at this.'

Cutting deeper, Peter had found quite a large piece of glass bound with scar tissue to what looked like a branch of the main facial nerve. He had stopped humming. Noel did not say anything. The whole theatre was very quiet, as Peter took a fine scalpel from Sally to start freeing the nerve branch. Noel held the inner end with a nerve hook while Peter very delicately cut and pulled at the tangled lump of scar tissue, like unpicking a knot in string. One tiny mistake, and this boy could be left with a partial paralysis on the right side of his face.

He did not need the echo of Dr Bremmer's voice to tell him, 'Better do a hundred-per-cent perfect job.' He was going to.

Sally handed him a pair of forceps, and he brought out a

piece of glass nearly two centimetres long. Immediately he and Noel, working under the microscope as one person with four hands, joined the two ends of a divided nerve branch with very fine sutures and then closed the wound carefully in layers.

'You were right,' Peter said as he stitched up the last zigzag of the scar. 'If I hadn't gone in there and found that glass, it might have caused a lot of trouble some day.'

'But when I originally voted for surgery on this chap, I didn't know it was there,' Noel reminded him. 'I just believe that if a patient desperately wants an operation, you should do it.'

Noel was planning to make his consultant career in cosmetic surgery, where the money was. On how many unnecessary face-lifts would he waste his skill?

Peter saw Mark on the ward after he came round. He could not smile, but he reached out a hand for Peter's and squeezed it hard. His dark brown eyes looked sleepily contented, like a child waking to security.

'Everything went well.' Peter gave him back his hand, which was large and strong, but bitten sore round the nails.

Outside he told Janet, 'Watch this one. He may get depressed when the first euphoria wears off. You know his history?'

'Oh, yes. But he doesn't seem the type to try that again.' Everybody had different theories about suicide. 'Surgery go well?' She and Peter had known each other since this unit started. Big Janet had been the first staff nurse applicant and later, the first promotion to sister.

'Bit tricky. I found a piece of glass bound in deep scar tissue.

Had to separate part of the facial nerve, but the end result seems successful. I think I've done a good job.'

'You always do. How's Phil?' Janet was Catherine's friend too, and she knew the family well.

'Everything seems all right now. I should have been aware that something was going on.' He sighed. 'I fail my children by being so preoccupied here.'

'You can't do everything.'

'Why not? If I can't, I should change my way of life.'

Janet grinned. 'Give up the Milner, or give up your family?'

'Give up being so bloody inadequate.'

'Oh, look,' she said, 'the patients are bad enough. Don't *you* start.'

Mark's parents, who almost never travelled south, came to see him at the Milner Unit, his father lurching into the ward as painfully as if he still had his old arthritic hip joint.

'From braking in the passenger seat.' His mother laughed too loudly, to cover her shock at Mark's face. 'He hates me driving him.'

'I could have driven here.'

'Not two hundred miles, Marcus.'

'You say so.' Like a barrister's 'As your Lordship pleases'.

Mark's dressings were off his face now, the new scar and stitches exposed. His mother was satisfyingly sympathetic. She liked operations. When she was teaching full time, she had brought each sixth form to a Birmingham hospital for a tour and a careers talk, so she knew quite a lot. She asked some rapid fire questions, which Mark answered as best he could, 'as one who was present, but not participating'.

His father, sitting on the edge of a hard chair with his leg stuck out as if it would not bend, asked, 'Why did you have the scar monkeyed with?'

'I hated it.'

'Looks much worse now.'

'Oh, of course it does, Marcus, give the boy a chance. It's got to heal.' His wife reached over to put chocolate and paperbacks on the bedside locker, and her husband winced and jerked back his foot.

'Why didn't you tell us?' he asked, so kindly that Mark almost answered, 'I was scared.'

'I didn't tell anybody,' he said. 'Not even Judy.'

'Why?'

'I was in a bit of a state about it, I suppose.'

His parents had seen Dr Bremmer. They knew that he had tried to drown himself – how could they not? – although Mark had dreamed about keeping it from them.

'Stupid sort of thing to do,' his father said, still smiling but not kindly. 'What's wrong with you?'

'Nothing is wrong now.' Mark would not be able to smile for days, so he had to say smiley things with a serious face, and hope they could read his eyes.

'That shrink thinks you should have some therapy.'

'He would. That's his job.' Mark did not like the psychologist, who fancied he knew him better than he knew himself.

'Perhaps the man is right?'

'I don't think so.' Jean put her head on one side and looked at her son fondly. 'He just went into one of his glums, didn't you, Mark, like he's done all his life, that's nothing new.'

'Jean,' her husband said patiently. 'He tried to kill himself.'

'Not really. He's always made these dramatic gestures. He

gets it from me.' Like many unregarded women, she was given to parading herself: You know me . . . there I go again, etc.

Why didn't she throw her arms round Mark and beg, 'My son, my son, don't kill yourself, I need you!'

'He'll be all right,' she said encouragingly, and Mark's father grimly said, 'I can only hope so.'

'You're angry with me.' This could sometimes work as an irritant when the old man was being extra dry.

His mother protested, 'Oh, no, no, no, no!' His father ignored it.

They stayed quite a long time, and Fiona, who was one of the young nurses in training, brought extra cups and cake for them when it was teatime. Before they left, the visit improved, because Peter Freeman came in: clean white coat, fresh-coloured skin, eyes friendly, Mark's hero whom he could proudly introduce to his parents.

They said more or less the right things, thank God, although they were not awed by Mr Freeman's fame, or bowled over by the glow about the man, which only Mark could see.

His father said to the surgeon, 'I'd like a word with you, if I may,' which meant in private outside, but no harm could come of it. The operation was done. Mark had achieved his goal, for once. Not even his father could take that away from him.

Before Mark jumped off the dock and struck out towards Spain, Judy had made up her mind to tell him that she was leaving. Duncan, the quiet friend from BBC Bristol who had been her background lover for quite a while, was tired of waiting. But now, being a tolerant, unselfish man who tried to see the other person's point of view – part of his attraction for Judy, after two years with Mark – he agreed that you don't walk out on a man who has just attempted suicide.

'Wait, darling. Just till he gets straightened out. It won't be long,' Judy promised.

But then she must be there for Mark before and after the operation. He could not go back to the flat alone, and after the stitches were removed from the new scar, she could not leave him while he was so distraught about how it looked.

If Duncan had thundered, 'Choose between him and me!', how could Judy have decided where her immediate loyalty lay? Fortunately he was not that sort of man. He fretted quietly, and Judy was reasonably nice to Mark, without sleeping with him unless it was absolutely unavoidable, because it was immoral to have sex with someone you were going to abandon.

When the stitches came out, Mark's new Z-plasty scar was sealed tightly with thin adhesive strips across the wound. After two weeks he returned to the Milner Unit, the tape was removed, and the already healing wound carefully cleaned.

'How does it look?' Mark kept asking.

'Fine,' the nurse said brightly.

Peter Freeman came in and studied the scar in a long silence.

'What does it look like?' Mark could not tell anything from the surgeon's concentrated face.

'Just as I expected. Do you want to see it now, or wait till you get home? Now? All right, but remember what I told you. It's a new wound, and until it heals completely, it's going to look worse than the old one.' This kind of warning could not penetrate the elation Mark had felt since the operation.

Mr Freeman sent him to look in the mirror over the sink of the treatment room. Mark turned round at once.

'It looks terrible.'

'That's what I told you. And I have to tell you also that it will probably look even worse before it looks better. It will take a long time.'

'Put some tape on it.' Mark's voice had an edge of hysteria.

'It needs the air now.'

'I can't go out like this.' Mark turned angrily back to the mirror. The right side of his face flared sore and swollen. The high irregular line of the scar was red and lumpy. He looked as if he had been whipped.

'Of course you can, Mark. If anyone says anything, tell them exactly what you've had done. Listening to grisly surgical details will take their mind off the look of it.'

Within a week Mark was back at the Milner Unit in a crisis.

'It looks worse. People stare at me. Women grab their children. Look it's a darker red now, and it's very sore and tight, here at the end. Something's gone wrong. I'll never be able to smile again.'

The crisis fell flat. Mark was given the usual reassurances. It seemed to be a busy day at the clinic, with a lot of people in the waiting room, a child crying somewhere, phones ringing, bustle and trolleys in the corridors. Mr Freeman's encouragement was too studiedly patient. Mark wanted to retort, 'You're angry with me,' but did not think he would get away with it.

He believed that he and Peter had become friends at the Milner. Noel Grant hated him, that was obvious. And mutual. But Mr Freeman – would he ever get the chance to call him

Peter? – did like him, although he would not tolerate hero-worship.

One evening when the surgeon had come to the ward to see him before he went home, Mark had said, 'I wish my father had been like you.'

Mr Freeman dismissed this briskly. 'We all dream of other parents. I used to wish *my* father was like the great surgeon who taught me most of what I know. Later I worked in Sheffield at the same hospital as his son, and he told me the old man was tyrannical, stingy and totally unreachable by his family.'

Now, when Mark came back to see him in turmoil and Mr Freeman had no time for him, he suggested that Mark might talk to a counsellor. Mark agreed, to please him. 'As long as it's not Dr Bremmer.' He hoped that Mr Freeman would ask, 'What's wrong with Dr Bremmer?' so that Mark could tell him, but professionals did not get tricked like that.

The counsellor was in the main hospital now, bringing succour to disfigured people like Mark. He saw her in a small hot room in the Social Work Department. Amazingly she turned out to be Mr Freeman's secretary from the Restora Hospital, the woman with good legs and a dreadful birthmark over the left side of her face.

If she said, 'You're doing fine,' Mark would walk out. But she said, 'Your face looks painful. Does it still hurt?'

'Yes.' A small whine crept into Mark's answer.

'And I expect you're disappointed with what it looks like. Have you been going out?'

'Just to the shops. I haven't been to a pub, or anywhere I'm known. It's bad enough with strangers.'

'But it's going to take quite a while for your scar to settle

down. You've got to be out and about among people, and
you said you had to look for a job.'

'In a mask?'

She laughed. 'No. In control. That's the trick. Suppose you
go to the pub tonight. It's Friday. You'll know people there?
All right, go in with a smile, and they'll smile back.'

'They'll dive for cover.'

'No they won't, Mark. Go up to them and start talking.
Get their eyes hooked, so they won't be looking at the rest
of your face. Do your friends know about the operation?'

'I suppose the word's got round. Probably all wrong.'

'So tell them the facts, and they won't have to worry about
asking or not asking. You're in control, see?'

'I'm not, Catherine.' She had asked him to call her that.

'I know, it's not so easy. You'd rather just go in – with
your girlfriend? – and sit in a corner and be left alone.'

'Till this obscenity is healed.'

'How about a dab of cover make-up?'

'I'm not a queen.'

'A lot of men use it. I'll tell you what it's called anyway.
You can get it at any chemist.'

'*You* don't use it.' Mark stared directly at her stained
cheek.

'Only sometimes as a social thing,' she said. 'I don't put
it on for work, because I'm trying to help other people to
accept their own disfigurement.'

'Have *you*?'

'I hope so.' When her smile melted down, you could see
what it really meant to have one side of you painted scarlet,
from the lower lid to the chin. 'Though you can't ever really
come to terms with it and say, "I don't care." You're lucky,

Mark. Your blemish is going to heal and fade, and in the end go almost right away.'

'That's what Mr Freeman says. What do you think of him?'

'He's one of the best in his profession,' she said at once.

'I mean as a person?'

'Oh, well, I'm prejudiced, I suppose.'

'Because you work for him. I thought, when I met you at the private hospital, it was odd you had the same name as him.'

'Be odder if I didn't.' She radiated the enormous smile that both spread her stained cheek wide and diminished it. 'He's my husband.'

'Could have knocked me down,' Mark said to Judy. They had gone to a pub, but an unfamiliar one, dim and grouchy, where no one spoke to anybody.

' "Be in control," she said.' Mark had liked the woman Catherine at first, but he could not forgive her for being married to Peter Freeman, living with him, screwing him, nagging at him as if he were an ordinary man. He was giving Judy a mocking version of the 'counselling'. 'You're my homework.' He leaned forward. 'Look into my voodoo eyes and I'll contro-o-ol you.'

'The scar looks awful,' Judy said honestly.

After several drinks, they began to fight on the way home, and continued in the flat, which was depressing and claustrophobic because Mark had spent too much time here.

'I'm fed up.' He ripped an expensive poster off the wall and stuffed it into Judy's wide alabaster vase.

'So am I. I can't live with this colour scheme much longer.

These sinister curtains – and you've made the place a dump, being here all day.'

'I said I'd decorate.'

'You said. You didn't.'

'I've been sick! I've been a patient.'

He was shouting. Someone banged on the front door, and Judy's sister Daisy came in. 'Oh, good, are you having a fight? Don't stop for me.'

'What are you doing here?' Judy gave her a sister's welcome.

'I need food. What did you have for supper?'

'We ate in a pub.'

'I need a bed.'

'Why?'

'I've been staying with Crackers, but he threw me out.'

'With those scaly hands? I don't know where you pick up these vile men.'

'At least mine don't try to kill themselves,' Daisy said nastily.

'They would if they had any sense.' Judy stuck out her tongue and went to make coffee.

'No offence, Mark.' Daisy moved to kiss him and went, 'Yuck!' when she got close to his face. 'I'm really into suicide. I can relate to what you did.'

'You ever tried it?'

'Not yet, but it's one of my alternative agendas. You genuinely wanted to die, huh?'

Mark said, 'Yes,' because he had told everybody that. But sitting here with Daisy, slung about with bags and cords, her greenish hair pulled up into a loose clump with pigeon feathers stuck through, it came to him that the answer might be 'no'.

'Good for you.' Daisy smiled sweetly. 'I really admire that for transcendence. When Judy gets sick of you, let me know.'

Judy had met a man who needed a delivery driver. 'He runs a small printing firm, and he has to drive the van himself until he finds someone.'

'Who'd take on a driver with a smashed-up face?'

'Derek would. I've told him about you. But not,' she laughed, 'how you came by the scar in the first place.'

Mark got the job. It felt good to be working. It always did at first, until the novelty faded to boredom. Most of his deliveries were to the rear of shops and offices, with few people about. If anyone stared, Mark stared back, which was easier because of his status as driver of a white van with SOMERSET PRESS on the side in bright blue lettering. Take me or leave me. You want the goods, I bring them. Was this what counsellor Mrs Freeman had been getting at?

Most of the time he was on his own in the van. The job was all right, and his new scar did seem to be settling down, flattening ever so slightly, paler in certain lights.

'Don't you think so, Judy?'

'For God's sake, stop brooding over it. It's healing. That's all. Come away from the mirror.'

Judy was a bit chilly and snappish these days. Resentful of his new independence?

You don't love me. Mark had whined that so often since they had been together, that he was as sick of it as she was. 'I love you, Jude,' he tried, very simply and sincerely.

'No. No you don't. You shouldn't use that word.'

'We used to love each other – what happened?'

'You were such a child,' Judy said. 'Now you're outgrowing me.'

Did she think that? Was she afraid that one day he would grow up and leave home? Poor Judy, he felt very tender towards her.

Time for a gesture. When Mark got his pay, he bought white glossy paint and some very expensive material for new living room curtains – splashed with flowers, clean-looking, blue and pink and green on a pure white background. He put the bulky package on a shelf behind his sweaters. After Judy came home, he would spread it out on the bed and sound the trumpets.

Judy came in tired with a bag full of food, because now that Mark was working he didn't do the shopping any more. She did not ask, 'How did it go today?', so he told her.

'Had a pretty good day today. Must have driven about a hundred miles, back and forth, and got the rush orders out on time.'

'Good, you've done well, Mark. You're tougher than you think.'

'Of course I am. Tougher than anyone gives me credit for.'

Mark was buzzing with excitement. In a moment he would go into the bedroom, spread out the beautiful fabric like a bright-hued waterfall, and lead her in there with her eyes shut.

'Except me. I know you can make it. Look.' Judy sat down. 'I couldn't say this before, but now I've got to tell you.'

'No. *I've* got something to tell *you*. Wait there for a moment.' He went towards the door.

'No, Mark, don't stop me.' Judy jumped up and grabbed his arm. 'Listen, I've been a coward. I should have told you before. I've made up my mind. You're all right now, so I'm going with Duncan. He's got a house. You can keep this flat, and I'll pay my share of next month's rent.'

Mark had jerked his arm away. He stood silent against the bedroom door and let her talk. Then he said, 'Who the hell is Duncan?'

'You know, he came to supper, when Daisy was here.'

'He's a poof.'

'First I've heard of it. Oh, Mark, you know this hasn't been working with us. You're sick of the fights, and so am I.'

'Why didn't you tell me before?'

'I couldn't. You'd tried to drown yourself. Then the operation.'

'You stayed with me because you were sorry for me?'

'In a way. I felt I had a – a sort of duty to stay with you.' Judy was the only person who could use words like duty seriously.

'You're a patronizing bitch,' Mark said. 'Serves me right for getting mixed up with an older woman.'

He was very angry. Not wanting to rage and explode and kill her, but cold with anger, chilled to the bone with a future lost in the frozen wastes of outer space. 'You can't take the car,' he said.

'I'm not going to. Duncan has an old Volvo wagon. I'll drive that.'

Judy left the next day. After she had gone, Mark took out the heavy packet of curtain material and spread it out on their bed. He lay down and covered himself with it, pulling it over his face to smell the clean crisp cottony freshness.

Then he got up and folded it carefully into the brown paper. The next day he put it on the front seat of the van and took it back to the shop.

'My wife didn't like it.' This must be how it felt to return a wedding ring.

They gave him only half the price he had paid for it, because it was cut off the roll. 'It's a remnant now.'

He did not bother to try to return the white paint.

Chapter Nine

*T*owards the end of August Peter took Annette back into the Milner Unit to renew his grafts on two of the badly burned areas. The child had been walking for some time, but tightness over the left groin was giving her an uneven gait, and the right elbow, burned down to the bone and one of Peter's main worries all along, could not be straightened fully because of scar contraction.

Annette was admitted to a four-bed ward near the nurses' station in C wing. When Peter came in to welcome her, Deirdre Leigh, inspecting the new set-up with the eye of a seasoned hospital mother, asked him why her daughter had not been put into a single room, as before. 'Her old room is empty. I took a look.'

'Annette was isolated because of infection, Mrs Leigh.

When that danger eased off, she was still so ill that we didn't want to move her.'

'It was nicer,' Deirdre mused, unfocused, as if he had not spoken. 'So quiet and private.'

Peter glanced at the other beds, in case anyone had taken offence at this, but two of the patients were off somewhere and the rodent ulcer lady in the opposite corner was asleep.

'You both went through hell in that room,' he said. 'I should think you'd want to forget it.'

'*I* do,' Annette said chirpily. She was a different child from the passive, suffering creature of six months ago, a joy to Peter's heart. 'This is more fun.' She had arranged her books and photographs and stuffed animals round her bed, staking out her territory. 'And all my same nurses are here, all my best friends.' She gave Peter the full beam of her innocent, blithe smile and clear blue eyes.

'As long as you like it here, pet,' her mother said in the slow, acquiescing drone she used for doctors and nurses with whom she did not agree. 'You're all that counts.'

Once Deirdre had got used to the new situation, she found some advantages to being on a ward. Annette, recovering from the new grafts, attracted attention as the youngest patient in the unit, and Deirdre was the only long-stay mother. Other patients and their families treated her with some respect, because she knew the doctors and nurses and physiotherapists better than they did, and could tell tales of past adventures, and was intimately acquainted with the valley of the shadow. Deirdre began to use make-up again, which she had not bothered with in the hospital before.

New patients came and went, in and out of this clean bright

ward to which Deirdre brought a touch of home. Skin cancers, a varicose ulcer, short-stay lacerations, a severed thumb – Deirdre was able to give them reassurance before surgery and sympathy afterwards, and those small services like arranging pillows and bringing fresh water or amusing a small child so that the replanted thumb woman could talk to her husband in peace.

Mr Freeman had even taken her to talk to a burns mother in the children's building, who was having a hard time summoning that strength of hope and faith which Deirdre knew was an important part of healing.

'Look at my Annette.' She told the tearful woman how appalling the injuries had been. 'Sixty per cent of her body. Everyone expected her to die. I faced that, but I never believed it in my heart.'

'Didn't you ever want to give up and run away from it all?' The poor young woman was weeping into her coffee in a corner of the cafeteria.

'I couldn't. And nor can you. Nor *will* you.' Looking back, Deirdre could not really remember making a conscious effort to be brave in that crisis time when Annette had been so ill. But it would be no help to this young woman disintegrating inside her baggy mauve track-suit to say, 'I was a zombie.' So she said, 'Women are strong, Nicole. We have to be.'

And then suddenly, with Annette's discharge planned for the end of the week, time went backwards. The elbow graft, which had looked promising at first, had not taken. More surgery would have to be done.

Peter and Noel went through the curtains round Annette's bed, where Sister Janet had the elbow exposed. The graft was mottled with black, yellow and white patches and was not sticking to the wound. Janet had lowered Annette's head, but she could still see the inside of her arm held out on the splint.

'What's wrong with it?' she asked Peter. 'Didn't it work?'

'Not well enough, I'm afraid. You know how it is with grafts. They don't always do what they're supposed to.'

'What will you do now? There can't be much room on my bottom for any more donor skin.'

'Don't worry,' Peter said. 'We'll fix you up. Just stay with us a bit longer.'

'You'd been hoping to start school with the others, hadn't you?' Janet began to redress the elbow.

'Oh, well.' Annette was not passive now. She had become quite avid for life as she grew stronger. But she did not cry or rage at the disappointing setback of more surgery. She accepted it with pathetic maturity, as if the terrible assault of the fire had robbed her of what was left of the rest of her childhood.

'What will you try now?' Noel asked Peter, when they had left Annette with the curtains drawn back and the dressing trolley gone, and the mother sitting by the bed, saying things like, 'This is a drop in the bucket to what you've been through,' more to encourage herself than her daughter.

'I don't know,' Peter said candidly. 'I thought the thick split-skin graft would work, but a thinner one might have taken more certainly.'

'And left you with the same problem of flexion contracture,' Noel said.

'Any ideas?' Peter asked him.

'Yes, sir.' Noel was never at a loss. 'Something you might

try – I've seen it done at the Frenchay on the back of a knee – multiple Z-plasty. Tricky, but perhaps worth trying?'

In his mind Peter began to see the elbow under the theatre lights, felt in his hand the instruments with which he could remove the failed graft, carefully, delicately, so as not to injure the deeper healed levels of the burn, saw exactly where he would make the first of the new diagonal incisions . . .

He looked quickly up at Noel. 'You want to do it?'

Noel did not waste time demurring. He said at once, 'I'd love to.'

'It was your idea. I'll assist. Get a time fixed with theatre and tell Mrs Leigh.'

Deirdre felt really quite rotten. The third operation on Annette's poor tortured elbow was thought to be a success. They all seemed happy about it, but Deirdre was not happy.

'We've put all our trust in this place, Ted, and in Mr Freeman. And then he goes and lets a junior doctor cut her about, a man still in training. It doesn't seem right at all.'

'He's done a good job, Dee, and he's not in training. He's a qualified surgeon, is Mr Grant, that's why he's not called Doctor.' Ted had been talking to a knowledgeable porter during the dreadful slack hours of waiting, when the shiny automatic doors to the theatre wing had swung closed behind his child, and she could be dead under the anaesthetic for all he knew.

'He's not old enough.' Deirdre felt the same about fresh-faced Mr Freeman, although he was older than he looked. She would have preferred surgeons to be greying and distinguished, with a deep slow way of speaking.

'You're tired, Dee, that's all. Come home with me tonight and get a good night's sleep in our comfortable bed.'

'With you in it, groping? I said I'd stay here tonight, so I must.'

'Shall I bring Campbell in tomorrow?'

'I don't think Annette's up to it, Ted. Has he asked to come?'

'He doesn't say much, you know what he's like. He's got two jobs, though, walking people's dogs in the park.'

'You make sure he doesn't bring them in the house.'

'Of course, old dear, never fear.'

'I suppose the place is a mess anyway. What's broken?'

'Nil. Come home and you'll see. It's a palace, Alice.'

When Ted had gone, although it was good to get him out of the ward with his fidgeting and walking about, recrossing his thick legs, trying to say something nice to the other patients but not knowing what, Deirdre felt more depressed and down than before. She had more or less given up smoking last winter when she had to spend so much time at the hospital, where notices browbeat you at every turn: THANK YOU FOR NOT SMOKING; but the persistent craving started up in her throat now. She must have a cigarette.

She went out through the small side door near Annette's old single room which she had used in those old days when she wanted to nip out for a breath of air without having to go through the front lobby. There was a small staff car park out here, and a quiet path between late-flowering shrubs.

Where the path crossed an open grass slope between the Milner Unit and the main buildings of the Royal, there were three wooden benches, each labelled with the name of the person who had donated it. Patients and visitors sat here, and nurses sometimes, like white gulls briefly settled, but it was colder this evening, with a wind off the sea, and only one bench was occupied.

For some reason, perhaps because it was the nearest, Deirdre sat down on this one, Fergus T. Ansell, beside a young man whose thick blowing hair covered and uncovered a reddened diagonal scar. Malignant melanoma? Deirdre was familiar with those.

She took out a cigarette and the young fellow lit it for her, and one for himself when she offered the packet. They exchanged a few meaningless remarks. She was sitting on his good side, and he kept his face in profile, looking over the roofs and chimneys and spires all the way down to where the sea would be if you could see it for the clutter of the harbour.

'You got someone in there?' He jerked his head towards the unit.

'My little daughter. She's in again for more skin grafts, six months after the fire.'

'The child who was so badly burned? I've heard about her.'

'You've been a patient, then?'

'Mr Freeman operated on me. Peter Freeman.'

'He's our doctor too.'

They talked for a while about Mr Freeman, in whom the young man seemed quite interested. He asked about the surgeon's family, and it bucked Deirdre up a bit to be able to display her knowledge of the great man. She had talked to Mrs Freeman a few times – poor woman, I'd shoot myself if I had that birthmark – and the boy and girl had been brought in to see Annette when they were at the hospital with their father: shy girl, outgoing boy, the reverse of Deirdre's two.

'Brilliant, isn't he?' The young man forgot not to turn his face to her. 'He's famous, you know. It was all in the papers.'

Deirdre shrugged, to show that she did not need tabloid sensationalism to tell her about Peter Freeman.

'Did he operate on your face?' she asked, not from interest but because talking was better than the brooding depression that was on her today.

'About six weeks ago. I had this old scar, from a deep wound when I ran through a glass door as a child, that had been cobbled together by some half-baked casualty officer who didn't know her job. Mr Freeman did plastic revision.'

'Oh, yes?' Deirdre looked at him, but she was thinking of something else.

'I know, I know.' He put the palm of his hand over his cheek. 'It still looks terrible, but they won't admit it. "Doing fine." It makes me furious. It looks much worse than it did before. People stare, and my girlfriend's left me because of it.' He closed his eyes for a moment and dropped his hands into his lap, biting his lip. 'I had all sorts of questions for Mr Freeman today, but the OP clinic was taken by Dr Grant.'

'Mr Grant,' Deirdre was able to say.

'Whatever he calls himself, I'm not impressed.'

'Nor me.' Deirdre sighed. The short relief of talking to another human being who did not work at the hospital was dragged down again by her grievance against Noel Grant. 'I didn't want him operating on Annette.'

'Is she all right?'

Deirdre nodded. 'It wasn't right, though. It should have been Mr Freeman. You know what they do, don't you, in the National Health. They let people practise on you, like a hairdressing school. I'll bet Mr Freeman's private patients don't get the registrar building new silicone bosoms for them.'

It occurred to her that the young man, having noted her own meagre front, might be thinking, 'Pity he couldn't do it for you, lady.' And there had been a time, long before the fire, when Deirdre had dreamed unattainably of having an operation like that, long, long ago when it was permissible to want things for yourself.

'I tried to say I wanted Mr Freeman to do Annette's operation,' she went on, 'and they're quite polite, but they don't take a blind bit of notice, do they, and you feel that it's all taken out of your hands.'

There was a lump rising in her throat that swelled up into her hot face and pushed tears dangerously near the edge and filled her mouth with chaotic words.

'You don't count, do you, and there's no end to it all, and oh – and oh –'

She had been so careful, at the hospital, never to let herself go. She had played her part faithfully, star mother, selfless, inexhaustible, rallying to each new crisis. But as the young man sat slumped in his pea jacket, listening or not listening, it all came pouring out of her like vomit. Things she would never tell anyone. Some things she did not even know she thought. She wept. She had no tissues, and the water streaming from her face blew away in the wind. 'Why me?' she cried. 'Why should it happen to me?'

Quite soon, it was over. The tears had dried up, and she did not want to say any more, did not know why she had said as much as she had. She found a crumpled tissue at the bottom of her pocket, lit a cigarette and went back to the ward, stubbing out the cigarette in a tub of geraniums on the way.

Noel had done an excellent job on Annette's elbow. The first dressings had not been changed yet, and Peter could only hope that the complicated pattern of incisions would look as good in two days as it had in theatre. He had Annette on a new broad spectrum antibiotic sent down urgently from the maker by helicopter, but would the same infection problems still creep in?

He wished he could worry to Catherine, but she and the children were still at the cliff cottage, and he would not join them until the weekend, because of evening appointments and early-morning operations. He looked in on Annette before he went up to the Restora. No sign of infection, no swelling below or above the splinted elbow. But the child's face was flushed, and Mrs Leigh said, 'I think she's running a temperature.'

'Only slight, on the chart.' He put his finger against the carotid artery.

'Are you worried, Mr Freeman?'

He knew her too well to lie. 'I am a bit,' he admitted.

'So am I.' Mrs Leigh looked pale, and her eyelids, not made up today, were pink and swollen as if she had been weeping. Who would blame her?

Going out to the car park, Peter met Noel in the corridor.

'Got a moment, sir?'

'Of course.' They leaned against the wall. They were both tired.

'I had a bit of trouble with that crazy character,' Noel said.

'Which one?' Although Peter thought he knew.

'Mark Emerson. He came to the dressing clinic. Disappointed to find only the minion there, of course, instead of the great mogul.'

'I'll see him next month.'

'Good thing he lives so far away. He can't keep popping in whenever he's got nothing else to do.'

'How does the scar look, Noel?'

'Like you would expect at six weeks. You did a beautiful job, but he refuses to believe it. The surgery he so desperately wanted hasn't improved his outlook.'

'I was right after all, Noel. I should never have operated on him.'

'And let him take another shot at suicide?'

'I wonder. Let's not confuse a sensible decision not to gratify the obsession of somebody who expects a magic scalpel to transform his life totally, with an order that says, "Go away and kill yourself." That would have been his responsibility, not mine.'

'But you'd have felt guilty as hell.' Noel laughed and pushed his tall, slim body away from the wall. 'Only good thing – it would have got him out of our hair.'

Dusk was beginning to settle into the countryside, and the street lamps were on in the main part of the small town where Peter lived. His avenue was darker, overhung by trees, and lighted windows set back inside gardens. His own house was quite dark. There was no one about, but, as he slowed to turn in through the gateway, he had a glimpse of a man moving away under the trees on the opposite side, close to the garden walls.

Why should he imagine it was Mark Emerson? The boy lived sixty miles away, and could have no reason to be in this road. Nevertheless, after he had gone into Liberty House and turned on lights and poured himself a drink – not even a dog to welcome him – Peter switched off the porch light and went outside again, walking on the grass, not the drive, and stood half behind the gatepost to look up and down the empty road.

After Judy left, anger kept Mark going, in a blurred, haphazard fashion. He drove the van for Derek because it was better than lying in bed all day. He kept bits of the flat clean, and ignored the rest. Scouring the sink and washing the vinyl floor with too much soapy water could be done furiously, with a scowl and gritted teeth. The few things that Judy had left behind and the presents she had given him – mugs, funny little pictures, the fox mask, an alarming belt buckle, a pan to grill steak on top of the stove – he either broke or threw out of the window into the yard where the dustbins were.

After he did this, he would take a look in the mirror and see the zigzag scar suffused with blood, witness to the intensity of his pain.

Driving the van aggressively, Mark fumed about treachery and ingratitude. After all he had done for her . . . changing his face, suffering through the operation . . . taking the job she suggested, although it was a comedown after working for the paper. He went 'Up yours' to scared pedestrians, and loomed behind small cars, flashing his lights.

When the rage and resentment ran out of steam, sadness and loneliness slithered in, as he had known they would. Where was everybody? During the last months he had lost touch with old mates, and the crowd that he and Judy used to mix with and call friends. Growing obsession with disfigurement had turned him in on himself and Judy. Now there was only himself. His job was solitary. That was what he had wanted. Derek and the typesetters did not bother him. Deliveries brought only a brief contact with someone who signed his slip and said, 'Put the stuff there.'

He thought about Judy's sister Daisy, who admired him. She had once said, 'When Judy gets sick of you, let me know.' Daisy was a weird kid, but kind enough in her sloppy way, and she and Judy were permanently at war. Mark could defect to the other side.

He had no idea where Daisy lived, but he knew some of the places where she hung out. She was not at likely market stalls, and had not been seen at any of the ruined barns or campsites on the hill above the abbey ruins, where the children of delight came and went. He looked for her at the handicapped children's playgroup where she had once been sent by the Magistrates' Court for community service, and at the youth club in Bridgwater, where she used to teach tie-dyeing.

In the end it was Daisy who found him. When he came out of the Somerset Press office with a bunch of order slips, she was sitting in the passenger seat of the white van, waiting for him. Her uncle, the only family member Daisy had anything to do with, had had a birthday card from Judy that said she was now living in Clifton.

'So you're free now,' she told Mark. 'You can be any of the selves you want to be.'

'I'm lonely as hell,' Mark said. 'My life is in shreds, and I hate myself almost as much as I hate your sister.'

'Oh *dear*.'

Daisy moved briefly into the flat and his bed, with her

seaweed hair that always smelled wet even when it was dry, and her tough bare feet and generous body. One day she took him to see her American healing friend who made his home quite comfortably in a green bus without wheels, tucked into a hollow behind stone walls and thorn trees on the north-west corner of Dartmoor.

Daisy called her friend Goo-roo, but his name was Bob, which seemed too unmythical for his way of life. He had done some years of medical training in the United States, but believed that his herbs and thick soups and relaxing imagery were more effective than anything clinical he had done. He did not perform healing on Mark's scar, because he said it was doing all right for itself without interference.

'It looks ghastly.'

'Only to you, kid. To me, it looks like the everyday mystery of repair cells quietly doing their job. You're a living miracle, Mark.'

'Why?'

'Anyone is, with a healing wound.'

He was small and trim with a neat beard and basin-cut hair the colour of yellowed nylon, and nimble feet and hands. He had cats and dogs and goats and chickens and ducks and a bicycle and a hand-painted Citroën 2CV that looked like a deck chair. He knew a lot about animals and birds and the way they healed themselves with whatever their surroundings had to offer. He knew how they preserved life only to continue their species, and died without struggle when it was time to get out of the way. He had learned a lot about the moor too, and the people who had once lived here and grown away from the animals with tools and wheels and ideas of conquest.

Wandering about with him, Mark picked up a black and

white flint and was going to throw it at one of the predator birds that hovered above the moor, gliding on air streams.

'Don't!'

'I couldn't have hit it.' Mark felt criticized and defensive, but Bob had spotted that the flint was a hand tool.

'Look, you can see where they bashed at it to narrow the sides, and then ground it down.' It was roughly triangular, fitting the palm of the hand, the jagged edges still razor sharp. 'Neolithic, I guess. Maybe two thousand years BC.'

'You want it?' Mark felt that this was Goo-roo's part of the moor.

'No, you keep it. I'm always finding stuff.'

Mark wrapped the flint in a leaf and put it in his pocket. It was the only valuable thing he had ever owned that had not cost money.

Inside the bus Daisy told Goo-roo about Mark trying to drown himself, because she thought that was the most interesting thing about him. Bob felt that the suicide urge might be explained as past-life nostalgia, and offered to regress Mark to former death experiences in search of cathartic release.

Mark lay on his back on one bunk while Bob hopped on to the bunk opposite, with his legs crossed beneath him, and told him to fly up on to the roof of his house.

'Which house?'

'Any house you know.'

'I don't know what the roof of my block of flats is like.'

'Belt up,' from Daisy, 'and get out on any old roof.'

Once there, he rose out through the top of his head and soared, like the birds of prey on currents of air, high and far, until Bob murmured, 'Now . . . come down with your eyes shut. Slowly . . . slowly . . . now feel your feet on the ground. There. Don't open your eyes. You're in a former life. Look down and tell me what you're wearing on your feet.'

With his physical eyelids closed, Mark opened the eyes of his imagination. 'Sandals.'

'Oh, for God's sake,' Daisy broke in impatiently. 'When people see themselves in sandals, or turned-up Turkish slippers, you know they're making it up.'

Goo-roo continued to guide Mark, beyond her chatter. Up a road into a dry gully, among a sweating crowd of men and women, using muscles strenuously. Mark knew himself to be half naked, straining at a heavy load.

'What are you?'

'A slave.'

'That does it.' Daisy got up from the floor and leaned her heavy breasts over Mark to wake him up to the present. 'Everyone wants to be a slave or a prince – whatever fits in with their sexual fantasies. Why has no one ever been a boring person who sells cabbages?'

Mark was disappointed. 'What about me being whipped to death?'

'That will have to wait.' Goo-roo uncrossed his legs like opening small folding scissors. 'You'll have to come back. This silly child won't take reality seriously.' He laughed uncritically. People were as they were. Things happened or did not happen. He looked about forty, but he seemed ageless. Mark liked him, and envied his way of life.

When Mark was ready to go, because he wanted a drink, Daisy decided to stay behind with Bob. Mark was on his own again.

*

Most of the business of the Somerset Press was local, but a regular customer had moved south with a large uncompleted order, so, when the catalogues were ready, Mark had to drive them down to Ivybridge.

Before starting back, he went into a café for lunch, and got talking to a bus driver at the same table. Although the scar on his face was still a hundred per cent worse than before Mr Freeman performed his work of art, Mark was gradually becoming less self-conscious. Rather than see people look at it and glance away, wondering, as obviously as if their foreheads were transparent, whether to ignore it or mention it, he tried bringing it up himself, as Catherine Freeman had advised him.

'Tell them the facts,' she had said, 'if they seem to want to know.' So sometimes he did; not always the same facts. He had come up against patients with face cancer while he was at the Milner, and so he hinted at this to the bus driver, for dramatic effect. They had a second pot of tea together, and Ron told Mark about life on the buses, and that the bus company, based at Kingscombe, was always short of drivers as the summer season ended.

Mark had to leave the Grafton flat next week, and had done nothing about finding another place. Suddenly it all began to come clear.

'Think they'd take me on?'

'Why not, if you've got a clean licence? You should see some of the chaps we've got in the driver's seat.'

It was crystal clear. Mark would give up the boring van, apply to be taken on as a trainee bus driver, and find somewhere to live – *in the same town as Peter Freeman.*

No more wangling time off to make special trips to the hospital. He would be there on the spot, dropping in as a seasoned patient, using the coffee shop, keeping watch on Peter Freeman, recapturing the thrill that had shivered through him under the wall with the overhanging tree, as he watched the doctor drive home and turn on the lights in his house.

Have you ever driven a heavy vehicle before?

Have you been convicted of any offences?

Do you suffer from: epilepsy, high blood pressure, blackouts, diabetes, asthma?

Do you use alcohol or drugs?

Has your licence been clean for at least three years?

Why do you want to work for us?

Mark completed the application form with the kind of answers he would want to read if he ran the South Devon Transport Co., and when they told him to report for Assessment, he gave in his notice to Derek.

He was certain he would get the bus job. Something had to go right for him soon. The enlightenment that had come to him in the café with Ron was still clear, guiding him nearer and nearer to the magnetic circle within which Peter Freeman moved and had his being.

Assessment was being driven in a long yellow bus to some deserted streets where the houses were boarded up for demolition, and told, 'Okay, take her over.'

Piece of cake, Mark had thought as the deadpan instructor drove him here. But the gears and steering were unlike anything he had met before. He was struggling with the whole weight of the bus, right up through the wheel. At last the instructor cracked his Egyptian-mummy mouth open to say, 'Use your lower gears.'

'Yes, of course, ha ha. Like my brother's eight-wheeler.' Mark had invented this mythical juggernaut and its owner in answer to the question, 'Have you ever driven a heavy vehicle before.'

'Pull over. I'll take her back.'

The instructor did not say 'Not bad' or 'You've got a chance'. He did not say anything, but Mark chatted and charmed him on the way back to the garage.

The mouth opened grudgingly. 'Come back and see the manager at two.'

'Oh – thanks.' Mark was not discarded yet. 'Thanks for helping me. I've learned a lot already.'

The instructor's face was expressionless, for a man who was being charmed. He looked hard at Mark's scar, then took the keys from the ignition and got out of the bus.

At the interview Mark returned to the childhood glass door story to explain the scar. Aylmer Harwell, in the small muddled office at the back of the garage, was youngish and out of his depth.

'Now, let's see where . . . caught me on a bad day. Is that a rule sheet? Shift charts are out there. Bit of a mess, but we're thinking computers.'

If Mark stayed with this job, he thought he could work his way up to manager within a year.

He was to start training in a few days. He bought a local paper and found himself a small holiday flat attached to the bungalow occupied by the widow of a naval engineer. 'Out of season rates don't start until the end of October.'

When Mark rang his mother to tell her about 21a Carlsburg Crescent and his new job, he did not add that he and Judy had split up, because he knew that would please his father.

But his mother challenged him, and so he told her it was he who had left Judy.

'That was rash, I think, and not very fair to her. At her age, women want to settle, d'you see.' She rattled sharply on about Judy and about the lack of commitment in today's young men, which served Mark right for having told her a lie. If he had told the truth, he might have got some sympathy, which was lacking in his life these days.

During the three weeks' training for the Class Three test, Mark went in a bus to different towns and villages every day, with a group of trainees from other depots. When they were not taking their turn to drive, they were supposed to listen to the instructor: 'Look at every side road. In narrow lanes, expect to meet a maniac doing sixty round every bend. Observe all mirrors every ten seconds.'

Mark and Rusty and Vic and the rest of the all-age, all-style crew played cards at the back of the bus and drank beer.

Annette was able to go home at last, with new pressure garments fitted to her groin and right elbow.

'Here we go again.' Her mother made a tight, efficient mouth. 'I know all about *these*.'

'The expert,' Janet said. 'We should get you to demonstrate to the student nurses.'

Annette was allowed to walk now and could go back to school, as long as she did not play games or dance or jump about, or put too much weight on to her left leg. She was happy. She would not have to be in hospital again for several months, for the small grafts still to be done.

Car accident emergencies eased off as the summer traffic slackened. The Milner Unit, like the main hospital, was busy enough but not hectic: burns, lacerations, machine injuries, cleft-palate repairs, pigmented moles, melanomas, some complicated finger work. A topheavy young girl came in shyly for breast reduction, and an amused, unselfconscious mastectomy patient told Peter that since her prosthesis had fallen out during a tennis match, and she had also met a man who had made her feel that perhaps she was not yet quite off the market, she was ready now to talk about reconstruction.

The Friends of the Milner had been working for months on their annual fund-raising event, and, on a warm September evening, some three hundred people gathered in Kingscombe's Connaught Hotel for a reception before the benefit musical performance at the theatre.

Peter was proud and happy. Many of his staff were there dressed in their best, with husbands and wives and friends: Richard Valentine with his wife and teenage daughter, Noel and Alison, his very young bride, and Catherine, who did not usually spend much money on clothes, in a stunning shimmery dress like many-coloured butterflies. She wore long iridescent earrings, one of her devices for drawing attention away from her face, which Peter privately thought was a lost cause when the face was so warm and engaging.

After the chairman's welcome, Peter gave a brief explanation of where the money was needed: new low-air-loss beds, the video wall screen for the theatre microscope, and the big project, the establishment of the endowment fund for the separate burns unit that was his dream for the future. The applause was gratifying. The chairman of the Regional Health Board proposed his health. Peter stood there like an idiot, but he could not pretend he was not delighted.

Normally he did not enjoy large social groups, but this was

different. This was the Milner, and he could talk and laugh and move about at ease among people he knew or did not know.

'You are the man of the hour.' The basal cell woman beamed all over him. 'The miracle worker.'

'I wish I was.' He had seen her last in the theatre bar at the opera, the night Annette was brought in and their long struggle together began. *Will you make me perfect?*

Catherine had done her face carefully with cover make-up, which had to be more discreet as you got older, if you did not want to look grotesque. When Mark Emerson, on the edge of the crowd, saw her coming to greet him, he said, 'Snap!'

'Why? Oh, you've got a little make-up on too. Good for you. I'm so glad to see you here.'

'Well, you told me to get out and about, so I bought a ticket for the reception. Can't afford the theatre, I'm afraid.'

'It was nice of you to come and support us. You look great.'

'Is this really all right, Catherine?' He put up a nervous hand to his face, but was grinning with pleasure.

'You've done a good cover job.'

'I couldn't let all the beautiful people who give the money see one of the Milner's failures.'

'Is that a joke? It's coming on beautifully.'

His grin had dropped. 'It still looks terrible.'

'Hang on, Mark.' Catherine put a hand on his arm. 'Your day will come.'

People were beginning to leave the hotel for the theatre, when Noel Grant drew Peter aside.

'Guess who's here, sir. That bloody young man with the scar – Mark Emerson.'

'So are quite a few patients. I'm glad he came.'

'I'm not. He's been knocking back the wine, and Alison says he was trying to put the make on her.'

'Saying what?'

'She wouldn't tell me exactly. That means it's bad.'

'If you're going to punch him in the face, be careful of my Z-plasty.'

'I don't go round hitting people.' Noel did not like it if he thought you were teasing him. 'I want you to tell him where he gets off.'

Peter found Mark near the bar, looking respectable in a dark suit and harmless tie. When he smiled broadly, Peter could see that the new scar was beginning to merge in with the creases.

'Hello, Mark.' Peter had already discarded Noel's hearsay evidence. True or false, young Alison was perfectly able to take care of herself. 'Didn't expect to see you here.'

'I'm a grateful patient, Mr Freeman, a Friend of the Milner now. I want to do my bit.'

'Thanks, Mark. You're a long way from home.'

'Oh, I've got a new job.' His smile was less broad, but still slyly there, the dark eyes knowing. Perhaps Alison Grant's maidenly complaint was justified. 'I'm living in Kingscombe now.'

Chapter Ten

Mark passed his Class Three licence test, did a few runs with other drivers to learn the routes, and then was on his own.

Ron had said when they first met in the café, 'Fair enough job if it wasn't for the passengers,' obviously a standard bus joke but partly true. Some of the passengers were chronic grumblers, seeing the bus service as part of the establishment, and Mark as its scapegoat. One or two of the more offensive commuters were going to get it back from him, but not for a while. He wanted to keep this job.

Most people were pleasant enough to a new driver on a route they used regularly. The young women assessed him quickly while they were paying or showing a pass, and gave off a subliminal whisper of sex. The old ducks fell in love with him, which was a nice novelty, since all Mark's grandmothers and aunts were either disapproving or dead.

His still quite lurid scar was on the side away from them. He did not want anyone to see it. He did not want old ladies to cluck at it, or young ones to lift their top lips. The scar was hateful, disfiguring, he couldn't live with it much longer. If it was going to go on being like this, Mr Freeman would have to do something about it.

Meanwhile he kept his profile to the passengers, and wore a grey uniform and a bright blue tie. He was his own boss, king of the road, in charge of his little domain, with the power to excommunicate anyone who caused too great a nuisance, except children, who might drink and curse and rip the upholstery and copulate on the back seat, but could never be thrown off.

The ineffectual Harwell brothers, Paul and Aylmer, who owned and managed the South Devon Transport Co., were no great threat. They were naïvely smitten with the ideals of public service, but less concerned about its mechanics. In Mark's first week, on a shopping run, he had driven gaily out of the garage into a lot of trouble. Pulling out to pass a line of parked cars, he braked hard just in time to avoid colliding head-on with traffic coming the other way. The road was blocked. Passengers were upset. Drivers swore at him; he panicked, tried to back out of the way, and knocked a parked car three feet into a motorbike, which fell over, narrowly missing a child in a pushchair.

Aylmer, the brother whose name was more dashing than his spirit, told complainants that Mark was suspended for three days. He immediately cut it down to two days, then to one, which his brother Paul cut to half a day, then half an hour, because they were short of drivers.

'Never reverse a bus,' Ron said to Mark in the canteen.

'*Now* you tell me.'

Too fast, too slow, the grumbles went, bus early, bus late, fares a rip-off. Mark acquired some patience, and also some new friends at last. Ron took him out with his crowd. Ron's ex-girlfriend, giddy Liz with electric hair, would sometimes agree to a drink or a curry and this and that. Twice she came to Mark's flat. She was surprising and energetic in bed, but she would never stay the night, or even have a sleep before she whizzed off, urgently, as if she had an appointment somewhere in another bed.

She wasn't Judy; but Mark tried not to think about Judy.

'Why invite pain?' Daisy said. She had turned up in Kingscombe at a bus stop, getting into Mark's bus and sitting behind him with her bags and clutter taking up the empty seat, and talking to him while he drove. 'Why give my sister another chance to hurt you?'

Daisy stayed on the bus until the end of his run, because she wanted him to drive her in his car across the corner of Dartmoor to the American healer's green bus shanty. Mark left her there with Goo-roo and came home alone. When the landlady's niece, Rose Marie, heard his car and saw the lights go on in his flat, she came round with some scones and clotted cream, and wanted to tidy up for him.

She was sorry for Mark, because he had told her that his face scar was from a knife attack when he was a security guard at Bristol Royal Infirmary. He was sorry for her, because although she was passively nice-looking, she was dim and cautious. One day he would ravish her. No, he wouldn't, because her aunt Mrs Power would throw him out, and he was quite comfortable at 21a Carlsburg Crescent.

He wanted to be liked by Mrs Power. He brought her home a bag of OAP bus tokens.

'I can't use these, Mark.' She peered into the bag through her bottle-bottom glasses. 'I'm not a pensioner.'

'Who's to know?' Mark said.

'*Do* you mind?'

Oh, God, she thought he meant she looked old enough. Well, she did.

On a school run one early morning, the children were being particularly obnoxious, fighting and shrieking and using words which shocked even Mark, especially with smaller ones on the bus.

When he shouted at them, they paid no attention. He stopped the bus, suddenly enough to throw those who were standing off their feet, and turned round and yelled at them furiously.

'Shut up!'

Silence. Then giggles. Hoots. Hoarse adolescent baying. 'Ooh, look – Frankenstein!'

'Shut *up*, you little bastards!'

'Drive the bus, Frankie. We like the back of your 'ead better!'

Mark complained to Aylmer and Paul. They promised to take him off the school runs, but they never did. Some of the time, driving the bus on a good day, with a dry road and civilized passengers, Mark could feel free and reasonably hopeful. Then his right hand would go automatically to his face, and feel the roughness of the hated scar. Or he might bend forward to put his cash box under the dashboard and catch sight of his face in the side mirror. Oh, God, in sunlight, it looked even worse.

His next clinic appointment, which he had fought the Milner secretary to get, was in a few weeks. He would tell Mr Freeman. He would insist. 'You can't treat me like this – you've got to do something!' The man was still a hero to him. He could do anything. But as Mark brooded more and more on the disappointment of his scarred face, the love he had felt for this great doctor was souring into anger.

He looked for Peter Freeman everywhere. Red cars in the traffic, the back of a light brown head going into a bank – now that he was in the same town, there was always the chance that he might see him. When he was not working, Mark kept watch.

Sometimes he went up the hill to the hospital and walked about between the buildings of the Royal and the Milner Unit. He would look round Peter's parked car to see what was inside – a sweater, a dog towel, a folder of papers. One afternoon he brought Rose Marie up here, to see the best view of Kingscombe. They sat on the bench called Fergus T. Ansell, and she talked about her job as Home Help Supervisor in the Council office, where she co-ordinated the women who went out to do washing and shopping and to clean behind the toilets of the aged.

'Hang on.' Mark had seen Mr Freeman come up the steps from the X-ray Department and go towards the car park. Leaving Rose Marie on the bench, Mark followed him at a distance. When the red car drove out, he drove behind it along the upper road and over the high bridge to the small private hospital where he had first talked to this godlike man who was to become the centre of his life.

Watching from a safe distance, he saw the doctor come out with his wife, and followed them inland, down the wide main street of their small town and round the stone market building to the avenue with the overhanging trees, where he saw them turn in at their white wooden gate that was always open, before he drove back to Kingscombe.

Rose Marie was still sitting on the bench with her passionless profile and unbruised lips, reading a paperback in the fading light.

'Sorry to be so long,' Mark said. 'I had to go and visit someone who's a patient here.'

'Oh, that's all right. I never go anywhere without a book.' She read in the car, in the cinema waiting for the film to start, on the ferry to Gull Island.

Once Mark had driven a group of children on an outing from the school that he knew Mr Freeman's son and daughter attended. He did not think either of them was on the bus, but when he returned with the children to the school he saw Catherine waiting in her small blue car, and saw the light-boned little girl with short curly hair jump down and run to the car and tug the door open and bang it shut behind her with the confidence of possession.

'Hey, Mark!' The long yellow bus swung into the garage with the unmistakable reckless roll, and Ron stuck his head out of the window. 'Coming down the club?'

'Not tonight.' Mark went on into the office with his cash box and his daily waybill.

Liz would be at the club, but he felt a stronger call towards the quiet avenue of big houses and enclosed gardens. The trees were changing colour now, and he could leave his car round a corner at the far end, and shuffle through leaves on the pavement with his hands in his pockets and his shoulders hunched. Under the bulge of the wall where the willow hung like a veil, he could stand on the far side of a green metal junction box and see what he needed, himself unseen.

It was almost dark when he saw Peter and Catherine Freeman drive out and turn towards the main road. He waited for a while and then walked very quietly through the gate, on to the front lawn. The dog barked and the boy's voice told him to be quiet. The barking continued while Mark went round the side of the tall brick house and stood back from a lighted window where he could hear the children's voices.

Light also came from lower windows half underground, and music. A thin young woman in big glasses came to a glass door on the raised ground floor and looked out. The dog was still barking. She opened the door and stood at the top of the garden steps with her hand on the big Labrador's collar.

'Who's there? Is anyone there?'

At once a basement door opened, and a man scrambled up the grass bank.

'Claudine – what is it?'

'Nothing. I thought I saw . . .' She sounded frightened.

Mark had slid back into the bushes at the side of the house. As he ran to the gate, he could hear the man shouting in the garden at the back, and the dog's deep wild barking.

'You must be so glad to get back to a normal life,' friends and neighbours told Deirdre, now that she had some time to herself, with Annette and Campbell both at school.

'You can say that again.' Deirdre was spending the morning in the shopping centre with her renewed friend Eileen, who had got a bit fed up with her when she was always tied to Annette, at home or at the hospital.

'You've been so wonderful, though, Dee, in all this terrible time. I'm sure I couldn't have coped with it.'

'If you have to, you just do it. Anybody could,' Deirdre said, although she did not really believe this. 'Shall I get us a cake?'

The small white chairs and tables gave the coffee shop an outdoors air, although it was inside the mall. There was a flower stall, and a pond with a thin waterfall, and harmless music coming from the glass roof.

'No more ops until the New Year,' she told Eileen. 'Small grafts, nothing much. I think the town hall is going to let me go back to work part time. Will you come and help me look at suits?'

'Oh, good.' Eileen approved of this. 'Something for yourself now.'

Ted and Campbell had been given a new lease of life too. They had Annette at home, and, except for the constricting pressure garments, as a normal family member. She let her father play draughts and cribbage with her, although she had had enough of games when there was nothing much else she could do. Every afternoon after school she helped her brother Cammy with his job, which was exercising a spaniel and a rough mongrel belonging to neighbours. Annette put up a notice in the newspaper shop, and they took on two dachshunds. As they walked along the streets where the trees were clothing themselves in reds and golds, they talked about the dog they might have had if they had been allowed to have a dog. When they got home, Annette checked Cammy's outsize shoes for dog mess.

He still had nightmares in which flames sprang up from a dark pit with a whoosh like fireworks and dragged him down in smothering heat and the stench of burned flesh, which was in his nostrils as he struggled awake. But now he could stumble from his room and into Annette's bed and cry and cower there with his big bony knees up to his chin, as long as he did not knock against any bits of her that were healing.

'Hush,' Annette whispered. 'It's all right.'

'You don't know what it's like.' As a big hulking eleven-year-old, it was a luxury to be able to blubber.

'I have dreams like that too,' his sister said, 'but it's worse for you, because you remember it more clearly.'

Ted Leigh, who did not accommodate himself quickly to change, had got used to being without his wife at home and taking a back seat in the terrible drama in which he could only be a supporting actor. It was hard to start sitting at a table for breakfast, instead of eating at a worktop standing up, and to figure out how Deirdre wanted him to be now that she was there all the time.

She was quite restless. He thought she ought to give up the pep pills that she had started taking when Annette had to go back to the Milner in August.

'The uppers saved my reason,' she told him. 'What do you know about it? You've never needed more than a couple of aspirin in your life.'

'But if you gave up the uppers, you wouldn't need the sleeping pills at night.'

'It isn't so simple. The chemistry of the body is a very complicated thing.'

'I'll agree with that. Head to toe, we'll never know, what makes life flow. High or low, friend or foe, we come, we go.' He sought to lighten the conversation.

One day at the appliance shop, he was lightened like a

helium balloon. The Area Director dropped in for a grumble, and surprised Ted Leigh almost out of his wits by telling him that he was in line to manage a bigger store with a higher turnover and a corresponding rise in salary.

'It would mean moving, though,' Ted told the family. 'We might go north.'

Campbell gave his hoarse chuckle.

Deirdre said, 'We couldn't move away from the hospital.'

Annette sat very still, her eyes going back and forth from one parent to the other.

'But she's only got to have a few minor grafts now. Mr Freeman said. It could be done at any good hospital.'

Annette suddenly shouted fiercely, 'No!'

Campbell slid half under the table and wrapped his arms round his ears.

'Don't carry on.' Deirdre looked at Annette narrowly. She pushed away her half-finished plate and lit a cigarette. She was smoking more now than she had before this whole dreadful business started at Christmas, and drinking a bit more too, but that could be because she was seeing friends again and back in the social whirl.

'Where Dad goes, we go,' she said surprisingly, 'and if Annette has got to have her precious Mr Freeman, she could always come back here for treatment. What are the possibilities, Ted? What are they offering you?'

'Swansea, it might be. Hereford. East Anglia was even mentioned.'

It was heady. He had something exciting to tell them about work for a change. They all talked at once, planning, speculating about his future. His future! It just showed: you never knew which way your life would go.

Never let go
'Cos you never know
What might be round the corner.

'I must say' – Deirdre lit another cigarette from the stub of her last – 'I won't be sorry to leave this town.'

'I like it,' Annette said. 'I'd miss the sea.'

'They've got sea in Wales.' Over her mother's flushed cheekbones, her eyes were glittering. 'And on the east coast, from what I hear. I'll be glad to leave this place where we've all been through so much unhappiness and fear.'

'Ah, as to that,' Ted said. 'But you can't blame Kingscombe. Accidents can happen anywhere.'

'Oh, can they, then?' Deirdre leaned towards his bland face so ferociously that Campbell, sitting beside his father, shifted his chair back. 'But only when a certain person is too bloody lazy to mend an electric heater when he's been asked and asked a dozen times, and then brings an old firetrap oil stove in to a room full of children – is that an *accident*?'

'Dee, I – Dee, but –' Ted's mouth would not make words.

Campbell said, 'Jesus!' and blinked his eyes tightly to shut out his mother's face. Annette's left hand had flown protectively over the angle of her right elbow. Her blue-grey eyes, like stones underwater, stared unseeingly, slow tears welling and falling down her stricken face.

'Have I said something?' Deirdre laughed and got up and began to clatter plates together.

Towards the end of November, Annette was back in the clinic with some pain and a low-grade fever. When the pressure bandage was removed, Peter saw that although most of Noel's elbow zigzag was all right, one end had broken down.

'Too much physiotherapy,' Noel said.

'She's got to keep the full movement. Before you get defensive about your masterpiece, let's see the report of the wound swab.'

When he told Mrs Leigh, 'Annette has acquired a strep infection and there's some staphylococcus as well,' she said, as defensively as Noel, 'But I've been so careful.'

'It's nothing to do with you. Just one of the risks. We'll take her in and splint the elbow, and she'll need daily dressings and a topical antibiotic as well as penicillin.'

'I can manage her at home. I could get the nurse to come in.'

'I'd rather have her here.'

'You do think it's my fault.' She seemed unusually edgy.

'No, no. You've done very well.' Peter made the right noises. He was preoccupied with Annette, but he had learned long ago – not from Tom Sutcliffe, who was quite rude to mothers – how much attention parents needed.

Deirdre Leigh insisted on staying in the unit again, although Annette was not ill and kept telling her to go home. The mother looked very tired. When Peter came to the ward to say that the end of the elbow scar would have to be repaired, she said, 'By you. Not by Mr Grant.'

'Mr Grant did an excellent job last time.' God, you stuffy bastard, he thought. No wonder people accuse doctors of trying to play God.

'What makes you think this will work? Why not let it alone to heal by itself?'

'And leave this beautiful girl with an ugly scar for the rest of her life? All along, my concern has been for the best possible appearance.'

'You promised to make me perfect.' Annette smiled at him.

'I promised I'd do my best.' Peter turned to her mother. 'And we're not giving up now.'

'Oh, no, I never said . . .' Deirdre dropped her head and was the docile, co-operative mother he had known before. Peter added, 'As long as Annette can stand one more operation on that poor old elbow.'

'I'll have to, won't I?'

'How about me?' Her mother's smile was stretched and her laugh shaky. 'No one asks me if I can stand it.'

'Poor Mum,' Annette said. 'I'm fussing about not being able to start my ballet classes, but she was going to go back to work.'

'She will,' Peter said. 'You've been so strong, Deirdre.' With mothers he had known for a long time, he sometimes broke his prudent rule about no first names. 'Just one more hurdle to get over.'

Deirdre Leigh looked at him blankly.

After the operation, Night Sister Joyce said that Annette's mother had stayed awake all night, sitting by the sleeping child, going outside for cigarettes, pacing the corridor. Although she looked exhausted the next day, she had put on eye-shadow and cyclamen lipstick, like a brave flag of victory over no sleep.

Outside the ward, when she asked Peter, 'Everything all right?', he answered honestly, 'I can't be sure yet.'

'And if it's not?'

'Then we try again . . . and again.'

*

And again. In the little lavatory along the corridor, Deirdre leaned on the edge of the basin and stared in the mirror at the grey-skinned old woman of not yet forty.

I look awful. I look as if I'm dying. She rubbed some of the bright lipstick on her finger and was smoothing it frenziedly on her cheek, when her whole being broke down, and she slid to the floor and washed all the make-up off with floods of uncontrollable tears.

She sat with her poor aching face in her hands and her knees drawn up and emptied herself into crying for an agony of hours. People came and tried the door, and went away.

At last she struggled up and washed her face, then went out to her car and drove away. She cashed a cheque at the bank. I must look ghastly. The travel agent, finding her a last-minute reservation, said, 'I'm sorry, has there been a death?' Deirdre nodded.

When Campbell's mother stumbled into the house, looking ill, or drunk, she said to him in a strange, angry voice, 'What are you doing here?'

'I told you. Half day at school. Teachers' meeting. How's Annette?'

She looked at him as if she did not know what he was talking about, and headed for the stairs.

'Has she had the – ?'

After a while he followed his mother up to her room. She had put a suitcase on the bed, and when he opened the door she turned round in a fright from an open top drawer, and he saw that she had her passport in her hand, and some papers.

'What are you doing, Mum?' He tried to sound calm, but he was in a panic at the way she looked.

'I'm going away.'

Away – what did she mean? Her hair was like string. Her eyes looked at something beyond him. 'But Annette – ' She could not go away. She must be playing a joke on him, as she used to, in better times.

'Now don't you start. I've had enough.'

She had gone mad. He must do something. Here he was, alone in the house. 'I'll make a cup of tea.' That was what people said. Downstairs, he filled the kettle full enough for an army, like his father did, and while he was waiting for it to boil, the front door bell rang.

His mother came stumbling down the stairs in her winter coat, with her big loose tapestry handbag and the suitcase.

'That's the taxi. I'll be out in a minute!' she called. 'Now, Campbell, I want you to be a good boy.'

He flung himself across the kitchen and put his arms round her waist, hanging on tightly, the only way he knew to stop her.

'Let me go!' She got herself free and stood in the hall, looking at him with a kind of sorrow. 'You'll be all right,' she said hopelessly.

'Will you be back tomorrow?'

'The kettle's boiling.' She dragged the suitcase down the hall, wrenched open the front door and went out, banging it shut as he followed. When he opened it cautiously, the taxi was driving away.

When Ted Leigh went to the hospital after work to see how Annette was after her operation, he found his son Campbell sitting as far away from the bed as he could get without trespassing on the territory of the other patients on the ward.

'Your mother's what? She's gone?' Ted whispered. He glanced anxiously at Annette, but she still seemed to be in too much of a fog to realize that anything was wrong. When she said once or twice that evening, 'Where's Mum?', Ted told her, 'She's not very well.'

'And that's the truth, from what you tell me,' he said to Cammy on the way home. 'I wouldn't want to tell Annette a lie.'

At home he fried some sausages, to make up to the boy for what he had been through. He fried them swimming in fat, and then fried thick slices of stale bread in the fat. When one of Campbell's customers rang up to know why he had not been round for the spaniel, he too told the truth. 'I went to see my sister in the hospital.'

'Not again? Oh, dear, I am sorry. Give my best wishes to your mother.'

'Yeah.' Cammy said.

The next day, while Ted was still trying to get up the nerve to ring the police and report his wife missing – *How long has she been gone, Mr Leigh? About twenty-four hours. That's nothing, we've had 'em gone twenty-four years* – Deirdre's sister June called, transatlantic.

'How is Annette?' she asked. She had this Canadian accent, which said hoo for how.

'She seems very well, after another small operation, but we've a bit of an upset here. I'm sorry, June, but there's quite a worry about Dee.'

'I know. She's here. That's why I'm calling.'

'She's in *Canada*?'

Ted's mother-in-law Mrs Last was quite helpful. She brought in food and did some laundry for Ted and Campbell, and visited Annette every day, keeping up the reassurance that her mother was exhausted and had been sent away by the doctor for a rest, poor Mum.

She did not pretend to Ted that she was sorry for Deirdre. For once, she allied herself with him against her daughter who had 'done this to me once too often'.

She was at the house when June called a few days later to say that Deirdre had gone totally to pieces and been admitted to a psychiatric hospital on heavy tranquillizers.

'How many more times does she think we can take this?' Mrs Last asked Ted.

'I suppose she can't help it.' Ted did not know what to make of it all, and he did not see how he was going to cope with everything.

'There's a lot of us would like to have a nervous breakdown when the going gets tough.' Mrs Last could sound as if she were tossing her head without actually tossing it. 'Right, Campbell. Fetch me a clean apron and a bucket of ammonia water and I'll start on these windows. This place is a pigsty.'

Annette's elbow was doing very well, and the infection appeared to have subsided. She was allowed home after Mrs Last had convinced Mr Freeman that she could look after Annette as well as Deirdre had. 'Or better,' she added, 'I venture to say.'

When Ted took a Saturday off and was home all weekend, Mrs Last went back to her own flat, saying she had a hundred things to take care of, although Annette and Cammy and Ted thought it was because she was sick of them. She had always looked down on Ted and his ways, and, after being on his side for a while because she was angry with Deirdre, she began to complain that standards had slipped in this house, and to correct the children's speech and table manners. After she left on Friday evening, they gleefully overboiled the supper cabbage, which in Mrs Last's reign had been required to keep its goodness by barely being shown to the gas flame.

Annette ate hardly any of that supper, and the next day she would eat nothing, because of pains in her stomach. The pain grew worse. On Sunday she began to vomit, and the pain was very bad. Ted spoke to Noel Grant and then to Mr Freeman, who sent an ambulance, and Annette was admitted to Intensive Care at the Royal with a severe infection and a stone in her left kidney which would have to be surgically removed.

'Septicaemia.' Peter came from Annette's bedside back to the Milner for his morning meeting with Richard and Noel and the houseman Harry Baker. 'She's extremely ill.'

'Not good, eh?' Richard knew Peter well enough to know when he was seriously worried.

'I'm afraid not. After all she's been through . . . poor child, I think we could lose her.'

'What are they giving her?' Noel and Richard discussed the pros and cons of Annette's predicament in a fairly terse and clinical way. Peter had to do that too, because if he talked about how he really felt, it would sound to these colleagues as if he had let himself get caught up in a sentimental saviour complex about one patient of the hundreds for whom they were responsible.

Catherine was doing letters and accounts at the Restora today. If she were here, he would grab her and find a quiet place to tell her that he was afraid Annette would die.

The routine of work must go on, and it was his outpatient clinic today. There were about a dozen people to see, starting with a child whose fused fingers he had separated a month ago. The mother and the little boy were content, but Peter saw the possibility of loss of circulation in one finger. He got the nurse to take the child out to the playroom and told the mother there was a five per cent chance that he might have to shorten the finger.

'I wish you hadn't told me, Mr Freeman.'

'But then you're prepared if the worst happens and delighted when it doesn't.'

'But now I'm riddled with anxiety.'

She left, ruffled. It might have been better not to have told her. But the same thing had happened in his first year as a consultant. He had not told the parents of a circulation risk, and when he did have to take off the top joint, the excitable father had threatened to sue him for misrepresentation.

He looked at some healing grafts, and his extrovert breast reconstruction patient came in for a post-operative check.

'I should have had it done months ago. Why didn't you make me?'

When she had told her new man that she was going to have a reconstruction, the commitment implicit in this undertaking had scared him off.

'How arrogant,' she said to Peter. 'He thought I was having it done for him.'

'You had it done for yourself, didn't you? The only good reason for cosmetic surgery.'

Although it was a relief to give attention to other patients, Annette was in his mind all through the clinic. Only three more people to see. Oh, Lord, not today. Hurrying in late to the consulting room, he had not noticed the name Mark Emerson towards the end of the list.

Mark came in wearing a grey shirt and trousers and pullover and a bright blue tie with the running horse device of South Devon Transport.

'Driving a bus? Good for you.' A responsible job for this erratic young man (would you ride in a bus driven by this man?).

Mark slumped into the chair on the other side of the desk. 'It's a job where people don't see the right side of my face,' he said sulkily.

'But the right side of your face looks excellent to me.' Peter put on his glasses and came round the desk. 'Faces nearly always heal well, because of the good blood supply.'

'It's worse than it was before.'

'Look.' Peter sighed. 'We've been through this dozens of times. I've told you, it will take another six to twelve months to pale, and give you the maximum benefit. Everything looks fine, and I won't need to see you for about three months – say February or March.'

'*Three months?*' Mark had been sitting looking up at Peter. Now he turned his head impatiently and thumped the desk.

'Unless something goes wrong, of course.'

'Something's gone wrong now. It hurts in the cold. It's still awkward to shave. It looks like hell. I hate the way I look.'

'You look all right to me,' Peter said truthfully. 'Just be patient, and I know you'll be pleased with the end result.'

'That's not good enough, Mr Freeman.' Mark swallowed and his face flushed, reddening the scar. 'It's not right, and you've got to do something.'

'I've told you.' Peter sighed. 'There's nothing –'

'Oh, yes, there is. If the operation's a failure, you could cut it away and give me a skin graft, I know you could.'

'A graft? That's not at all appropriate.'

'Why not? You do it for other people. I've talked to them. That child with the burns – Annette. I know her mother. You've done dozens of grafts on her. Why not on me?'

'Because you don't need one. Mark, you must calm down and listen to reason. The operation was not a failure. It's a success. The scar is *all right*. All it needs is time. Now, if there's nothing more I can do for you, I'll let you go.'

More subtle than saying, 'Get the hell out of here,' but Mark protested, 'You're angry with me!', like an overgrown child.

'Oh, for God's sake.' Peter could not keep patience with him.

'You don't want me here.' Mark jumped up, pushing back his chair, and slammed out of the room.

Peter sat with his eyebrows raised, taking deep breaths. I should have said, 'You've got two more minutes,' he thought, sometimes the only way to contrive a calm exit for such a touchy patient. He had heard that the Queen, unable to throw people out, heads for the door a few minutes before it is time for her to leave, so that she can allow herself to be briefly detained.

I thought he could give me a perfect face. On the way to the garage, Mark chewed on his anger. He could if he wanted to. He can do anything. A perfect face, a perfect me. Not much to ask of a miracle worker.

Every time I go there – a stab of pain pierced the empty prospect of being banned from the clinic for three months – he says the scar is fine, it looks better. All right, then. Why isn't my life better?

Why have Liz and I quarrelled? Why is she disgusted with me? Why do I still want Judy, although she hangs up on me and doesn't answer my letters? Why do the Bus brothers always pick on me?

The other drivers were no better and no worse than Mark. They all took an extra five or ten minutes for a kip at the turn-around. They all despised the passengers, and some of them, like that creep Rusty, were still drunk from Friday night when they turned up for work at seven o'clock on Saturday morning.

But Paul and Aylmer always came down unfairly on Mark. With these sheep tracks they called roads down here, every driver took a narrow twisting corner too fast once in a while and ended with the front of the bus embedded in a bank. Nobody could be eternally polite when passengers at every stop grumbled at you, 'The bus is late.' As time-served drivers themselves, the brothers must know that.

Service to the community. At the bus station Mark looked at the rota board and saw that he was to serve the community this evening in that old wreck Thirty-four with the dicey gears. The late run was bad enough even in a perfectly maintained bus, and that was as rare in this company as a passenger who thanked you for the trip.

On one or two late runs, Mark had had trouble with small gangs from the pubs threatening him when he told them not to annoy the other passengers. He had taken his precious sharp flint from the drawer at home, and now kept it with him in the metal box with his ticket machine and peanuts and the little biscuits that Rose Marie baked.

After his clinic Peter had a graft to do on the small deep burn of an elderly woman who had fallen against her electric cooker.

It was done under local anaesthetic, with a sign on the theatre door warning PATIENT AWAKE, in case anyone came in with an inappropriate remark. A tape recorder played Viennese waltzes – the old lady's choice. Then to the Restora for another graft which had to be fitted in at the end of the day, because two of the powerful older consultants there were still slightly hostile to plastic surgery.

Before he went to change and scrub up, Peter looked in on the graft patient, teenaged Louise, in remission from leukaemia. As if the leukaemia were not enough, an inexperienced doctor had injected a chemotherapy drug into the tissues outside the vein wall, so that the surrounding skin had died. It would need quite a large graft, to extend to healthy skin, and would probably leave her with considerable scarring.

She knew this, but was euphoric from her pre-med, and more optimistic than Peter. Not like Mark, with his unrealistic demands and expectations, but still, one more patient who wanted to believe in miracles.

Smiling and joking gently with Louise, Peter felt as Tom Sutcliffe must have done when he brought his starry-eyed young assistant down to earth with, 'The more you do, Peter, the more you'll find you can't do.'

In her room at the cliff cottage at Farne, Evangeline had stayed awake until her father came. Below her window the river channel followed its complicated ribbon pattern, always the same at each low tide, winding and braiding its swift, deep course out to the sea. On the hard wet sand, streaks of silver arrowed towards the moon.

Her parents were in the kitchen. Evie got out of bed and

went down with the yellow dog Archie to the sitting room. She put a log on the fire and her father came in to her.

'Waiting up to see me, darling? That's nice. I'm sorry I'm so late.'

'I wanted to talk to you.'

'Good. Anything special?'

She had planned all day how she would say it, but now she could not say it in any way, any of it. She dropped her head and had to murmur, 'Not really.'

'Everything all right at school?'

'Mm-hm.'

'And with Phil? It was worrying about him last term, wasn't it? The headmaster was really angry.'

Tell him now.

I can't. It was like being tied up with a rope, and sobbing inside. Why did Phil have to be staying with a friend tonight? He could have helped her to tell it. Not to her mother, because she would blame her birthmark. To her father.

'Why didn't you tell him, Ev?' Phil had asked in the summer, after he hit Amanda.

'Why didn't *you*?'

'I don't know. He's so – so straight somehow. It'll be all right now. I've told Amanda and her gang that if they *ever* start up again . . . I'll get John and Nick and his brother and we'll beat 'em up so badly their mothers won't know 'em.'

Her father was looking a question at her, so she went to the mantelpiece and showed him the delicate sea-smooth length of wood she had found, and painted with the head and shoulders of a young girl with hair that streamed backwards as if she were lying along the top of the water.

'Ophelia.' Her father knew. 'It's beautiful. Let's look for

more wood tomorrow. I wondered if we should also paint some of the little flat stones?'

Evie shook her head.

'Why not?'

'Because they've been there since the beginning. It has to be the wood – something that man took from the trees and the sea has taken from man.'

Later, after her mother had come up to bed, Evie went downstairs again. Her father was sitting at the kitchen table, reading. She slid on to the bench opposite him.

He took off his glasses and rubbed his eyes.

'You got problems, Daddy? I heard you telephoning. Is it something at the hospital?'

'It's Annette.'

'The burns girl? I thought she was all right now.'

'She was.' He looked at her. 'You got problems, Evie?'

'Everybody has.'

'What can be done?'

'Nothing.'

'Let's go to bed then.'

Chapter Eleven

Mr Freeman would not see Mark, but there was nothing to stop Mark seeing him. When he was not on the buses, he was sometimes with Rose Marie, or with Ron and his crowd, and electric Liz, who had sparked back briefly to him; but a lot of his free time was spent secretly waiting and watching.

If the doctor did catch sight of him, it wouldn't matter. He was committing no crime. He had as much right to be on the hospital premises as any other member of the public. The avenue where Peter Freeman lived was not a private road, nor was the road to Torquay where, on an afternoon off, Mark trailed the surgeon to the outpatient building where he or Mr Valentine held their weekly clinic.

After Mr Freeman had gone inside, Mark followed and found the waiting area for plastic surgery.

'When is this clinic over?' he asked the woman behind the desk. 'Because I have to fetch somebody who's got one of the last appointments.'

He could go away and have a meal. Better than waiting in his car or sitting here along the wall, parading his scar among the other freaks.

When Mr Freeman left, Mark kept a discreet distance behind the red car. The doctor, like most people who were skilled with their hands, was a fast, expert driver, missing no chances but taking no risks. At a red light, a difference between two lanes of traffic brought Mark's car alongside. He turned his head away, but Mr Freeman had his window open, and he could hear that he was singing.

It was after six o'clock, but Mr Freeman did not turn off the main road to go up towards his home. He went on into the town, and left the through road to follow some of the old steep streets near the harbour. Narrow terrace houses had been done up here and painted in Mediterranean colours. There were small expensive shops and bow-windowed restaurants with candles already lit on tables inside. What if Peter Freeman was on his way to see a girlfriend? What if Mark could find out something about his secret life and use it as a weapon to force him to operate on the scar again?

The red car turned into a dead-end street bounded by a big church. Mark braked and got out, to see the house where it would stop. At the end, the car went through an iron gate into a small crowded car park. Mark walked cautiously forward and saw Mr Freeman go into the church. As he pulled open the heavy door, the sound of voices in chorus came out to greet him.

When Mark was in his flat or driving the bus, he schemed

how he could get his own way, and a lot of the time his mind was filled with thoughts of Peter Freeman, his saviour and his doom. Sometimes he was an enemy, sometimes a god, sometimes almost a second self whose routine Mark knew as well as his own.

One day when he was on the early and the late runs, with time off in the middle of the day, he changed into his salesman's suit and went to the Restora Hospital. In the lobby, which was flower-filled and luxurious, the silky female guardian politely challenged him.

'I'm a patient of Mr Freeman,' Mark said, 'here to make an appointment.'

He headed towards the pink perfumed lift, but the female said, 'Just a minute, sir,' and made a phone call. She talked softly for a while, raising her eyebrows at Mark. Then she admitted, 'Mrs Freeman says you can go up.'

Catherine was not as friendly as she had been at the Connaught Hotel reception.

'Mr Freeman told you he wouldn't need to see you until after the New Year. You must accept that. If something's wrong, you should make an appointment at the Milner Unit.'

'They won't let me.' Mark had tried that. 'So I'm here as a private patient. I can pay,' he told her aggressively.

'I've no doubt you can.' The dark red stain on her cheek was more pronounced than usual. Her smile was not as wide today. In fact she was frowning at him with her soft brown graceful eyebrows. 'But unless there's something wrong, like bleeding or swelling or unusual pain, I'm not going to make an appointment for you either.'

Bitch.

'There is something wrong,' Mark said bitterly. 'I've told

Mr Freeman, but he won't listen. Will you tell him for me? I want him to give me a skin graft.'

'Did you tell him that?'

'He refused, but you could ask him again for me. Please, Catherine. You said you'd help.'

'I did,' she said quite sternly, 'but not like that. You have to accept that the doctor is doing what's best for you.'

'Ha!' Mark laughed, staring at her stained cheek. 'He's wrecked my life.'

'Come on, Mark,' Catherine said more gently. 'I know you're upset, and if you want to try to sort out your feelings, why don't you and I have another talk? I could see you later on at the Milner if you like.'

'I'll be working.'

'Well, perhaps you could suggest a time when you'll be free?'

Mark looked at her with contempt. 'How can one disfigured person help another?'

All right, then. If he was not allowed to see Mr Freeman at either of the hospitals, he would see him at his home.

After work next day Mark went back to his flat to change. Perhaps the uniform had put off Mr Freeman the last time in his consulting room. Not right to pay a social call on a famous surgeon dressed as a bus driver.

The phone rang while he was in the shower. It was his mother, asking him why he never rang them, although Mark had explained that the flat had a pay phone, for summer visitors, and he never had the right change.

His mother thought it was time he paid them a visit. 'Your father is quite back to his normal self. Better than before, as a matter of fact, though if he wasn't, there wouldn't have been any point having the hip operation. If you come up at a weekend, you and he could have a round of golf.'

'I work on Saturdays. Overtime pay.'

'And Georgina says you've got to come up next month for the children's Christmas play.'

'Who says?' Mark asked. 'Georgina or you?'

'It's *The Wizard of Oz* this year,' she rattled on.

Mark groaned. They had done *The Wizard of Oz* when he was at school. His mother had a photograph of him as the tallest Munchkin, standing up against the backcloth with his eyes shut, as if he were facing a firing squad.

'I'll come when I can.'

'We can count on you at Christmas?'

'I don't know. I'd have to see how they work out the rota.'

Later, when he was dry and dressed, his father rang, just as he was going out.

'I'm sorry we're not going to see you.'

What was this – a peace overture? They had never formally declared war. Mark did not know whether the old man actually realized that they had always been at war.

'How are you, Dad?'

'Fine. Walking a lot. Very important for the new hip. I want to show you a path they've opened through Park Wood up to the old fort at the top of the hill. You should come before it gets too cold.'

'I'm busy, you know.'

'So I hear. A bus driver, eh? A bus driver. I'm proud of you.'

He may have thought he meant well, but he could not keep the sarcasm out of his voice.

Although he was feeling defiant and reckless, Mark did not

have the nerve to drive his car through the wide white gate of Mr Freeman's house. He left it in the road and walked along the stretch of gravel to the front door. He had never been so close. The porch light was on and he saw the name LIBERTY HOUSE on the arched fanlight. He had not known it was called that. It made the white panelled door seem more approachable.

Mark went up the steps. There was a bell and a brass knocker in the form of a dolphin. Which? Knocking was bolder, so he knocked. The door was opened by the little girl who had ridden on his bus, wearing jeans and a skimpy pullover.

'Hullo,' she said. She was shy but composed. A doctor's daughter, trained to deal with social or professional situations. 'My mother's out.'

Good. If Catherine had opened the door, Mark would not have got his foot over the sill and into the hall, as he did now.

'Is your father in?'

'Oh, yes. At least he's in the garden.'

'May I come in?'

She stepped back, and Mark went into the hall, his eyes hungrily grabbing at details to remember. The hall ran through the middle of the house, past the open doors of inviting rooms, and ended at a glass door at the top of steps into the garden.

Mark stood there for a moment, trying to see through the gathering dark. He heard voices, and, with a stab of excruciating jealousy, he saw Mr Freeman's son run through the shadows across the grass, and Mr Freeman, in the thick white sweater he had worn in the newspaper picture, dribbling a football craftily away from the boy, who shouted and charged at him.

They were quite rough with each other. The father fended the son off and knocked him down, and the son got up and plunged to tackle him round the legs.

The little girl moved past Mark and pulled open the door. 'Daddy! Someone to see you.'

'Who is it?' Mark was standing too far back to be seen. 'I don't know.'

Peter Freeman turned and came towards the door, still laughing. When he saw Mark, the laughter vanished and he came quickly up the steps and took Mark's arm and pushed him back into the kitchen.

'You go out with Phil, honey,' he said to his daughter and shut the kitchen door.

He was very angry. He was such a polite, well-mannered person, you would not think he could be like this. Mark had managed to annoy him in the consulting room, but he had not seen him with his mouth set and his eyes crackling.

'What are you doing here?'

'I tried to see you at both the hospitals, and they wouldn't let me, so I thought . . .'

'I told you to stay away until your next appointment – and that will be your last.' He was leaning against the worktop, his arms folded. Mark did not know where to stand, or whether he could sit down on one of the chairs at the table.

'I had to see you, Mr Freeman.'

'Are you here as a patient, or what?'

In fantasy, an unreal Mark said quietly, 'As your son.' The real Mark heard again his father's thin dry voice on the telephone: 'A bus driver.' Pause for inaudible grunt. 'I'm proud of you.'

What chance had Mark ever had? If this man here had been his father . . .

'Listen to me, Mark Emerson.' Mr Freeman stood upright and came to lean his hands on the table opposite Mark, his head down between his shoulders like a lightweight bull. 'I have an obligation to you as a patient, but you also have an obligation to me as your doctor. Stay away. Don't come here. I don't want you bothering me or my family, and if I ever hear of your hanging around when I'm not here, I'll turn you in to the police.'

'I've done nothing wrong.'

'Not yet. Just take care you don't. Now come on, I'll see you out.'

He opened the door and pushed Mark along the hall. As Mark turned by the front door to protest, he saw that the two children had come in from the garden and were staring at him.

'In the United States,' Richard Valentine said, 'I read that movie stars and pop singers hire people called "threat assessors" to monitor nutty phone calls and letters, and see if there's a risk, like John Lennon's killer, and the man who shot Ronald Reagan. You'd better be careful of this fellow.'

'Oh, he's no threat. Though he seems to think I'm a threat to him, in some way.'

'Joe Bremmer says he's a borderline psychotic.'

'I think he's more of a spoiled neurotic – pretty obsessive too – who can't stand frustration.'

'Self-induced frustration, at that. Crying for the moon.'

'I've tried to get through to him. Catherine's tried, God knows. I'm afraid we haven't seen the last of him.'

'Are you seriously worried about him?' Richard's plump

face was topped by thick glossy black eyebrows which he lowered now to look keenly at Peter.

'I don't want to be. He's a damn nuisance, but I don't want to have to worry about anything now that Annette is over the worst. Poor child. It's always so heartbreaking when someone has to go through months of agonizing treatment, and then die anyway.'

'She's going to be all right.'

'It'll take time. But she's a survivor. Amazing.'

Peter made a mental grimace at Tom Sutcliffe droning on with his 'There are no miracles'.

Oh, *no*?

Peter had left theatre after a long operation with the maxillo-facial surgeon to repair the excised jaw of a cancer patient. Harry Baker put his head round the door of the changing room.

'Mr Freeman?'

'Yes, *what*?' Peter wanted to wash and change and get a cup of coffee and sit down.

Harry was not so nervous now. He had become quite an old hand in the unit, but was still too deferential to consultants, which he would have to get over.

'Sorry to bother you, sir. Your wife called about an hour ago. She wanted you to call her back as soon as you came out of theatre.'

Evie had disappeared. She left the school at some time during the day, but there was a muddle and nobody rang Catherine, because a girl had said that Evangeline was ill and had been taken home.

'When she wasn't on the bus, I rang the school.'

'My God, what does Phil say?'

'He went straight to judo with the Robinsons.'

'Can you get hold of him at the sports centre?'

'I tried, but the class is somewhere else. He probably wouldn't know anything anyway. They never see each other at school now that he's in the other building.'

'Where are you, Cath?'

'At home.'

'I'll come.' Peter gave Noel some hasty instructions and drove home like fury, his stomach a cavern of swirling terror.

Things had been bad, then things got better, then they got bad again. At the end of the summer term the group that Evie thought of as Amanda's gang, although different people came and went like wasps going in and out of a vile grey papery nest, got bored with other crimes and started on Evie again.

Last winter they teased and gloated over her mother's face. Then they dropped that, and Evie could coast along at school quite happily, but when it all started again in the summer, it was worse, because it was Evie herself now who was on the rack.

Evangeline Freeman was a stinking little creep. They put death notes through the air hole in her locker. The teasing turned to bullying, not for any special reason, just bullying for its own sake. So that if her parents asked her whether people still said things about her mother's face, she could answer no with truth. If you were bullied at school, you did not tell a teacher, and you certainly did not tell your parents, for all kinds of complicated and confusing reasons. But you did tell your older brother.

When Evie finally told Phil a few of the tortures that

Amanda and her gang invented, Phil hit Amanda – Aman-*da*! – really hard in front of a lot of people, and she went home with concussion and came back with the story that she had been blind for two days and might lose her sight for ever. Oh, Aman-*da*!

So things got better again, and when Evie went back to school in September, she thought everything would be all right, because she was nearly nine now and life changed so fast, and a person who had been an enemy one term could be your best friend the next.

Wrong, Evangeline. It was worse. A girl called Hilary with a face like a rat had joined Amanda. After a quiet month or so, they pounced. There were four or five of them and they were bigger than Evie. 'Lie down on the floor.' If she refused or tried to run away, they pushed or knocked her down, so she might as well lie down in the first place.

They did this in a horrible little place they called the Tabernacle, which was a disused storage space behind the kitchen, with stained walls and a leaking roof.

The weather was bad, but not bad enough for boots, and their shoes were dirty. They made Evangeline lick the mud off their shoes. Worse, Amanda took off her shoes and made Evie kiss her feet. She had to say, 'I worship you, goddess.' If she wouldn't or couldn't, Hilary banged her head on the floor. Afterwards Evie was sick.

She could not tell Phil, because he had threatened Amanda in the summer: 'If you *ever* . . .' He had got into terrible trouble then. Now he would do something so bad that he would never be forgiven. He might even kill Amanda.

Yesterday Amanda had said to Evie, trumpeting through

her nose in her goddess voice, that the time had come when they were destined to tread in dog mess.

'Tomorrow, O slave, or the next day, or perhaps we'll wait till Monday to give you more time to look forward to it.'

Evie would have to crawl on her stomach and lick dog mess off their shoes. She could not tell anyone. There was only one thing to do. She went away.

By the time Phil came home, Peter and Catherine had talked to the police, the headmistress, some of the teachers and as many of the parents of Evie's friends as they could track down.

Phil was stunned. 'Gone? She can't be *gone*. She's playing a joke.' He searched the house frantically, and then the garden. 'She would never have gone without Archie.' The Labrador had made the search with him, barking idiotically at nothing in the bushes at the end of the garden.

'But she left from school, Phil,' Catherine said. 'She wasn't on the bus.'

'The bus.' Peter put down the telephone after one more fruitless call. 'Oh, my God.'

'Mark Emerson.' Catherine looked at him. In her drained and pale face, the stain was paler too.

'One way to get my attention.'

Peter's harsh laugh made Phil ask agitatedly, 'What is it, Dad? Mark who? What's he done?'

'It's all right.' His mother put her arm round him. 'Stay calm. We all must. You'll have to tell the police, Peter.'

'Not yet,' he said grimly. 'I'm going after him myself.'

He rang the unit. The secretary had left, so he asked Janet, the sister in charge, to find Mark's file and give him the new address.

'Mr Freeman,' her deep voice said when she came back to the phone, 'is something wrong?'

'Evie's run away.'

Janet did not cry out or ask questions. She said sensibly, 'If she's scared to go home, she might come here, you know.'

'She might.'

'Want the Emerson phone number?'

'No – well, give it to me anyway.'

He would not telephone. He would just turn up, and keep turning up until Mark was there, or get the police to break in.

'I'm coming with you,' Phil said.

'You stay and take care of Mum.'

'Or she of me.' Phil was too realistic to be conned by parental clichés. 'Dad,' he said quietly, 'this may be pointless, but do you remember, last summer . . .?'

'What? I must go.'

'But do you remember that time when I hit a girl at school, and there was all that fuss? I didn't hit her for fun, you know. Well, it was fun, in a way. She'd been – well, she'd been teasing Evie.'

'I thought all that had stopped.'

'It did, after I hit her.'

'Are you sure?' Catherine grabbed at this clue.

'*I* don't know. I don't know what goes on among the little kids.'

Amanda's name, Bronovsky, was unusual enough to be the only one in the phone book. Catherine went off to find her. Peter went to find Carlsburg Crescent. Phil stayed in the house to answer the phone and wait for Evie.

Peter drove across the upper bridge and down to the western side of the town. He was in a wretched state, ripped apart by anxiety, burning with anger when he thought about Mark, desolate and dismayed by the hopelessness of peering at children on the pavement, trying to see into cars, lighted windows, buses.

Because he had no clues, the idea of Mark as suspect drew him with increasing strength. The closer he got, the more intense his anger, so that by the time he had found Carlsburg Crescent and No. 21a he could storm out of the car to the bungalow without knowing what he was going to say.

A mild, elderly lady opened the door. 'Mark Emerson? He's in the apartment. The door is round the back.'

'Did you see him come in?'

'I don't spy on my tenants,' she said reprovingly.

The door to the apartment at the back was not locked. Peter pushed it open and walked in. *Evie – Evie, are you here?*

'Mark!' he called fiercely. 'Mark Emerson!', and charged into the small sitting room, where Mark and a young woman were sitting with a tray of coffee and cakes on a low table between them.

Mark jumped up with a broad grin. 'Mr Freeman!'

'Do you know anything about my daughter?' Peter was still at full steam and could not stop himself. He strode to the window to look out at the garden, and turned round. He had to take a deep breath. 'My daughter's missing. She didn't come home from school, and I don't know where she is.'

The young woman followed his movements with slow eyes. Mark's grin had faded to bewilderment. The image of the depraved kidnapper that had lured Peter here had dwindled to only a confused young man with a scar.

'I mean – ' Peter blundered on. 'I thought you might –

I mean, because of the way you – I wondered if you might know anything,' he ended feebly.

'Why should I?'

'I don't know.' Peter spread his hands.

'Did you think I had something to do with it, Mr Freeman?'

'Well, I – '

'I'm not a child molester, but you can look round the flat if you want.' Mark insisted on taking him into the bedroom, the kitchen, even opening the door of the tiny bathroom. Peter was desperate to escape.

'I'm sorry about your daughter. She's probably with a friend. I used to disappear all the time, and forget to tell anyone.'

'Thanks. I'm sorry to have disturbed you.'

'To have suspected me,' Mark corrected.

His smile was now rather self-satisfied. The doctor had made a fool of himself. Mark was top dog. He had been wrongly blamed. He was righteous.

'Would you like a cup of coffee?' the girl asked, impersonal as a waitress.

Peter stopped at a public telephone and rang Phil.

'No news, Daddy. The police rang. They've got her on the computer.'

'Can you think of *any* other friends besides the ones we've tried?'

'Nope.'

'Oh, Phil.'

'What are we going to do?'

'Something. I'll think of something.'

'When are you going to come back?' Phil sounded nervous.

'Are Claudine and Leo downstairs?'

'No.'

Damn. It was dark now. Peter hurried home.

Janet rang after midnight.

'She's here.' Evie had been picked up by a driver, walking towards Farne, and had asked to be taken to the hospital. 'She's all right,' Janet told Peter quickly. 'She's exhausted.'

'I'll be there.'

'I've got her in bed and she's asleep already. Shall I ring you when she wakes? She's in no state to talk,' Janet decreed, as if she feared they would grill the child as soon as they got her home.

Evie had been trying to walk to the cottage on the cliff, so at the weekend they all went there, although there was a November onslaught of fierce wind and rain. Enough talking had been done. Amanda Bronovsky had been removed from the school. Catherine had wrestled with the ignoble anger that accompanies relief. Peter had fought the double-edged pain of his daughter's suffering, and her silence. The headmistress had remarked, 'The trouble with you busy professional people is that you don't know what's going on under your eyes at home.'

'She's retiring at the end of the year,' Phil said, 'so please don't move us to another school.'

At low tide Peter and Evie walked inland through the woods and struggled back on the sticky sand of the estuary against a squally off-shore wind.

'As an afterthought,' Peter said, 'why did you introduce me to that horrible girl that morning, as if she were your friend?'

Evie stamped her boots into some pools, and threw seaweed stalks for Archie that blew back into her face before she answered, 'All that stuff about Mum. I wanted her to see that I had a lovely father.'

Evie had always been inclined to compete with her mother for her father's love. When she was quite small, she used to push in between them when they embraced. Because Catherine, in the aftermath of her deranging anxiety, had reproved her for going off, Evie was being a bit cool towards her, playing up the idea of herself as current heroine, which they had tried to avoid.

'You mustn't – ' Peter began, but retreated from the impossibility of arguing against the innocently incestuous instincts of a little girl. 'Come on, let's try to run. It's going to pour in a minute.'

'If I run away again,' Evie panted with discouraging good cheer, 'it will be with you, Daddy.'

Chapter Twelve

'My mother will be here to take me home,' Annette told people at the hospital; but when the time came, Ted had to tell her that her mother was still seeing the therapist in Toronto and would not be allowed to travel yet.

'Between you and me, Ted,' Deirdre's sister June had said on the phone, 'poor Dee's really blown apart this time. It's going to take another bomb to get her out of the crater.'

'If you ask my opinion,' Deirdre's mother said, 'she's not letting herself get better. It must be costing June a fortune,' she added, not without satisfaction, since June had gone to work in Toronto against Mrs Last's advice and married a Canadian with more money than she deserved.

When Annette was finally discharged, after a frustrating delay caused by a thrombosis in her leg, Mrs Last helped out again, grudgingly. Campbell brought home the kind of boys she disliked – noisy and ravenous and uncouth, like Cammy himself. Annette's friends began to come round again when they heard that she was well. Annette, on whom so many fierce demands had been made in the last year to be stoical and sensible, reverted happily to giggling and pop music and hilarious nonsense sessions in her bedroom. Mrs Last found that the most humdrum remark, like 'Pass the Jaffa Cakes' or 'Where are you going?' could bring on a paralysing storm of giggles and gasps.

'Where is that girl who was so grown-up at the hospital?' Mrs Last would demand, and Annette and Lisa and Becky would shriek and rush round the house, looking in cupboards, under the sofa, in the rubbish bin.

It was a relief all round when Annette went back to school, and good Mrs Last could return to her unruffled flat with the satisfaction of a martyr's duty done.

If Ted left work punctually, there were only a couple of hours when Annette and Cammy were on their own. Unless Annette's leg was sore, or it was too cold or wet for her to be out, she went to the park with Cammy and his dog customers, and then started the supper.

Ted kept a nagging ache in his heart for the loss of Deirdre, but the three of them muddled along very well. Mistakes and messes like burned or raw food, and spills and breakages, did not matter. Mrs Last had knocked herself out to clean the house as if the Queen Mother were coming to tea, but what was the point when they would soon be moving out?

Looking in Deirdre's dressing table mirror at the very ordinary man who looked unenthusiastically back at him, Ted wondered what the staff and customers would make of him in Hereford. He seemed to have aged a bit in this last year, and especially during the rock-bottom days when he and Cammy had somehow soldiered on when they believed Annette was dying. He could see grey hairs above his ears, and two new lines had etched themselves in between his nose and the corners of his mouth.

'I am old and grey,' he said to Annette, and she bought some Grecian 2000 darkener and combed it in for him with her clever hands that still showed scars between the patches of shiny grafted skin.

The children's friends came round for hot dogs and Annette's lopsided cakes.

'Come on in and take a pew, we're at home and so are you.'

They bought snacks and fizzy drinks and rented the kind of videos that were said to turn children into violent criminals. Best of all, with Mrs Last safely out of the way, they got a dog from the Kingscombe Canine Defence League.

It had a harsh mottled coat and one ear that had lost its spring. It shed grey and black hairs. It stole food from the kitchen. It slept on beds when they were out. It threw up on the way to the door. When it came in wet, it dried off along the chair covers.

'When my mother comes back, will we have to get rid of Pepper?' Campbell asked.

'She'll be so glad to get home, son, she won't care if you've got a monkey and three piranha fish.'

'Could we *have* an aquarium?'

They talked to Deirdre every week. Sometimes she sounded like herself. Sometimes she was depressed and sad, blaming herself for not being with them.

'We're all right,' they told her. 'Don't worry.'

She sent them Christmas cards covered with kisses and

emotional messages. 'To my wonderful husband,' she wrote, 'who I love with all my heart.'

When she comes home, I'll hold her to that, Ted thought.

Pepper had trodden on his glasses when he jumped into the chair to bark at the television. While Ted waited for new lenses, he used an old pair with heavy dark frames which he had worn in the days before men's faces got softer. Campbell cut his hair for him, and chopped too much off one side, so the barber had to trim it very short all over.

'A skinhead!' Mrs Last exclaimed in dismay when she dropped in to check them over. 'What *are* you people up to?' She bent to open the cupboard under the stairs, always her first port of call. 'Where's the vacuum cleaner?'

'It died,' Annette said. 'Dad's getting a new one through the shop.'

'The sooner the better.' Mrs Last drew breath as she stood up, and Cammy finished for her, 'The house is a pigsty.'

'Is this place on the market? I wouldn't want to show it to buyers in this state.' She got at the dishcloth and began to swab worktops.

'We've had several prospects.' Ted was not worried. He was getting used to things falling into place again. 'We're renting a flat in Hereford until this house is sold.'

Pepper was so sensible and streetwise that he was allowed to patrol the neighbourhood on his own. His paws thundered against the front door, and he was let in, wet, swashbuckling, panting with pleasure to see Mrs Last and dribble on her skirt.

Annette had made a de luxe fish pie, out of which her grandmother picked the mushrooms and ranged them along the edge of her plate. Looking up at Annette, who was watching her across the table, she said sharply, 'Don't hang your mouth open like that, child. You look like the village idiot.'

'Like what?'

'You know what I mean. There – you're doing it again. Too much television.'

'No – wait a minute,' Ted said. 'You're right. Her mouth isn't quite closed. Seeing her all the time, I never noticed.'

'Though one would think you would, with those heavy-duty spectacles.'

'What? Noticed what, Dad?'

'Something's not right here,' Mrs Last said complacently.

When Ted Leigh brought Annette in, Peter could see that the grafted skin below her jaw was tightening and beginning to pull down her lower lip slightly.

'Tell me the worst.' Annette sat on the edge of her chair, luminous blue-grey eyes, so much brighter and clearer now, fixed on Peter's.

'The graft is contracting. I'll have to renew it soon before it gets any worse. I'm sorry to have to put you through one more trial.'

'I'm sorry to make more work for you.' Annette gave him back the same consideration. They saw each other as equals.

For some time Mark Emerson had not been seen hanging round the hospital, or Liberty House, thank God. Being suspected of kidnapping had either shown him he was playing a risky game or seriously discouraged his pursuit of Peter.

He had telephoned once, at home, with the excuse of asking about Evangeline.

'She's all right.'

'I was afraid she might – '

'No problem.' Peter had given him a short answer, and when Mark tried to talk, had cut him off abruptly.

The Fidelis Choir was giving a Sunday evening carol concert in the big lecture room at the Royal. Patients were brought from all the wards in dressing gowns or day clothes, on crutches, in wheelchairs, half a dozen on stretchers pushed against the back wall.

There wasn't room for visitors, but in the middle of 'Love and Joy', Peter saw an all too familiar figure. The double doors were open to let the sound flood out into the hospital. Mark sidled in and was stopped by one of the social workers. He must have said he was a patient, because he came on in and worked his way through the crowd to stand on a step under one of the high windows. He listened intently to the carols, his eyes on the place where Peter stood with the tenors.

Then it was Peter's big moment: his solo as King Wenceslas, with one of the sopranos, his tenant Claudine, singing the part of the page.

'Thou shalt find the winter's rage,' he sang, 'freeze thy blood less co-oldly.'

A pause. The conductor was using definite breaks between verses to bring out the story. Then Claudine, pure, recognizably French:

> In 'ees master's steps 'e trod,
> Where the snow lay dinted.
> 'Eat was in the very sod,
> Which the sent 'ad printed.

Someone laughed. Heads turned to the window to see where the intrusion had come from. Into the pause Mark's voice threw coarsely, 'Some sodding saint!'

The conductor's baton rescued them: 'Therefore Christian men be sure . . .'

In the small consternation, Peter saw the social worker come through and pull Mark off the step to get him out of the door.

The scene at the concert had been satisfying to Mark: shocking everyone, catching Mr Freeman off guard in a secret role, not his everyday ones of family man or doctor. No scandal there, though. And nothing damaging to be discovered about the daughter who had run away.

What now? What could he try next? Mark thought about Peter Freeman day and night.

His parents were going to the Scilly Isles for Christmas. Mark felt resentful, although he would not have gone with them if they had asked him.

Couldn't have anyway. On the rota board of the South Devon Transport Co., the reduced service offered over the holiday featured Mark's name unfairly often.

He found Aylmer in the office, crouched over a takings box like a money lender.

'No, no, wait a minute, c-calm down,' Aylmer begged, his lightweight moustache quivering like a timid animal. He stuttered a few excuses: Mark was one of the newest drivers. He was not a married man. Such an obliging bloke . . .

Ron gave Mark a better reason. 'Aylmer doesn't like you.'

'Because of my face?' Mark thrust the scarred side of his face towards Ron, who looked away, embarrassed, and mumbled something.

Because of my face.

Was that why Liz had gone off him again? Rose Marie had talked about taking Mark home for Christmas dinner with her family, but after the incident at his flat with the apparently deranged doctor, she had said no more.

'Since your parents have gone missing, I'm surprised you didn't want to go to Rose Marie's house at Christmas,' said her aunt Mrs Power, who usually got the wrong end of the stick. 'It doesn't seem natural for a young man to be on his own.'

She roasted a chicken for herself and Mark, and they ate it off her good lace tablecloth at midday with the curtains drawn, because she did not like anyone to see her eating.

When Mark left to get changed and go to the garage, she told him, 'You're quite a nice-looking young man. It's a shame about that ugly scar. Can't you have something done about it?'

Apart from a horrendously drunken night on New Year's Eve, which left Mark half paralysed in brain and body, the last decade of the twentieth century opened with no renewal of spirit.

He was not yet tired of the buses, although he could not see himself still at the wheel for ten or fifteen years, like some of the old turtles who worked here, but he was becoming increasingly irritated with passengers, and they were more critical of him. Even the old ladies who loved him and offered sweets would say, 'Come on, Mark put a good face on it. We need something to cheer us up on a morning like this.'

'You're late . . . you're early . . . slow down . . . get a move on . . .' The litany would drive you crazy.

The Bus brothers were more critical of him too, and when something was wrong, Mark usually got the blame. One of the buses had a fault in the air valve of the passenger door, which left it always slightly open, so that brake pressure was weakened. This had been reported by several drivers, but it had to be Mark who put his foot down hard on the brake pedal to avoid a car coming out of a side turning, and slewed round into a telephone pole because he could not stop in time. The pole fell forward on to the front of the bus, dented the roof and shattered the windscreen.

'I'll want a seat belt fitted next time I ride with you, mate,' a passenger said as he got off to board the relief bus.

It was not Mark's fault, but of course it was seen as Mark's fault.

One morning the traffic was even worse than usual. Everyone was going to be late, but one of Mark's regular commuters, the manager of a wine market in Kingscombe centre, was infuriatingly edgy.

From his seat behind Mark, he fretted, 'For God's sake, man, step on it!' and 'Pass, pass! Why don't you pass that crawler? Come on, you've got loads of room. Speed up and you'll get the light. Oh, God, you've missed it!' He howled.

'All right.' Mark stopped at the red light. 'You drive the bloody bus.' He got out and was never seen again.

For three days he did not answer his phone. When he did, it was Paul telling him not to come back.

'Haven't you noticed? I wasn't going to.'

There were other bus companies in South Devon. Mark was qualified. Perhaps he could find something with a better salary.

He wrote to Aylmer, asking for a reference. Paul rang back.

'Reference? Oh, yes, I'll give you a reference. I'll see to it that you never drive another bus in the West Country.'

Without a reference – perhaps with the bad news already out over the bush telegraph – it might be hard to find another driving job. Trying taxis, Mark was taken on as a night driver by a small firm with only a few cars. He was mugged by a couple of yobs on his second night, and had to refund the twenty-seven pounds, because he had been told not to take any fares out to the Hanscombe Cross area, but had forgotten.

'See you tomorrow?' the boss asked.

'Shove it.' Even with his sharp flint tool, he would have had no chance against those thugs.

He had left the flint in the box with his ticket machine when he walked off the bus. He could not find Ron's number, so he rang Liz.

'I hear you got fired,' she said before he could speak.

'I left because I – '

'And now you need a job and some money and you're fed up and will I meet you for a drink.' All of which was true.

'I want you to give a message to Ron,' Mark said with dignity. He did not say that the flint was four thousand years old. He did not trust Liz or Ron, or anyone.

When he got the flint back, he carried it in a pocket, until he cut his finger quite badly by putting a hand in to feel his treasure and getting hold of the cutting edge. After that he kept it handy in the glove compartment of his car, since the whole world was now against him.

Mrs Power reminded him that he was a week overdue with the rent. Paul wrote to him, saying he owed the bus company five hundred pounds for his training. Mark went to the Job Centre, and answered some advertisements in the paper, knowing, from his apprenticeship in Classified at the *Grafton Mercury*, the extent to which they lied. At the few interviews he had, low spirits made him present himself at his worst, and he felt as negative about the interviewers as they felt about him.

He was bored and frustrated and lonely. He went up to the hospital, but did not get a sight of Mr Freeman. Sometimes, in the evening, he walked up and down the avenue where the doctor lived, but the tree that hung over the wall was bare now, and he could not wait in its shadow opposite the brick fortress of Liberty House.

When the lights were lit in every room, it was painful to know that he could not go and bang the dolphin knocker and be taken in. He hated them all, secure in there against him.

He rang Liz again a couple of times, uselessly. He asked Rose Marie out for dinner at a restaurant she liked. She was quite greedy, like many passive people who did not waste much time talking at meals. Afterwards, in the car, Mark wanted to take her back to his flat.

'It's too late.'

'Never too late for a good time.'

'What do you mean?'

They had not yet done much more than kiss and fumble. She had lain on the bed with him but with her clothes on.

'You know what I mean,' Mark was losing his temper, 'and you want it as much as I do.'

'Speak for yourself.' Even heating up a bit, which she was, she did not abandon the clichés.

When Mark started the engine, she opened the door on her side. He pulled her back into the seat. 'How are you going to get home? I'm not going to drive you.'

'I'll find a taxi – or wait for a bus. They tell me the buses are safer now.' It was the only time he had heard her make a joke. 'Let me go, Mark.'

'All right.' He could not be bothered with it any more.

'Goodnight. And thank you for the dinner.' She leaned

forward to kiss him, moving her head sideways so that her kiss landed on the other side of his mouth from the scar.

At the end of January Mrs Power told Mark that if he could not pay the full rent, he would have to leave. 'You'd be going before Easter anyway, because of my seasonal visitors.'

Mark rang Judy. Twice he hung up when Duncan answered, but at last it was her, with, 'Hul-lo?', her upbeat way of answering the phone.

Just to hear her clear, expectant voice flooded him with loss. Although he had meant to be tough and practical, he said, 'I'm in bad shape, Judy. I need money and I haven't got a job. I – ' He struggled to pull himself together. 'I wondered if you knew of anything up your way.'

'I'm sorry, Mark. Look – this is no good. I can't help you any more. You've got to make it on your own.'

'Well. I just wondered.'

When she said goodbye, she added, 'How's the scar?'

Why did she ask that? Because she could not think of him without seeing it, dominating one side of his face.

The scar was him. He was the scar.

Peter was dictating operation notes when the secretary came in.

'I'm sorry, Mr Freeman, it's Mark Emerson. This is the third time he's rung, and he says it's an emergency. He won't speak to anyone but you.'

'All right.' Peter switched off the dictating machine and picked up the phone. 'Yes, Mark.' He made it a statement rather than a question, not too inviting, polite, but businesslike.

He was not prepared for the desperation that poured out.

Mark gabbled, sobbed, rambled, some of the time without making any sense.

'I've got to see you, Mr Freeman. I've got to see you,' was the clearest message that came through.

'Hang on, hang on. I'll see you, Mark. It's almost time for your final appointment anyway.' Peter had noticed it ahead in the diary.

'I can't wait till then.' Mark's voice trailed off, as if he were going to pass out.

'Are you all right?'

'Yes . . . no.'

'Have you taken pills or anything?'

'Oh, no. No, I wouldn't do that. I've got to see you.'

'Can it wait till tomorrow? I could see you first thing. Be here at eight thirty.'

'All right.' Mark's voice was suddenly flat and toneless.

'Look, you're obviously very upset. Would you like to speak to Dr Bremmer, the psychologist you saw before?'

'I don't care.'

'I'll get him to give you a call.'

Later Joe Bremmer reported back: 'I got hold of him, but he wouldn't speak to me. He hung up.'

'I'm seeing him at eight thirty tomorrow. If you're around, Joe, I wish you'd drop in here.'

Mark looked as bad as he had sounded on the phone, wild-eyed, dishevelled, the pallor of his face accentuating the redness of the scar.

'Sit down,' Peter said, to stop his agitated pacing. 'Tell me what's wrong.'

'Everything. Everything's gone wrong.'

Still walking about, turning, gesturing, he spilled out a

litany of disaster and loss. No job, no money, no friends, nowhere to live, no one to turn to. 'Except you, Mr Freeman – you've got to help me!'

'It sounds really bad. I'm so sorry.' Peter tried to calm him with a low, steady voice. 'What happened?'

'It's my face. I know it is.' Mark spoke in a breathless rush, hardly able to articulate the words. 'It's no use. I can't look like this. I can't live with this evil.' He was standing against the wall now, leaning his head back and rolling it from side to side like someone in intolerable pain.

'Your face is all right.' Peter was not afraid of this frenetic young man who had been harassing him for so long, but he was afraid for him, and he wished Joe Bremmer would show up. 'The scar is already paler and smoother. You must see that.'

'I see it every day, and so does everybody else.' Mark jerked his head away from the wall and stood with clenched fists, breathing hard. 'It's no use. Listen, Mr Freeman, Mr Peter Freeman, the man I thought was a – was a bloody hero. Listen, miracle man. I want you to put my face back the way it was. I was all right then. My life was all right. You've got to – you've got to –' He suddenly bent double, clutching himself as if he were in abdominal agony. He sobbed, 'You've got to make me look the way I did before!'

Peter went over to him. He put his hand under his chin to lift his head.

'Come on, Mark, you know I can't do that. And if I could, it wouldn't make any difference.'

'God . . . damn . . . you.' The dark, troubled eyes devoured Peter's face.

'That's enough. Come on, sit in the chair, and I'll give you something to calm you down.'

Mark jerked his eyes away from Peter's and lunged for the door.

'Mark, no – stay here, listen to me –'

The young man pulled his arm free with a cry of despair, and was gone.

Peter followed the sound of his running feet down the short corridor and round a corner, hesitated where the corridor divided right and left, and heard one of the outer doors bang. By the time Peter was outside – 'Can I help you, Mr Freeman?' asked a porter coming from the car park. 'Are you looking for someone?' – Mark had disappeared.

He drove until he had left behind the houses and shops and villages and the walled fields, and was on a deserted road in the open country that was the beginning of the moor.

No one to turn to. Now he knew what that really meant: agonizingly alone, his last hope gone, cut off from the only man who could help him, cut off for ever. He knew this road. It was the rough narrow way that he had driven with Daisy, going to see the American guru in the bus. He would go to him now, spill it all out, force him to understand how it felt to know that the surgeon, the man who might have saved him, would never agree to cancel his terrible mistake, to destroy the hideous blemish that poisoned Mark's life.

As he drove, heedlessly, his rage and confusion came together in an explosion of thought that blew everything else out of his mind. He knew the answer.

Following the road that dipped and turned and rose across the empty contours of the moor, he could feel himself doing what he was going to do, could feel already free in the ecstasy of pain and oblivion.

Below the remembered tumbled pile of rocks on the skyline, he turned off on to the grass track, bumping more slowly over the turf until the car stopped by itself. The flint was wrapped in a towelling rag that he used on the windscreen. Now – now! He slashed deeply, once across the scar, then in the other direction to wipe out the evil, to cancel his face with the sign of the cross.

Chapter Thirteen

Goo-roo Bob was outside with an axe, chopping logs small enough to go into the little stove he had fitted into his home, with a tin chimney that made the bus look like a tramp steamer.

He heard a car going slowly on the road above, and heard it stop. Being in a hollow and screened by thorn trees and a wall, the green bus could not be seen from the road. After a while, when the engine did not start again, Bob wandered up to see whether someone was lost.

Daisy's friend, the young man with the scar and the suicidal urge, was slumped in the front seat with a blood-soaked towel pressed to the side of his face. He was barely conscious. As Bob pulled him out, he could only just stagger down the slope, and let himself be pushed into the bus and on to one of the bunks.

With the poor young man almost insensible from shock and exhaustion, Bob gently pulled the bloody wad of towel away to reveal an injury as terrible as any he had seen in his old Hell's Angels days of cut and slash. Because no large artery had been severed, the towel had stopped the bleeding from the vicious cuts. They began to ooze again fast now, fresh blood welling up from the middle of the wound where the slashes crossed.

Bob put a thick pad on Mark's face while he collected what he needed. He gave Mark a cocaine injection from the small store of drugs he had brought from America and kept for emergencies, and washed the wound thoroughly with one of his herbal mixtures. The pain opened Mark's eyes, and he tried to sit up.

Bob pushed him back. 'You're okay,' he murmured to him while he worked. 'You're here. That's good. I can help you, kid. But these cuts are going to need stitching.'

Mark struggled against his restraining hand. 'Not hosp'al,' he said with difficulty. 'Don't . . . turn . . . me in.'

The few words he could manage were thick and almost unintelligible, because he could not close his slobbering mouth, but Bob said, 'I get you.'

He cut some strips of adhesive tape and laid them across the cuts, pulling the edges together tightly, then covered the whole large wound with a pad and more tape, and left Mark to sleep, while Bob meditated himself down from the practical level to the source whence the healing energies arose.

Mark could barely remember how he had found his way to the healer, nor how long he had been in the car with the towel pressed to his face, and blood everywhere. He lay in the nest of the bunk, sleeping and waking and sleeping again, and waking to pain. When he groaned and cried out, or tried to claw at the bandage, merciful Goo-roo injected more cocaine, and he was lost into a suspended space in which he hoped to be able to stay for ever.

He lay in the bunk for an endless time, until gradually the heat and swelling went down and the intensity of the pain subsided. No more drugs, but eating and talking were still very difficult.

At last, moving slowly, he began to get up, and then to go outside, and later to take on a small share of the work, helping with the animals and the vegetable garden, but he could not bend without waves of anguish invading his whole head and face. He wandered short distances, looking vaguely for the wild plants and herbs that Bob said were so easy to recognize.

He and Goo-roo meditated together, with the cats and dogs, attracted by their relaxation, gathering to lie close, and Bob showed Mark how to create images of the infinitesimal healing processes of his own flesh.

After about a month Bob eased the plasters off the wound and stood back to assess Mark, who sat on a stool near the stove with his unshackled face tilted up.

'How does it look, Bob?'

'You want to see?'

'You tell me.'

'Lum-py,' Bob said thoughtfully. 'But I guess that's because of the infection we tangled with early on, remember?' Mark grunted from the side of his mouth, although he did not remember whether he remembered or not.

'Pretty rough, and – I guess you'd have to say, pretty damn ugly.'

'A different me?'

'Yeah. I don't know what your future plans are, Mark, but I guess you'll have to – '

'Get going now? Sure. You must be sick of me.'

'You'd better stay a while.' Bob knew it was no use suggesting a doctor.

Mark shrugged. He had not looked at the future. Up to now, Goo-roo had said, 'The present is enough,' a simple recipe for eliminating anxiety which everyone should learn. Mark picked up the pan of mash and potato peelings from the stove and went out to the chickens. Peter Freeman could wait. He would still be there for Mark.

Daisy turned up on a motorbike one day, with a bag of stale cakes from the bakery where she was working. Bob went to meet her when he heard the bike, and Mark could hear them talking outside the bus in the cold untrammelled air of the moor. He was lying on his bunk, thinking about who he was if he was no longer himself, and Daisy immediately jumped up and snuggled down beside him, soft body and soft loose clothes enfolding him in the old sloppy comfort.

After a while, she sat up and looked at him, her seagrass hair hanging over her face. Mark reached up and tucked one side back behind her ear to force her to see him clearly.

Her mouth had fallen open in a silent gasp of horror. She turned her face quickly away. Mark muttered, 'Look at me!', and when her eyes came slowly round they were staring and blank with fear.

He put up his sleeve and wiped the eye which watered all the time, and bared his teeth at her in what he meant as a grin. Grinning was difficult, because of the partial paralysis that Bob said was caused by damage to the facial nerve.

'Like me?' he asked in the slurred voice that came from one side of his mouth.

Daisy was struggling to get her face together. 'Have you looked in the mirror?'

'You're my mirror. Your face tells me about mine. Pretty gross?'

'Oh, Mark.' Daisy's face was collapsing into tears. 'Why did you do it?'

'So it's gross. I wanted that.' He could still say this in a fairly calm, self-satisfied way.

When Daisy had gone, and while Bob was bringing the goats back to their shed from where they were tethered farther down the stream, Mark took down from a shelf the hand mirror that Bob used to trim his hair and beard.

He knew it would be shocking. He had not prepared himself to see a monster.

The ragged cruciform scar, ridged with hideously overgrown bright new flesh, had dragged everything on that side of his face out of shape. The eyelid was pulled down, showing the wet pink lining and a web of broken blood vessels at the bottom of the white. The nostril flared sideways. The corner of the mouth, beginning to drool again as Mark stared into the small mirror in a turmoil of fevered emotions, was drawn up into a ghastly sneer.

When Bob came back, stamping the cold out of his feet and beating his hands and wondering why the lamps were unlit, Mark said from the bunk, 'I'm leaving now.'

'Why suddenly?' Bob saw the mirror in the net that hung under the window. 'Mark, you can't. Wait, for God's sake. You've seen how you look. Let it settle some more. Give me a chance to look for someone safe who maybe can fix it.'

'I was fixed before. Leave me alone.' Mark looked around him in a blurred farewell to the benign claustrophobic interior of the bus, the aromatic iron pot at the back of the stove, Bob bending over one of the oil lamps and turning the wick down until the flame was steady, his brown lined face softened in the golden light. 'Let me go.'

'How are you going to live? That world out there is brutal. Haven't you been hurt enough?'

'It's my turn now. I know what I've got to do.'

'I hate like hell for you to go, but it's your life.' Bob brought the lamp over to Mark and examined his ruined face long and solemnly. 'You'll have to watch out. I'll give you some stuff you can use for cover when you have to.'

He put some dressings in a bag and showed Mark how he could hold a large pad over the scar with a bandage diagonally over his head and chin, covering the distorted eye. 'Been in a crash. People will accept that.' He gave him some money, and Mark put on the heavy black jacket and dark woollen cap he had worn every day since it got cold.

They walked together up the slope to where Mark's car was parked beside Bob's 2CV. As if he knew that Mark had nowhere to go, Bob was carrying the old brown blanket in which Mark had liked to wrap himself into a cocoon on the bunk.

'Thanks.' Mark's new constricted voice gave one of its grunts.

'Any time. Come back if you want.' Bob dropped this casually, but he meant it.

The car, idle so long, started on the fourth attempt. Gooroo stood on the grass at the edge of the road, not waving, just watching as Mark drove away into the gathering night.

*

Because they knew Annette's story, Ted's firm had been very accommodating. The new manager of the Kingscombe shop had taken over early so that Ted could be with his daughter when she had the second graft on her chin. The manager in Hereford, who was retiring, agreed to stay on until Mr Freeman said Annette could move up there. By a stroke of incredible good luck, the outgoing tenant of their new flat was willing to stay on and pay rent for a few weeks.

Ted's compassionate leave was unpaid and money was tight, but he sang: 'There's new hope in my heart every day. Everything's going our way.' Deirdre's depression seemed to be finally responding to a new drug. She was coming home. 'If you'll have me,' she said shakily on the phone.

'Can't get along without you, Dee.'

'You've managed, though.'

'Don't kid yourself. Me and Annette and Cammy have made a right mess of everything,' he said, because his colossal pride in what the three of them had done for each other would not be dimmed by hiding it from Deirdre.

'It won't be the same, though, not being in our house.'

'Stop being so bloody negative. We'll make the flat into a home.'

'There won't be room for the three-piece suite.'

'You don't even know. Get yourself back over here and then you can complain and criticize to your heart's content.'

'She'd better go easy with us.' It was a new Campbell, emancipated, bossy. His big feet still fell over everything, he still wore the maroon baseball cap indoors, his neck still sprouted thin and grubby from the greasy sweatshirt, and there was still a chilly gap above the dangling strings of the track-suit bottoms; yet Deirdre would see an overgrown boy who was no longer a skulking hulk, but, as he said of himself, 'man of the house'.

'What does that make me, then?' Ted had wanted to know.

'You're the woman, because you've got to do all the stuff for Annette and that.'

His sister had come home with a clear acrylic mask on the lower part of her face to keep pressure on the new scar margins. Other children made jokes about the IRA and bank robbers, but Annette did not care. She was so glad to be back at school and leading a fairly normal life.

Ted had to look after the mask and the tight bandage on her right elbow, and sometimes help her with dressing and washing.

Annette, now thirteen, complained, 'It's a bit weird being bathed by your father.'

'Think of him as another woman,' Cammy said, which was how the woman-of-the-house joke had attached itself to Ted.

When Annette was on the ward in the Milner Unit, Ted had sat there most of the day, with not much to say, and been consulted as an equal by Mr Freeman, who used to be mostly Deirdre's business. When Annette was at home, the doctor still insisted on being told of any change or small problem. It was Ted's decision now whether to call, and Mr Freeman was never too busy to talk. He did not make Ted feel a fool for asking dunderhead questions or worrying over trifles. He always signed off like a matey colleague: 'Good to talk to you.'

For a few cold nights Mark slept in his car on an unlocked campsite, which had running water and a windbreak of dark fir trees.

Wearing the camouflage bandage, he got himself a night

security job in one of the business estates outside Kingscombe. He did not have to see anybody, and it gave him a place to sleep, on the long narrow couch in the visitor's waiting room, with an alarm clock waking him every two hours when the time clocks had to be punched.

As soon as the last employee left, Mark put on the kettle in the storage room off the secretaries' office and took the covering from his face. The secretaries had a mirror behind the storage room door, and there were others on the walls of corridors and toilets as he patrolled the silent building with his beautiful sharp flint in his pocket, for want of the gun he ought to have had. He looked into all the mirrors to remind himself that he prowled the corridors as reliable Security Officer Emerson, in the company of an anonymous monster so ghastly that he could walk only at night.

Mark was restricted by his duty to the clocks. The monster was free.

One evening on his way to work, his bandage swathing his face ('Poor man,' his female boss had condoled. 'I'm glad to give you work after the bad luck of your accident'), he saw a broad-beamed woman walking alone past shuttered shops. Looking back over her shoulder, she turned down a narrower street between blank-faced buildings.

Mark left his bandage in his pocket and followed her on foot in the soft prowlers that Goo-roo Bob had brought back from the Red Cross shop. He made no sound and kept his distance. When the woman turned round again, she saw him and began to run.

She ran in heels, knock-kneed, heavy bottom swagging from side to side. Mark caught her easily before she reached the corner where traffic passed along a brighter street. He put his arms around her and pressed her against the wall, keeping the right side of his face turned away.

She did not say anything. Her head was jammed against an iron grille over a small dirty window. Mark pinioned it tightly with an arm across her neck. Then he turned his face to hers.

The scream was choked and strangled because of his arm. He could see the horrified eyes in her ugly fat face. When she looked as if she were a moment away from death, he loosened his arm and moved his body back. She screamed wildly and stumbled like a rhinoceros for the lighted street.

Because she had seen him, he could not risk going to work. He did not want to anyway. This was better. Her face had told him what he needed to know. He was an outlaw, cast out from the pretences of the civilized world in which he had struggled to live. The raging beast within could finally show its true face.

Chapter Fourteen

*A*fter Mark's frenzied stampede away from the clinic, Peter had not expected him to keep his outpatient appointment two weeks later; but when he didn't turn up, he asked the secretary to ring him. A new tenant answered the phone. She did not know anything about Mark.

What would become of this poor deluded young man who had tried to make Peter his saviour? Where had he gone?

'Good riddance,' Noel said. 'The farther away the better.'

'I worry about him,' Peter admitted.

'You can't afford to, sir.' Noel, who had applied for a senior registrar post in a larger unit in Edinburgh, the last step before becoming a specialist consultant, was still determined to toughen Peter up before he left. 'There's always another customer coming through the door. And another and another and another. Forget the psycho.'

Peter might forget Mark, but he would never forget Annette, even long after she was out of his hands. The latest chin graft was successful, and the other patches of shiny new skin on her body and limbs were gradually blending, although the scars of the burns and grafts would need to be watched for years.

'I'll come back to Kingscombe to see you,' she told him. 'My Mum and I told Dad we wouldn't go to Hereford unless we could do that.'

'You'll come here once,' Peter said. 'After that, you'll find some whiz-kid plastic surgeon up there and that's the last I'll see of you.'

'Never.' She dropped lightly off the treatment table where she had been sitting, to stand in front of him and search his face with her sea-goddess eyes, this child, this beautiful child who had been his challenge and focus for more than a year, so dear a triumph to him that even if he never saw another patient, his life's work was fulfilled.

On a dark night without a moon, an independent woman in her thirties opened her front door at about ten o'clock to take her dog for a walk before she went to bed.

She had been doing this almost every night for years. New houses were being built as the town crept further up the hill, but she still thought of it as a country neighbourhood, and did not bother to lock her door when she walked down her road to the diminishing green common space. She thought she had left lights on in her house, but when she got back, she saw that she was wrong. All the downstairs lights were off.

She went a few steps into the dark hall and put out her hand to the light switch. Ever since she was a child, hating to go up to her room alone because her father would not allow lights on upstairs when everyone was downstairs, she had cringed with the certainty that one night, another hand would come to cover her own on the switch.

It had taken thirty years for it to happen, and when it did, it was worse than her most dread imagining. The man's hand did not cover hers. It was already on the switch, and when she reached out unerringly in the dark, her hand was over his.

She could not switch on the light. She snatched her hand away and screamed. Her small dog, which had been lingering in the front garden, came in barking. She heard a crunch and a yelping grunt. She screamed again and the man turned on the light and she saw his face.

Kicking the dog in the ribs had been a mistake, because it distracted the woman's attention. She knelt down, making high-pitched cries that matched its feeble whines, trying to see where the dog was hurt.

Mark leaned down and pulled her upright in front of him, so that she must see his face again. He slapped a hand over her scream. It would spoil everything to have kindly neighbours in pyjamas trotting in.

The dog moaned. He kicked it aside and forced the woman into the front room, where the curtains were drawn. He switched on the light by the door and pushed her back into an armchair where she lay, paralysed with terror.

Every woman has a secret desire to be raped by the devil. This one watched him with horrid fascination. Then a spasm shuddered through her, and she closed her eyes. 'Go on, then,' she said brokenly.

'Open your eyes.'

The arms of the chair restrained her, and his body blocked her from getting up.

'Look at me!'

She rolled her head from side to side against the back of the chair. Tears oozed out from under the closed lids. Her body jerked as he slapped her hard on the side of the jaw.

'Look . . . at . . . me.' His slobbering face was jammed close to hers, he could smell the foulness of his breath that she smelled.

Rape – anyone could do that. This was power. With his thumbs and fingers he forced her eyes open, and he drank in the staring horror, the ultimate revulsion, before he flung himself away from her and disappeared, a hideous secret beast, into the night.

The next evening, he moved closer to the hospital. he had no plans beyond the eventual goal: to show himself to Peter Freeman. One last test for the hero. He must see me *as I really am*. He must see the worst of me, and accept the blame for unleashing the monster.

The Phantom of the Opera had been on to a good thing. Everybody in Paris was baffled, disgusted, sickened out of their minds by the horror that lived under the floorboards. But no one ignored him.

Noel Grant and his wife lived in one of the large Victorian houses that had been turned into flats by the Royal, in the road that ran along one side of the hospital. Alison went to evening classes. Mark had followed her in his car to the brightly lit concrete of the technical college. When she returned from her class, she had to leave her car a hundred yards away from her house. As she got out of the car, prettily huddled in a black and white coat with a huge collar that made an angelic white cowl round her face, Mark pulled her into the dark garden of one of the houses that had no gate across the entrance.

She hit out at him, but she was very small and it was not difficult to subdue her. He did not knock her down. He was not going to attack her. She only had to look at him.

At the hotel reception in September, Alison had seen him and talked to him as a good-looking guy with a scar who had tried to give her the business. She would not recognize him now. She did not need to. She was a stuck-up bitch married to a supercilious prick for whom Mark did not exist. Pretty Alison must look at evil. Beauty and the Beast. She must see this grotesque twisted face and confound herself with her own degraded desire.

But she knocked the torch out of his hand before he could shine it on his face. He hit her and she went down, bleeding from the lip, and the Beast pulled the wide wool scarf over his face and escaped by his secret ways to the burned-out engineering shed where his car was hidden.

When Annette's leg began to hurt again, she kept quiet about it. The swelling had gone down before. It would again. She put on the support bandage under her warm trousers and propped the foot up on the chair in front of her at school. She was not going to fuss.

When her mother arrived next week, there was going to be nothing wrong with Annette. That would be the best homecoming treat she could give her. A hundred-per-cent healthy Annette, to make up for the tiresome sick Annette who had caused her mother's breakdown. The leg would have to cure itself by neglect, like the occasional headache or dizzy fit, which Annette saw as only her body's attempts to remain addicted to being a pampered patient.

When her father was called urgently to fetch her home from school, he kept nagging, 'Why didn't you tell me?', but it was all too complicated to explain, and her mother's welcome home treat had gone up the spout anyway.

Annette was back in her old room at the Milner, the single room at the head of B wing.

After she had collapsed at home, coughing up blood, and Ted had rung Peter in an incoherent panic, things had moved fast.

When the ambulance got her to the hospital, the anaesthetist passed an endotracheal tube to keep her lungs inflated by machine. Peter stayed with her all night. Ted sat in a corner of the room, not moving or speaking, keeping out of everyone's way.

'Don't wait till Friday,' Ted had told Deirdre abruptly on the phone. 'Get on the next plane.'

'I don't know if I – '

'Annette's very ill. A pulmonary embolism.'

'You told me that.'

'Dee.' She thought he was going to say, 'Don't start,' but he said wearily, 'Just get on a plane, that's all.'

'You sound as if she's dying.'

'Come as soon as you can.'

Deirdre had hung up and turned to her sister June in dismay. 'Ted talks as if Annette is dying.'

'She can't be. You don't die of an embolism, do you? Children don't *get* pulmonary embolisms anyway.'

'Ted said to come now.'

'You want me to try and change your reservation?'

'Well, *I* can't do it, Ju.'

It would be a long time before Deirdre would be able to tackle things like travel agents. Her illness might have left her, but it had taken with it all her confidence and courage. She could not even make a phone call without doing her deep breathing for two minutes.

'Are you all right?' the young stewardess asked when she picked up Deirdre's tray, almost untouched.

'Yes . . . no, not really,' she said, but she was on the inside seat by the window, and the girl did not hear.

The woman sitting next to her heard. 'Is anything the matter?'

'What? Oh.' Deirdre was busy putting up her tray table. Her shaky fingers had trouble with the latch. 'I'm upset, that's all.'

'Oh, dear.' The woman gave her a tissue.

'My daughter may be dying.' It sounded as unreal as it felt, like a line in a badly written play.

'Have you talked to the doctor?'

'Only to my husband. I can't make sense of it.'

'No wonder. You need to see for yourself what's going on.'

'Yes, you're right.' Deirdre sniffed and swallowed. 'Always expect the best. It's just my husband . . . She's been very ill, you see, so it makes him overanxious.'

'Mm.' They nodded at each other. The woman smiled encouragingly.

Deirdre felt worse. 'Excuse me.' The man and woman had to stand in the aisle while she struggled out and went to the toilets to be sick. They were all full. People had got up as soon as they had eaten their meal, as if the food had gone right through them. While Deirdre was waiting, she swayed and almost fainted.

'All right, madam?' She managed a twitch of a smile.

It's just that my daughter is dying.

You need to see for yourself.

The woman's voice had been so sensible. She must be right.

As the plane lumbered steadily on, Deirdre sat tense in her seat and urged it to go faster. She was hurrying to Annette to keep her going, as she had always been able to do. She remembered the way Annette's eyes used to open mistily and then clear into focus. '*Mummy*,' she would whisper, as if her mother had been gone for hours instead of just outside a moment for a smoke.

Deirdre fell asleep against her will. When she woke and saw where she was, she could not at first remember why. As all the details returned, it was discouraging that the long flight was still drumming on, nowhere near landing.

At Heathrow an airline official took her to the place where she would get the bus to Reading. At Reading Station she bought a double vodka and a massive Danish pastry that no Canadian would accept. In the train, which seemed to go faster than the plane, she did not lean forward tensely or grip the edge of the table. She was too tired.

Ted and Campbell were at Kingscombe Station, Ted looking smaller than Deirdre remembered. They were awkward with each other. Ted was waiting for Deirdre to ask about Annette, and Deirdre was waiting for him to tell her.

At last in the car park, Campbell said in that awful accent he had picked up at school, 'Annette was dying. Now she's not.'

Relief stormed up as anger. 'She can't have been *dying*? Is this one of your jokes?' He was gaunt and ugly, with evasive eyes and hopeless hair. His clothes had shrunk on him. He had trodden his shoes over at the sides.

'Dee, she was.' Ted licked his lips. 'But she's survived. Mr Freeman says it's because she's so young.'

Mr Freeman – him of course. What had he been doing to let Annette get so ill? By the familiar shabby car, Deirdre's legs buckled, and Ted had to catch her.

'Oh, my God, my God.' The anger was washed away in tears now as she clung to Ted, gripping his solid body painfully. 'Oh, my Annette!'

'She's going to be all right,' her husband said gruffly. 'We'll go to her now.'

Annette would have to stay in the hospital for a while, and after that, she would be able to travel north with her mother and brother to where her father would have started his new job. He and the children had already done most of the sorting and packing of their possessions in the Kingscombe house, which was just as well, since Deirdre, although she claimed to be 'my old self again', was still touchy and excitable, and seemed to have lost much of her former confidence.

'She isn't her old self,' Cammy told Annette. 'And a good thing too. I was scared she'd start bossing us about again, just when we've got life the way we want it, but she doesn't do that no more. She's sort of – lost her what's it – lost her edge, sort of.'

'Poor Mum.' Propped up in the bed to play cards with her brother on the bed table, Annette sighed. 'She seems a bit lost. I hope she'll cope with Hereford, like we will. I feel older than her now, do you?'

Cammy gave his cracked laugh. 'Let's 'ang on to that.'

'What's the joke?' their grandmother demanded from the windowsill where she was disciplining the flowers and cards. 'I wish you wouldn't mumble. What's funny about Hereford?'

Annette giggled. Cammy said, 'There was a young lady of 'ereford . . .'

'You're out of hand,' Mrs Last pronounced. 'I've a mind to come up there and keep an eye on you. Get a nice little bungalow in the Border country.'

'The Welsh will burn it,' Cammy muttered to Annette, and the two of them were off again in the ridiculous sniggers and whispers that drove their grandmother to distraction.

Annette, although weak, was fairly well now, but her mother insisted on staying with her in the hospital most of the time, as she had before. Peter had been glad of her last year during the long ordeals of surgery and recovery, but since her breakdown she was not the same steadfast support. She was nervy and difficult. He had to make a conscious polite effort with her, especially in Annette's room, where the child must be kept quiet and at peace.

Deirdre was critical of Peter, where before she had been so co-operative and trusting. Why had the original neck graft tightened? She would waylay him in the corridor, usually when he was carrying something. Could that tightening have been avoided? She had never felt happy about it from the time of the first operation.

'Then you knew more than I did,' Peter said patiently, shifting his load. 'Some grafts contract as they heal. Others don't, as you know.'

'I'm not the expert.' Deirdre would start biting at the skin round her fingernails. 'You are.'

She had been badly shocked by the disaster of the pulmonary embolism. They all had. But it did not help to keep asking him why he had not foreseen it. Why had he discharged Annette? Why didn't he know when the leg swelled up?

'Because she didn't tell anyone.'

'What would you have done if you'd known?'

'Removed the clot and ligatured the femoral vein.'

'Why didn't the child say anything?'

'She was happy at school. She didn't want to come back to the hospital.'

'Why? I thought this was her second home. Didn't she trust you?'

And on and on. Annette might need a mother, like every child, but Peter wished she had stayed in Toronto.

One Friday, after a late emergency repair operation on a badly torn hand, Peter looked in on Annette, as he always did before he went home.

'Only one more week,' he reminded her.

'I know.' Her colour was better. The clear light was coming back into her blue-grey eyes. 'Mum and I have been making wishes for our future. Look at the new moon out there.'

Peter went over to the window, where a curved bright sliver rode between two low cloud masses, gilded by the lights of the town.

'I'll miss you very much.' He turned to go towards the door, but Deirdre Leigh had got up from her chair to put a hand on his arm and say, 'You'll see plenty of us.'

'I hope so.' He gave her what Catherine called his ghastly grin, when he had to force a smile.

'Will you really go on taking care of Annette, as you promised?'

'Of course.'

'But what if it's an emergency?'

'That's different. We've discussed that.'

'What if the Milner gets much busier and you haven't the time to – '

'Look, please.' Peter went to the door. He wasn't going to get into this with her in Annette's room, and he still had to stop in to see two patients at the Restora before he went home.

'People shouldn't really make promises.' Standing, skinny and off balance, between the bed and the window, Deirdre spoke like a disillusioned sage. 'Life gets its own back.'

'Yes, well . . . goodnight, Mrs Leigh. Goodnight, Annette. Sleep well.'

When he had gone, Deirdre looked out at the moon again and made another futile wish. Standing by the window, she asked the crescent moon to help her not to say the hasty wrong things that put Mr Freeman and everyone else against her.

She drew the curtains. When she turned round, Annette's eyes were closed. Deirdre leaned against the windowsill and looked at this clean, square, too-familiar room with distaste. Why was it all different now? When Annette had been in the Milner before, Deirdre had felt that she belonged here. Everyone was her friend. She was a valued member of the team. Even though the burden of Annette's long sickness had in the end been her undoing, she looked back with regret to the days when she had been a 'star mother', even able to help other parents caught in the same sort of crisis.

Now she felt in the way, unwanted here, perhaps despised by staff people like that bustling juggernaut Janet, because she had failed her daughter. She had run away and left them all to carry on.

Well, *you* try going mad, she wanted to tell them, and see if your first instinct isn't flight.

She had said that to Campbell when he had asked her, 'Why did you go to Canada, Mum? I don't get it.'

'*You* try going mad,' she had snapped, 'and see what you do.'

'She didn't go mad, as she calls it,' Ted told the boy, who Deirdre thought should not need protecting from the truth at his age. 'She was ill. And now she's all right.'

Everyone said she was all right now, but they still treated her with caution – Ted and the children and even her own mother. No one laid any blame, and they were all quite careful not to say, 'We managed perfectly well without you,' although it was obvious that this was what they felt:

'Oh, no, Mum, we do it this way now.'

'That's our dog, Pepper, we told you. He sleeps on my bed.' Campbell had fixed her with those small, canny eyes, daring her to object.

In the long weeks of her therapy, she and Dr McKenzie had talked about guilt until it was coming out of her ears, and what he called 'loss of vawl-yew', trying to make her see that everybody had that, even people like Peter Freeman; but some can compensate for it better than others.

Annette was awake. She was looking at her mother from under her lids.

'Want me to read to you, love?'

'Is Dad coming in?'

'Not this evening.'

'All right, then.' A second-best to playing cribbage with Ted.

Deirdre turned on the bedside lamp and switched off the main light. She read rather badly, stumbling and clearing her throat, losing her place when a nurse came in to give Annette a pill and check her pulse and blood pressure.

Quite soon, Deirdre looked up from the book and saw that Annette was asleep. She had been reading the boring teenage story to nobody.

It was not even seven o'clock. The long evening and endless night stretched ahead like a yawn, offering only the choice of the armchair or the camp bed in the day room. Deirdre would have liked to take a taxi and go home, but she had made such a fuss about needing to stay with Annette that she could not do that.

There was another choice. The best therapy for loss of vawl-yew, not included in the repertoire of Dr McKenzie, was to nip out to the Crown two streets away and have a drink.

Annette was sleeping soundly. Deirdre left the bedside lamp on, put on her Canadian down jacket and went out of the room, looking up and down the corridor before she went round the corner to the side door. It was bolted, with the light outside turned on. Deirdre turned out the light, unbolted the door, went out and crossed the car park to the shelter of the path behind the shrubbery that would take her out to the street.

Chapter Fifteen

*W*hen it grew dark, Mark had wandered up to the hospital to see if Peter was still there. Not seeing the red car in the larger parking place, he had moved round outside the radiating wings of the Milner, keeping his face wrapped up in the wool scarf against the cold and against the curious. Since there had begun to be stories about what the papers called the Kingscombe Monster, Mark was proud but extra careful. The police would be looking for him. They did not know who they were looking for, but he could not risk being picked up before he had confronted Peter Freeman with the truth of his accursed face.

And after that, what? Whether he was caught or whether he went free, Mark had not thought about what would happen. What future could there be for him? There was a kind of black freedom about having nothing to look forward to.

Peter's car was in the small staff car park at the side of B wing. There were bushes here and some sheds where mowers and tools were kept. Mark had quite often sheltered here when he was spying on Peter Freeman.

Each wing of the unit had several small wards and a single room at the top end where the wing met the central building. The window of the single room on this side laid a square of light on to the grass edge of the car park. The curtains had not yet been drawn.

As Mark waited by the bushes, he saw with a shock of pleasure the figure of Peter Freeman appear in the lighted window, looking up at the sky. Then he was gone, and soon Mark saw him come round the corner of the building from the front door and go to his car.

Mark watched him drive away, and was going to leave the hospital grounds and sneak down by back ways and disused yards and scrap heaps to where his own car was hidden. Perhaps he would hang about near Peter's house tonight, try to look in, listen to what music was being played, what television show the children were watching. He would spy on the family, living their evening vicariously, until the downstairs lights went out and then the ones upstairs, and Mark could prowl round the garden in the dark secretly, uncovering his wretched face to the stinging cold, slobbering, muttering to himself, unknown to the world.

As he turned to go, someone else came to the lighted window of the hospital room. A woman with high bony shoulders and straight dead-looking hair. It was the woman he had talked to on the bench in November, the mother of the burned child – Annette!

Annette was in that room, the favoured patient, the

cherished one who would have died, Mark had heard, without the skill and dedication of Peter Freeman. The one who got all the attention. Now, secure in that room – now was the time when she deserved some attention from Mark.

The mother drew the curtains closed. In the bushes Mark waited, sifting through a dozen crazy, hopeless schemes. While he was still trying to decide whether to stay here or to drag himself away, the side door opened and the mother, topheavy in a bulky jacket, came out and walked straight towards him across the corner of the car park. He moved behind one of the sheds, and she strode quickly along the path and down the slope at the side of the main hospital buildings.

There was no light outside the side door. Like a shadow, Mark slid towards it, found it unlocked and went inside. His heart was racing, knocking against his chest as if trying to escape. His breath rasped in and out through the slack twisted slobber of his mouth. The child, the child – this then was the ultimate. This was what he had been waiting for.

There was no one about. He raised his head to look through the small window in the door of the room, then opened it and was in the room, choked, dizzy with excitement.

Coming out of sleep, before she could be bothered to open her eyes, Annette knew that someone was standing by her bed. It wasn't her mother or one of the nurses. They didn't smell like this, and you couldn't hear them breathing.

The smell was disgusting, decayed and sour, like the stench when they took the dressings off a graft that had broken down.

She opened her eyes and saw him, leering at her in the light of the lamp. Lank, matted hair straggling over one eye, the other – oh, horrible – dragged down as if it were falling out, reddened and oozing into the fearful mass of knotted swollen flesh that made this the face of a beast, not a man. The loose sneering mouth erupted in bubbles of breath and evil, unintelligible words.

They stared at each other for a moment that would be imprinted on her mind for ever. He croaked a laugh and was swiftly gone from the light, in a stink of foul breath and dirty clothes.

Annette lay in stricken silence, her heart pounding, struggling to breathe. She lay paralysed, because he was *somewhere in the room*, beyond the pool of light, waiting in a corner, in the shadows. She could still smell him. The rasp of her painful breath struggled to the rhythm of his.

Slowly, she dared to move her eyes. The room came into dim focus, the walls, the chairs, the rail at the end of the bed. The door was ajar. She was alone.

Movement rushed back. Her fingers scrabbled for the bell that wasn't there. Breath filled her and she screamed, and went on screaming.

Peter was just leaving the Restora Hospital when Janet, who was on the late shift, called from the Milner to tell him that Annette had been terrified by the Kingscombe Monster. Her deep voice, usually steady and matter of fact, was breathless and agitated.

'I'll come back.'

'You don't need to. The police said they'll see you in the morning. It's just, I – '

'I'm on my way.' If something was wrong with Annette, he must be there.

A security officer from the main hospital met him at the

front door. 'Can't understand it . . . Never had any intruders . . . Had a check round the doors like I always do after dark . . .'

He followed Peter towards B wing and had to be assured half a dozen times that nobody was blaming him. Firmly quietened, he was sent back to work, because there were a few visitors about.

In Annette's room Janet was sitting on the edge of the bed with her arms round the still trembling child. The mother was pacing, grumbling, giving off short exclamations of distress and disgust. Janet had given Annette a sedative, but she was still sweating and wide-eyed, her pulse racing, her breathing shallow, with intermittent sobbing gasps.

When Janet got up, the child reached out both hands to Peter. They were cold and shaky. He held them firmly, careful of the graft scars, and they looked at each other. Annette's blue eyes were clouded with terror.

'Want to tell me what you saw?' Peter asked gently, although he wanted to rage and curse at the man for the outrage of his assault.

Annette shook her head.

'Oh, don't torture her,' the mother said impatiently. 'She's suffered enough. It's insane. I was only out of the room for a moment and came back to find her in this state. Total rest, she was supposed to have. Total chaos is what I call it. Any old vagrant creeping in and out – what kind of hospital is this?'

Peter stepped away from the bed, and she flung herself at him, grabbing his coat. 'You're in charge. It's your fault.'

Peter managed to get her out of the room, and she protested, 'Don't push me about. I want to stay with my child.'

'You're not doing her any good, carrying on like this.'

'I'm taking Annette away from here.'

'She's not ready to leave.'

'I'm not taking orders from you any more. We'll find another doctor, where we're going.'

Peter was upset with her, but so furious with the unknown man, whoever he was, whatever he was, that Deirdre was a mosquito irritant compared to the deep murderous hatred that he felt for the intruder.

He told Mrs Leigh to go home, which she refused to do, gave Annette an injection that weighted her eyelids almost at once, got wearily into his car and drove home, wishing he didn't have to be alone tonight.

Catherine had taken the children and Archie to her mother's. Peter was going to the cliff cottage at Farne to work on the paper he was to present to the British Burn Association, 'The Possible Salvage of Massive Burn Casualties with Cultured Human Skin'.

He let himself into dark, silent Liberty House, wishing he could hear Catherine call out to him, or the dog's bark, or Evie's running feet on the stairs. A note from her was on the hall table: 'See you tomorrow. Love. E.'

There was also a letter from his friend Dr Knox at the hospital which was pioneering tunable dye laser therapy on portwine birthmarks. They wanted to see Catherine again. There was a chance that some initial treatment might be started the year after next.

He rang Catherine at her mother's.

'What's wrong?' She could always detect an edge to his voice.

'Nothing. Nothing that I can't wait to tell you. Want

to hear some *good* news?' He told her about Dr Knox.

'Oh, Peter.' She was excited. 'I don't know what to say. All these years, and all the hard work learning how to live with it . . .'

'Now you'll have to learn to live without it.'

He changed into old clothes, and put some milk and bread and things he would need in a box. He rang Janet for news of Annette before he left.

'Asleep? Good. Make sure someone's in the room when she wakes. How's her mother?'

'Poor woman. I told her husband to come and collect her. Poor man.'

Peter took the box out to the car, turned out all the lights in the house and drove away.

Mark waited, muffled up, in his car round the corner near Liberty House, where he could keep watch. He mumbled to himself and wiped his constantly dribbling mouth on his sleeve. The bandage below his bottom lip was already soaked. He saw Peter come home, and then quite soon he saw the house lights go out, and the red car come through the gate and turn left and then right on to Market Street, heading towards Kingscombe.

Damn. He had promised himself that he would see Peter tonight, now, when he was still charged up from the intoxication of invading the hospital. He must finally show Peter his real self, and gloat over what he had done to Annette.

On the straight stretch through the copse of stunted firs, just before the downhill curves began, Peter Freeman's car took a left fork. He was not going back to the hospital. When the road levelled out along the coast, Peter turned left, with

Mark behind him. If he was going out to dinner, Mark would wait again patiently, and then – then what? If he followed him home again, Peter might call the police at the first sight of the mutilated monster, who would make headlines again tomorrow, after the outrageous assault on the child.

Mark had not planned what he was going to do. He had not planned any of this, tonight. He would wait and see what happened. When the moment came, he would know.

Although the evening was cold, Peter opened the window beside him, so as not to miss the first sharpening of the air outside the town. Kingscombe was on the coast, with the sea invading it in harbours and boat basins and the wide river mouth; but the man-made smells and sounds shut out awareness of the sea.

Halfway to Farne, he began to feel more like himself. Anger was an unfamiliar companion. He would let it go for tonight. Tomorrow he would have to go back and talk to the police, and Annette might need him, but tonight he was alone, with work to do, in uncluttered peace.

There were not many cars on the road. Soon, in April, the traffic and crowds would begin, the penalty for living in a beautiful place. After Peter turned off the main road to navigate the network of narrow high-banked lanes, there was not another car ahead of him or coming towards him. Through Charlton, left at the crossroads, and at last the steep chute down to the Farne estuary which made you feel that you were driving straight into the sea.

On the coast road Mark managed to keep Peter in sight without giving away that he was being followed. After the red car turned off round the curve of a stone wall, Mark was afraid of losing it in the maze of forks and crossroads. Where on earth was Peter Freeman going? Mark had to hold back, sometimes driving with sidelights so as not to be obvious, but the dark was his friend. When he could not see Peter's car, he could see its bright headlights tracing a course between the fields and small rounded hills.

Mark saw the lights swing left and disappear. Following slowly, he saw that the lane dropped steeply down to the sea. He switched off his lights and got out. Peter turned sharply at the bottom and the headlight beam illuminated the white wall of a low house on the edge of the cliff. Mark left his car in a gateway and walked slowly down the hill.

As always when he first arrived here, Peter walked straight through the cottage and out the other side to stand on the narrow grass terrace above the sea. No moon or stars, but a last greenish-yellow streak along the top of the cliffs above the estuary showed that the long stretch of sand was half covered with water, with the tide coming in.

He made himself a sandwich and coffee, took out his notes and the old typewriter he kept here, and settled down to work at the kitchen table. It was difficult to concentrate his mind. He could not dismiss the nightmare imagining of Annette waking to the sight of the grossly disfigured face she had described between sobs to Janet. He could not write about massive burns without being painfully reminded of the flayed child he had first seen.

He was restless and tired at the same time, not comfortable anywhere. He kept going to stand in the dark outside. All the light had gone. He could not see the opposite cliffs, but the tide was farther up now, and he could hear the sea breaking against the outcrop of rocks below the house. When he came back inside, his books and papers on the table under the lamp looked attractive, but he could not sit down to them. Better go to bed. He would get up early and go back to work.

Mark waited out the cold night in a doorless stone hut near the cottage, watching the windows. When Peter opened the door, the light ran out across the grass, and Mark could see the doctor's figure briefly before he stepped beyond the light and went to stand at the wooden rail looking over the beach. What was below there? If he was attacked from behind, was it a sheer drop? How far was it down to rocks?

When the downstairs lights went out and then the upstairs ones, Mark rested under the brown blanket on the grasses and weeds that had moved in to carpet the hut. He had slept in worse places since he left the comparative luxury of the green bus. He drank from the half bottle of whisky he had bought out of his dwindling store of Goo-roo Bob's money, and ate a large stale bun.

Peter woke in the early light. Sitting up to look out of the window, he saw wide pools and rippled glistening sand from which the tide was retreating. Unable to sleep any more, he got up and dressed.

Night-time ideas of leaving work for the morning look less appealing when the morning comes. Peter put on his thick white sweater and went down the rock steps to the beach to look for a small treasure of saltwood. He would paint a miniature seahorse on it to keep him away from Human Skin Culture a little longer, and give it to Evie when she came home this evening, just as she often brought a special gift for him.

He walked head down, looking among the rocks at the debris of very high water stranded under the cliff until another exceptional tide rolled it over, sorted it out and took some back to sea. The sky was a fusion of pastel colours, changing from minute to minute as the light increased. Above the trees higher up the estuary, streaks of cloud lay like sandbars between amethyst lagoons. He sang quietly to himself. Without the dog hustling everywhere and raising fountains of spray as he charged through the shallow water, the beach was blessedly peaceful. When the demands of the papers on the kitchen table eventually pulled Peter back indoors, he would be able to reward himself with the knowledge that he had made the most of the best of the day.

He walked out over the slippery bright green seaweed and across the growing sandbar, on to which the gulls were settling, to where the river current ran deep and swift, taking the shallower water with it out to sea.

After discarding several scraps of wood that were not perfect, he found a square piece shaped like a slice of brown bread, with close-striped grain across it. It was smooth and regular, edged with tiny pin holes where something had lived when it was part of a boat. Peter stood up straight with it in the wind and was knocked forward again on hands and knees by a body cannoning into his back.

He scrambled up, turning to face whoever had hit him, and caught his breath on a gasp of horror. It was Mark Emerson, but a horrible travesty of Mark Emerson, the monster he had perhaps crazily imagined himself to be when he was so paranoid about his face.

The inoffensive scar was now a dreadful criss-cross wound, half healed into knotted lumps and raw cavities, dragging that side of the face grotesquely out of shape, crude and harsh in the clear morning light. Mark was breathing heavily. When he brought his face close up to Peter's, he stank of whisky.

'*You!*' The shock had hit Peter like a hammer blow. This was the man the papers had been calling the Kingscombe Monster. This was the dreadful sight to which Annette had woken screaming, far worse than anything Peter had imagined.

'Take a good look.' The mutilated creature in filthy clothes staggered on the wet shifting sand, and leered at Peter with an eye whose reddened lid was dragged down and watering copiously into the sea wind. 'You're not . . .' The words were unintelligible.

'What are you saying?' Peter looked back across the sand towards the cottage on the cliff, two hundred yards away. This man was being hunted by the police. How could Peter get in touch with them?

Mark's voice came from the side of his twisted mouth, slurred and thick. 'You're not – the only one who can – use the knife.'

'*You* did this?'

'You wouldn't help me. I crossed myself out.'

'Good God!' Peter was seething. 'You bloody fool. You maniac. You did this to yourself, because I – because you thought I rejected you? You deliberately hacked yourself up.' He raised his hands as if he would strangle Mark. 'And then you used your – this dreadfully mutilated face to attack and terrify women. To terrify that poor child in my hospital – a little girl who's never hurt anyone – to frighten her so that she – that she – ' He was grabbing for words, hardly knowing what he was saying, incoherent with anger.

'Oh, yes. The child.' The corner of the top lip sneered, the bottom lip sagged and drooled. 'I came to tell you about that.'

'What do you want? Mark, for God's sake, what do you want with me? You've totally wrecked your face. You're not asking me to put it back together again?'

'No.' Mark gave a kind of frothy cackle. 'This . . . real me. Your fault, Mis – mister Freeman.' He wiped the bubbling dribble on his ragged sleeve. 'Your monster.'

'You're not mine.' Peter looked again at the white house above the rocks, wondering if he should make a run for it. He looked across to the other side of the estuary. No one on the sands there. No one on either side of the river but himself and the crazy, dangerous young man who must somehow be contained.

'Listen, Mark.' Peter moved away from him, his heart hammering, his breath taken away by the cold wind. 'Come back with me. You'll be in trouble, but I'll help you.'

'Turn me in?' Mark lurched towards him and stumbled.

'You're drunk,' Peter said, and turned away towards the house, his spine crawling with anxiety, but walking slowly enough across the wet sand to look as if he were not afraid.

A powerful arm came round him from behind and pulled him back towards the edge of the water, and, swiftly, something like a knife made a jagged hole in the front of his sweater. Peter yelled and felt a sharp excruciating pain under his chin. He put his hand up into the blood.

'You bastard!' He fought free of the clamping arm and whirled round to hit out in a storm of anger. Mark was crouched like an ape, holding something that looked like a triangular piece of flint. His other hand shot out to grab Peter's arm again.

He shouted hoarsely, 'Cut you! I'll cut your throat . . . you – won't get me –'

Half in and half out of the sea, Mark's foot slipped on a seaweed-covered rock. Before he could recover, Peter hurled himself upon him. He pushed Mark's face into the water and dragged the razor-sharp flint away from him, splitting the palm of Mark's hand. He stood up and threw the bloody flint far out into the water.

When he turned back to fight again, Mark had got up and was staggering drunkenly out into the strong, freezing current. 'My flint – damn you!'

He fell, half struggled up, and the tide knocked his legs away.

Peter had bent his head to dab at his bleeding chin with the front of his torn sweater. When he looked up, Mark was face down in the water, flailing uselessly as he was carried out towards the breakers.

Peter ran out along the sand and plunged into the icy, churning water. Half wading, half swimming, swallowing sea and tiring fast, he somehow managed at last to pull Mark by his jacket to the opposite side, and drag the heavy sodden body out of the water and on to the slope of the sand bank. He turned it on its side and pushed the head down and thumped the chest. Water trickled out of the slack, twisted mouth, but the skin was blue and there was no movement of the face. Peter realized that Mark's heart had stopped.

Frantically, he rolled him on his back and knelt beside him to do mouth to mouth. Two strong breaths, then heart compression, then back to breathe life into the lifeless boy. But the distorted mouth, pulled up at one side into the hideous calloused scar, was impossible to enclose with his own mouth.

Peter was aware of a dog barking and running towards him from far away. He kept working, pressing on the breastbone with both hands, trying to fit his mouth to breathe into the cold, misshapen mouth – because he knew you don't give up, however hopeless – listening for a breath, feeling for a pulse.

Mark was dead. The dog bounded up, scattering sand into the lank, drowned hair.

Peter raised his head and shouted to the man running across the sand, 'Get help!'

The man came closer to look.

'Get help!'

The man called the dog and ran back towards his car in the gap between the low cliffs.

Peter sat with Mark and waited, shivering, slumped on the sand, one hand pressed against his bleeding chin. He looked across the estuary at his white house perched on the cliff. He looked out to the open sea. He looked down again at Mark, and tenderly turned his heavy head over to one side, so that the scar was hidden in the sand.

FOR THE BEST IN PAPERBACKS, LOOK FOR THE 🐧

In every corner of the world, on every subject under the sun, Penguin represents quality and variety – the very best in publishing today.

For complete information about books available from Penguin – including Puffins, Penguin Classics and Arkana – and how to order them, write to us at the appropriate address below. Please note that for copyright reasons the selection of books varies from country to country.

In the United Kingdom: Please write to *Dept JC, Penguin Books Ltd, FREEPOST, West Drayton, Middlesex, UB7 0BR.*

If you have any difficulty in obtaining a title, please send your order with the correct money, plus ten per cent for postage and packaging, to *PO Box No 11, West Drayton, Middlesex*

In the United States: Please write to *Dept BA, Penguin, 299 Murray Hill Parkway, East Rutherford, New Jersey 07073*

In Canada: Please write to *Penguin Books Canada Ltd, 2801 John Street, Markham, Ontario L3R 1B4*

In Australia: Please write to the *Marketing Department, Penguin Books Australia Ltd, P.O. Box 257, Ringwood, Victoria 3134*

In New Zealand: Please write to the *Marketing Department, Penguin Books (NZ) Ltd, Private Bag, Takapuna, Auckland 9*

In India: Please write to *Penguin Overseas Ltd, 706 Eros Apartments, 56 Nehru Place, New Delhi, 110019*

In the Netherlands: Please write to *Penguin Books Netherlands B.V., Postbus 3507, NL–1001 AH, Amsterdam*

In West Germany: Please write to *Penguin Books Ltd, Friedrichstrasse 10–12, D–6000 Frankfurt/Main 1*

In Spain: Please write to *Alhambra Longman S.A., Fernandez de la Hoz 9, E–28010 Madrid*

In Italy: Please write to *Penguin Italia s.r.l., Via Como 4, I-20096 Pioltello (Milano)*

In France: Please write to *Penguin France S.A., 17 rue Lejeune, F-31000 Toulouse*

In Japan: Please write to *Longman Penguin Japan Co Ltd, Yamaguchi Building, 2–12–9 Kanda Jimbocho, Chiyoda-Ku, Tokyo 101*

P. 30   poofs
   44   bed-sit
   66   dupuytren

BY THE SAME AUTHOR

Dear Doctor Lily

'Lily ... is always on the look-out for life's lame ducks, like her friend Ida, who has a disastrous marriage to a GI. The twist is that in all her do-gooding, Lily neglects her own nearest and dearest. Wise, witty and perceptive' – *Daily Express*

One Pair of Feet

'A brilliantly funny account of the first and only year of her training to be a nurse' – Elizabeth Bowen in the *Tatler*. 'Monica Dickens gets better and better. It is a pleasure to record such steady and admirable progress in a world in which so much gets worse and worse ... The cheerful impudence, the power of observation and the family eye for a comic character are in better form than in her early work. And there are occasional touches of genuine pathos' – J. B. Priestly

Flowers on the Grass

Orphaned as a child, Daniel Brett could never settle down. After the sudden death of his young wife, he abandons home and security, setting off to find the freedom he knew as a boy. Monica Dickens's delightful novel follows Daniel's picaresque wanderings from a seaside boarding house to a hospital bed, introducing the strange characters he meets and recording his even stranger adventures.

The Listeners

If you are desperate, if you are at the end of your tether, ring this number ... The message on the poster seemed directed at him personally. Tim dialled. A voice answered, 'Samaritans – can I help you?' What follows is the absorbing story of Tim's struggle to come to terms with an alien society. It is also the story of the Samaritans, ordinary people who are there to listen and who care. Often that's all it takes.

BY THE SAME AUTHOR

Enchantment

In this compassionate story of real lives Monica Dickens explores the human need for role playing and escapism with an unparalleled warmth, insight and perception. 'A touching story ... It has all Miss Dickens's celebrated homely charm' – *Sunday Times*

Closed at Dusk

'Creepy ... a story of love, hate, and murder, tinged with the supernatural' – *Sunday Express*. 'Monica Dickens's prose is evocative ... [her] talents for storytelling have, if anything, improved over the years' – *Daily Mail*. 'She knows how to arouse our recognition and sympathy' – *Daily Telegraph*

The Heart of London

With all her sympathy and humour Monica Dickens shows us the rapidly changing face of London through the eyes of the people who live there – May Wilson, the district nurse, the Bannings, housewives like Mrs Boot and teachers like Grace Peel.

One Pair of Hands

An Uproarious backstairs view of the English upper classes in moments of comedy, drama, selfishness, and childish pique. Here is fun, wit, malice and – in the face of the tartars who rule on both sides of the green baize door – courage. 'Riotously amusing' – *The Times*

also published:

Man Overboard
My Turn to Make the Tea
No More Meadows